CW00762171

For more information, contact: hello@ainsleydoty.com
www.ainsleydotyauthor.com

First paperback edition June 2024

Book cover design by Karolina Loboda
Typesetting by Eric Forest

ISBN 978-1-7383327-0-0 (hardcover + dust jacket)
ISBN 978-1-7383327-3-1 (hardcover)
ISBN 978-1-7383327-1-7 (paperback)
ISBN 978-1-7383327-2-4 (ebook)

Proudly published by

MOOTE POINT
PUBLISHING HOUSE

www.mootepoint.com

THE
BLOODWOOD SOCIETY

BY AINSLEY DOTY

 MOOTE POINT
PUBLISHING HOUSE

DISCLAIMER

This novel contains brief references to suicide and child abuse which may be triggering for some readers and unsuitable for others. This novel also contains references to drugs; their descriptions and effects are entirely fictional.

For Kev,
the salt of the earth

THE BLOODWOOD SOCIETY

CHAPTER 1

F ar below where her bare feet dangled, a set of waves crashed against the rocky shore. The smooth limestone of the bluffs felt warm against her bare legs. The early-morning sun drew steam from the ocean's surface. First fog, the sailors called it. The salty breeze combed through her curls and ruffled the pages of the forbidden book.

Everly had been reading since dawn, eternally grateful that their overgrown lot was far from prying eyes. The textbook, like most others, had been banned by the Union decades before. It was anyone's guess as to why ornithology had been deemed worthy of censorship, but the fact that her dad's old bird book was illegal made it all the more fun to read. The fake book cover said, "The Democratic Union for a Sustainable Tomorrow: A Brief History." Most of the books in the study were legitimate; others wore masks.

It wasn't the colourful illustrations or the long Latin words that currently held Everly's interest; it was the notes in the margins. On this particular page about blackbirds—*icterids*—her dad had written:

grackles = plague

Not merely a flock. A plague of grackles. A murder of crows. These birds had bad reputations. They must've been criminals, too.

Everly looked into the sun. Based on its position above the misty horizon, study time was over. Her older sister would be ready for tea. Everly closed the book and trotted across the property. She pulled a fistful of leaves from the weed that had overtaken their garden. At least mint had a few uses, like flavouring toothpaste and soothing upset stomachs.

Everly entered the kitchen through the screen door, so riddled with holes it barely kept the grasshoppers out. Shelby was hunched over, adding pieces of wood to the stove. Everly could count the vertebrae under her sister's t-shirt.

"Shel, leave it," Everly said, a bit too forcefully.

Her sister, stubborn as always, smiled over her shoulder as she finished the task. "Happy Solstice," she greeted.

"Best day of the year for reading." Everly replied, placing the textbook on the counter.

"Agreed," Shelby said as she settled onto a stool. "Candlelight makes my eyes cross. What were you reading about?"

"Birds." Everly rushed to fill the kettle. She shouldn't have stayed out so long. A familiar tightness gripped her sternum, as if the house were slowly falling apart around her. Every surface of the kitchen was peeling like a sunburn—the linoleum floors, the whitewashed cupboards, the floral wallpaper. Fading away, just like her sister.

Shelby's skin was ashen and stretched over sallow cheeks. Her once auburn hair was dull and thinning. Harsh angles had replaced softness. For a nineteen-year-old to look so withered and frail was a crime against nature.

Everly was too distracted to notice the fragrance as she tore the mint and dropped the leaves into the boiling water. "How's the pain today?" she asked, handing Shelby a steaming mug.

"Manageable."

Everly pursed her lips.

"I'm good," Shelby insisted. "The new pills are better, I think."

The pills were garbage, but placebo couldn't hurt. Everly reached out the open window above the sink and grabbed a pair of navy cargo pants from the laundry line. There were holes where the knees used to be, and her toe got caught. She hopped around like a drunk flamingo while her sister watched, amused.

Shelby clucked her tongue. "Those pants are sanctionable, you know."

"It's on my to-do list."

"Speaking of sanctions…" Shelby pulled an unopened envelope

from her waistband. "You missed another class, you little brat."

Everly ground her molars. She'd been so careful to intercept the mail. "I just don't see the point," she grumbled, snatching the embossed envelope and hiding it behind her back. "Once I turn eighteen, I'll end up in the fishery with everybody else."

"Or you could go to college."

"What for?"

"Self-betterment," Shelby tried. "The Union controls the fishery, too, you know."

"Yeah, but if I can get my hands on a boat, I can sail away from here."

"To another Union colony. Where it'll be exactly the same. Come on, Everly. These fines are killing us."

Everly bristled. "What's killing us is useless doctors and bullshit medication."

"Tell me about it." Shelby blinked.

Everly arched her neck. The ceiling was also peeling. "I'm sorry, Shel. You know that's not what I meant. The Union has all of this amazing technology they're always bragging about, but they won't even get you a proper scan."

Shelby exhaled slowly. They'd had this conversation too many times. "The Union doesn't care about a traitor's offspring."

"But why make us live like this? It's 2075, but it might as well be the Stone Age. Dad told me that fifty years ago, everyone was connected— "

"Everly, please. What's the point in harping on about how things used to be?"

"But if the Union would just—"

"They won't."

Everly grimaced and looked out the window. How could her sister stay so calm? Her body was failing. Their parents were gone. Their lives were in ruins. All because of a war that happened before they were even born, one that put knowledge, medicine, and technology in the hands of a small, brutal few.

Shelby redirected. "Look, I know you hate that ridiculous

school, but it's the law. They won't let you work, so you might as well study. You can't buck the entire system all by yourself."

"I can try."

"Everly, I…I don't have the energy to keep fighting you on this." Shelby rested her chin on her knuckles. Blue veins snaked across the tops of her hands.

A fight—a real boomer with swearing and door slamming—would've felt good. The old Shelby would have wrestled her into submission.

"Okay, okay. School, yes, perfect," Everly lied. It had been months since she'd last set foot in the building. Most days were spent scrounging for food and bartering for medicine. Today, though, Everly had other plans. Shelby would not approve of those, either.

"Good," Shelby said with a tired smile. "If you hurry, you'll make the bus."

Everly threw on a navy button-down from the basket and grabbed her bag. Her oversized clothes felt like they were made of steel wool. She wanted to strip naked and jump into the sea. "I'll see you later," she called from the front door.

"Hey, you."

Everly looked back. Shelby raised her palm with her middle and ring fingers bent.

"Love you, too." Everly closed the front door behind her and struggled to get the latch to stick.

The twisted tree out front had barely produced any fruit, but she pocketed a couple of brown apples before jogging across the road to catch the armoured bus. As she climbed the steps, Everly considered riding it to the end of town, to look across the canal where the mainland beckoned from a distance. But it was pointless. The bus reeked of the docks—stale cigars and fish guts. A pungent reminder that Shelby was right. There was nowhere else to go.

The dirt road was lined with orange pines as Everly, the lone passenger, rumbled through the forest on tank tracks. Some of the trees were hanging on, despite the never-ending drought. Everything in town was equally dried up. Shop windows were covered in plywood, except for Union Surplus, with its navy blue garb and second-hand boots, and Union Books, which sold pamphlets and poorly-bound versions of history that left out the genocides. The bus stopped for a minute in front of the food dispensary so the driver could sneak a smoke.

Everly rested her temple against the glass. She jumped when a pair of knuckles rapped from outside.

"Hey, Dahl face," Jordan Knockwood said with a grin.

He had, by far, the most devastating umber eyes that had ever existed. Their friendship itself was an anomaly; a boy that beautiful should not know her name. But their dads had worked together before the university was 'restructured,' and the scrawny kid with a slight stutter had turned into someone who made it hard to keep her own words straight.

Everly cranked open the window. "What are you doing here?" she asked, trying to sound casual.

"Ran out of protein," Jordan replied, pointing to an oversized tin can of Union Tuna strapped to the back of his solarcycle. The one-wheeled machine had a sun-powered engine he'd spent years fixing up.

Jordan turned to nod at the bus driver, and Everly caught a glimpse of a swollen black eye. "Who did that to you?" she demanded.

"Who do you think?"

Her face flushed red, an irritating consequence of her whitefish complexion. "Which handlers?"

"Doesn't matter. They're all the same."

She exhaled slowly, surprised her breath didn't come out as smoke. "What did they get you for, anyway?"

"Curfew. I went fishing after dark. They caught me on the pier."

"Mudsuckers," she cussed. The Union thugs got off on harass-ing and beating innocent people for minor infractions, like trying to feed your family. For major ones, like theft or fighting back, they had no problem spraying brains across the sidewalk. Cape Fundy had to be one of the worst places; it couldn't be this awful everywhere.

"Where are you going, anyway?" Jordan changed the subject.

Besides the secretary in charge of attendance at the propaganda mill, he was probably the only person who'd noticed her absence from school. The boy paid attention; she'd give him that. "To the archive to do some more digging," Everly replied.

Jordan hummed. "Haven't you read that file a dozen times by now?"

"At least." Everly tried to ignore the subtext. She knew it was stupid, that no matter what evidence she found, it wouldn't change anything. But she couldn't just sit around while Shelby languished at home and her dad rotted away in a prison cell.

"Just be careful."

She raised her eyebrows. "This, coming from mister 'I fish when I want'? Dust off, pal."

Jordan flinched and looked around. The bus driver was unaffected. "Watch your mouth, Dahl. You know they don't tolerate that kind of talk. People have disappeared."

Everly brayed her lips like a pissed off pony. "I know. I'm sorry. I'll be more careful. Here." She grabbed one of the apples from her bag and dropped it out the window.

Jordan turned the gift over in his hand. "You sure?"

"Extra worms for protein."

Jordan smiled. "You've got something on your face," he said, thumbing his own cheek.

Everly touched her cheekbone and immediately regretted falling for the old joke. "Those are freckles, idiot," she said, trying to hide a blush with the palm of her hand.

He chuckled as he sped away, his long black braid swinging defiantly down his back. A sanctionable offence. People fought back in their own ways.

The driver finished his cigarette and lumbered up the steps on stiff knees. After a few more stops, Everly got off at the bottom of the War monument and walked the rest of the way to the archive, which was really just an old church turned into a government storage facility.

She paused on the sidewalk and stood on tiptoe to peek through the stained glass. The ancient clerk wasn't at her desk. The old bat was probably gulping screech in the back room; with any luck, she'd be gone for a while. Everly slipped behind the building and pushed open a window at knee height. A quick glance around to make sure no one was watching, and she lowered herself inside.

The basement felt like a catacomb. The courthouse used it as a dumping ground for all the closed case files in the region. Treason, mostly. It was divided into sections by rows of floor-to-ceiling shelves, all filled with cardboard boxes and alphabetized placards. As she made her way to the back, a shuffling sound moved through the stagnant air.

Everly twitched. She waited. No movement. No footfall. Probably just mice.

The boxes were layered with grime, except for the file she was after, making it easy to pick out. The lid read, "Case 14304 – Democratic Union for a Sustainable Tomorrow v. Nathaniel Dahl."

In hushed voices, the Union was often called another name. Their acronym, D.U.S.T., was among the most outlawed of words, especially when used to replace common obscenities. Their formal name was a total misnomer, as far as Everly was concerned—democracy was a thing of the past, and a union wasn't defined as a military state.

Careful not to make a sound, Everly carried the box to a fold-out table and lifted the lid. Ritualistically, she started with the photos taken of their house—her dad's Union badge, his glasses with a missing lens, an assortment of glass vials, some empty, some containing tiny rare feathers or hollow bird bones, and a pile of textbooks and maps scattered across his desk. Then came the investigation notes, so widely redacted they were practically illegible. But the overall thesis was clear. According to the Union, her dad was a traitor. The details didn't matter.

Two years ago, after he was imprisoned by handlers, Everly had expected—or at least hoped for—an uprising from the community. But, even though they knew Shelby was sick and the girls would be left destitute, lifelong friends and neighbours remained silent.

Disguise tyranny as law and order for long enough, and people eventually forget the difference.

The air became charged again, like the bricks in the two-hundred-year-old foundation had shifted. The hairs on the back of her neck bristled. Everly's hand hovered over a plastic evidence bag. She waited. Still nothing. Her mind was playing tricks.

Everly picked up the bag and removed the metal badge. Selling it was tempting, but not worth the risk. They were in enough trouble already. The badge was the size of a large coin, with a tarnished brass finish. The small magnifying glass set in the centre caught the light from the window and sent a prism across the table. Her dad, a biology professor, was forced to take a job with the Union as a low-level security guard. Cruelly, he'd been tasked with guarding the library. They'd locked him up over a few missing books.

With a sudden thump and a flutter of black feathers, a bird landed on the table in front of her. Everly nearly toppled backward from her chair. A foot in length from beak to tail, the common grackle was way too big to be hanging out in a sealed-off basement. She looked at the stained glass window. Closed. How long had the bird been down there? It whistled a pair of high notes.

"Shut up," she hissed.

The bird hopped closer. That was when she noticed the small roll of paper fastened to its leg. She reached forward to touch it, but the bird pecked her hand.

"Ouch! You—" With a flick of the wrist, Everly snatched the paper. "Ha!"

The bird blinked at her before fluttering into the joists. Everly unrolled the paper and held it up to the sunlight. The lettering was too small to make out, so she used the badge's magnifying glass to read the inscription:

> The warmer and wetter the weather,
> the better the fungi will grow;
> the closer two birds of a feather,
> the more that the moonlight will show.

Her mind swirled. It didn't make any sense. Not just the weird poem, but the undeniable fact that she'd seen the same handwriting just hours before. It was a perfect match to the notes in her dad's textbook. Questions filled her mind like billowing clouds, but they cleared when the floorboards creaked above her. Everly froze with the badge and the paper clenched in her fists. Something metallic scraped against the outer wall of the church, sending her guts into her ribs.

Everly pressed her back against the crumbling bricks as a pair of boots appeared in the window. There was a staircase to her right; she could bolt and try her luck with the Union clerk. Before she could make a move, the window opened. Her friend's face appeared.

"Jordan," she exhaled with relief. "The weirdest thing—"

"You have to come quick," he said, cutting her off. "It's your sister."

CHAPTER 2

The wind did its best to push Everly over as she fought to keep her balance on the back of the solarcycle. She didn't want to believe what Jordan had told her, but as they neared her house, she saw an Aeronautical Union Vehicle parked out front. The AUV had five circular rotors, each on its own axis. The official aircrafts were used for everything from herding cattle to hunting fugitives. There was nowhere they couldn't fly.

"What are they doing here?" she hissed as Jordan rolled the solarcycle behind a shed.

"I don't know, but it's never good."

As if on cue, the front door of Everly's house opened and two handlers appeared, dragging Shelby across the threshold. One had a beard, the other a large facial scar. Shelby was handcuffed. Her pale face was swollen and bruised. Everly started to move, magnetically drawn to the unbearable sight of her sister's suffering, but Jordan grabbed her arm.

"Let go of me!" she growled.

He released her, but blocked her path with his body. "If you go over there, they'll arrest you, too."

"For what?" she barked.

"Literally anything," he argued.

She knew he was right, but Everly wasn't in the mood to be reasonable. She shoved him away. "I can't just stand here!"

"Please, Everly! I don't want to lose you." Jordan's brow was creased, his jaw clenched tight. She'd never seen him so afraid.

Everly could barely think over her pounding heartbeat. "Alright," she conceded. "We'll go around."

Using the tall grasses for cover, they crept behind the weathered old house. When they reached the far side of the Dahl's property, they were within earshot of the handlers.

"Put her in the back," said the Beard.

"Please," Shelby begged. "I'm not well. If I—"

"Why are you still talking?" The Scar threw her to the ground. Groaning, Shelby curled up on the grass like a doomed baby bird.

"They're going to kill her," Everly wheezed.

Jordan scanned the area, but there was nothing to see—no neighbours, no escape routes. "What should we do?"

"Can you get across the road?"

"Yes, but—"

"Throw rocks, start a fire, anything to distract them."

"Everly…" Jordan put his hands on her shoulders, creating a space between them that felt safe. Intimate. But his eyes told a story with a tragic ending.

Everly's throat tightened; she didn't want to cry. Not now. "It'll be okay," she said like she knew it was true.

He dropped his hands. "Stay safe. If you make it out, go to my place and hide in the smoke house."

"Okay," Everly agreed. There were so many things she wanted to say, but there wasn't time. Everly blinked away tears as Jordan took off running.

Around the front of the house, the Beard dragged Shelby from the ground and dumped her in the back of the AUV. As he closed the door, a rock pinged off the bulletproof windshield. Jordan was fast and good with a slingshot. The rock hadn't done any damage, but the handlers were pissed.

The Beard fumbled with a remote. To Everly's horror, a drone rose from the top of the vehicle. It took off with an ear-splitting buzz. Jordan had a head start through the pines, but would it be enough? The drones had only three settings: seek, capture, and destroy.

The handlers un-holstered their weapons. As they crossed the dirt road and walked toward the forest, Everly could hear them chuckling.

Mudsuckers.

She tiptoed to the far side of the AUV and pulled on the handle. The door was locked. Shelby bolted upright in her seat. Her face dropped when she saw Everly outside of the window. Shelby started screaming, hitting her handcuffed wrists against the unbreakable glass. "Run, Everly! Get out of here! Go!" she bellowed.

Everly went numb. There was no way to get to her. No options. No hope of rescue. Only pain and submission and fear.

A cracking sound split the air. A bullet zipped by and lodged itself in the wooden siding of the house.

"Don't move!" the Beard shouted from the edge of the pines. Both handler guns were pointed right at Everly. The first was a warning shot; the second wouldn't be.

Suddenly, the solarcycle was below her. Only the rider wasn't Jordan. Everly had never seen this boy before. He was dark-skinned and long-limbed, his face mostly hidden behind a black hood.

"Everly, get on!" he yelled in a far-away accent.

Everly's head snapped back and forth. She looked at her sister through the window. Shelby was sobbing, the word "go" falling over and over from her bruised lips.

Everly dropped her ring and middle fingers and pressed her palm against the glass. Smeared with tears and blood, Shelby raised her cuffed hands and matched the sign.

The air cracked again. A bullet whizzed so close that Everly felt its vector. She jumped from the AUV and threw a leg over the solarcycle. They took off in the opposite direction of town on a road that ended at the docks.

"Who are you?" she shouted into the boy's ear as they raced away. Her arms were wrapped around his torso. Their bodies moved together with the inertia of the machine.

"I'm Micah," he shouted back.

"How do you know my name? Who sent you?"

Micah pulled back his hood, revealing short, coily hair. With one hand steering the bike, he used the other to shine a pen light on his neck. Just below his left earlobe was a tattoo, glowing against his Black skin—the shape of a crescent moon with the silhouette of a tree growing where the rest of the orb should be.

It took a second for her brain to compute, and when it did, she slapped her hand over her mouth. "You're a rebel," she gasped, feeling a mixture of awe and terror.

He clicked off the light and the tattoo vanished, invisible to the naked eye. "The Bloodwood Society lives," he said.

It was the name of the most notorious group on the planet. Late at night, with curtains drawn, her dad had told the girls stories about the last known counterforce on earth. The rebellion felt like folklore. Like urban legend. She'd never had reason to believe any of it, but the forbidden symbol had stirred something dangerous inside of her. It stood for hope.

The AUV appeared behind them, flying just above the ground and quickly closing the distance. The rattle of the rotors ached in her teeth.

"We're screwed," Everly shrieked.

"Shut up and listen," Micah snapped. "I can get us out of here, but you have to do exactly what I say."

Fisherfolk dived out of the way as the solarcycle sped through the crowded fishery. Micah side-swiped a pile of crab traps, sending the wooden contraptions flying into the air. The AUV swerved to miss the debris.

Everly bit her tongue and tasted blood as they sped through the fish yard and came perilously close to a group of townies. Micah manoeuvred the solarcycle onto the long ramshackle dock that lined the waterfront. The wood planks sounded like falling dominos as they sped along the seaboard, the frigid waves crashing between the slats.

"What are you doing?" Everly yelped.

"Saving your ass."

The end of the dock came into view, and Micah hit the hand brakes. They skidded and stopped inches from the final board. Two more AUVs swooped down behind them, landing weightlessly on the docks. A third hovered above the foamy water, blasting them with spray.

She tried to decipher which aircraft held her sister, but they were all identical. "We're surrounded," she cried.

"There's always a way out, but it'll cost you," Micah screamed over the mechanical chop of the rotors.

"Cost me what?"

"Everything. Your entire existence. You can never come back."

Nothing made any sense. She couldn't think. She needed more time. "What about my sister?"

"There's a plan, but it's a trade. Your life for hers."

Everly shook with adrenaline. She could surrender to the Union and face whatever punishment they had in store. Or she could take a chance on a total stranger. If he really was a rebel, that meant giving it all up. Walking away from her life and severing all ties. All with the blind hope that in exchange for her life, Shelby's might be spared.

"Why should I believe you?" she asked, every nerve alive and firing.

Micah twisted around to look at her. "Because we're your only shot."

Eyes burning, Everly met his gaze. She nodded her head, sealing the deal.

"Excellent choice," Micah said, jabbing a syringe into her neck.

The sudden pain made Everly fall backwards off the bike. She slapped a hand over the puncture wound. Before she could respond, a handler's booming voice filled the air.

"Step away from the vehicle with your hands up!"

Micah complied, leaving the solarcycle with fingers interlocked behind his neck.

Red dots danced across Everly's torso as she struggled to stand. Whatever he'd injected was travelling through her arteries at an impressive pace. The agony had a clarifying effect. Micah could be completely full of shit. He could have learned her name a thousand different ways. Tattooed his own neck. She could bribe the handlers. She and Shelby could go home. Pretend none of this had ever happened.

Everly opened her mouth to speak, but her tongue was thick

and the words wouldn't come. Sea water blasted between the boards. Through the chaos, Everly saw the drone appear above the fishery. Swinging beneath it was Jordan, hopelessly tangled in a synthetic net.

"Everly!" he screamed, struggling to break free. "Everly, run!"

She tried to call his name, but her jaw locked in place. The excruciating sensation surged upward and reached the space behind her skull. Her legs buckled.

Micah grabbed her around the waist and steadied her. "Hold your breath," he yelled in her ear.

In fractured tableaus, Everly saw the grenade. Watched Micah pull the pin with his teeth. Tracked it through the air. Watched it land on the dock. She saw Jordan, suspended above the blast as the pocket-size bomb went off.

Before blacking out, with her skin on fire and the icy-cold grip of the current dragging her under, Everly thought of her sister. Trapped inside the AUV as it exploded.

CHAPTER 3

Everly woke up screaming Shelby's name. When she tried to sit up, her forehead cracked against something solid. Terror ignited within her like a blowtorch. She was in a box. A coffin. The fear was ancient—*primordial,* her dad would have said. Her stomach twisted and threatened to empty. The blackness swirled with delirium.

A guttural cry erupted from her, a beastly sound she didn't even know she could make. Everly slammed her fists against the enclosure, but the walls held. She brought her hands to her heart; it rattled her entire rib cage.

Calm down. Breathe. Think.

Why would Micah go to the trouble of kidnapping her just to bury her alive?

Based on her level of thirst, she'd been in the box for a while. Seeing as she hadn't suffocated yet, odds were good she wasn't trapped under six feet of dirt. Everly pulled her feet beneath her and pushed with her knees. The lid cracked open slightly, revealing a latch by her thigh. She jimmied it loose and bucked her hips. The lid swung open. It crashed loudly to the floor.

She sat up, victorious, but her body quickly betrayed her, sending her into a fit of trembles and tearless sobs. The hyperventilation made her see stars. Everly could have gone on like this for hours, but the part of her that wanted to survive, to learn what really happened to her sister, took over. Two AUVs had exploded, but what about the third? Shelby might still be alive.

Everly wiped her nose with a grimy hand and scanned the area, taking in its stone walls and low ceiling. The air was thick and damp, and when she called out—"Hello?"—there was no response beyond the steady hiss of white steam rising through cracks in the ground.

Everly swung her legs over the edge and climbed out. The inside of the box was filled with a human-shaped mould that fit Everly's outline exactly, as if she were a porcelain doll carefully packaged for transport. The creepiness level was impossible to measure. The outside was untreated wood, covered in bark. She looked around and counted thirty-two boxes total. All empty. Was she the only one, or were there others?

The stone floor was slick with algae. A troop of mushrooms grew along the wall. Their gills emitted a clear, blue light that brightened the cave enough to find her way around. Bioluminescence. Her dad's dusty textbooks had finally come in handy. Everly was starving, but nature's most beautiful creations—jellyfish, coral snakes, poison dart frogs—were often the deadliest. There was no point in introducing radioactive fungi to her system, tasting colours for a while, and finally choking to death on her own tongue, so Everly moved on.

She surveyed the room, but there wasn't much else to see. She was alone, but if she waited around too long, someone was bound to show up. There was only one way out of the tomb-like cave, and unfortunately, it was through a menacing hole in the wall that billowed with white steam.

The stench of rotten eggs hit hard as she entered the tunnel. She gagged and committed to mouth breathing. In the darkness of the tunnel, Everly could barely make out her own feet. To keep her balance, she trailed her hand along the damp walls. After a few minutes and eighty-five careful paces, the ground transitioned from mud and rocks to wide, swollen planks.

A pair of boards bowed slightly underfoot. Between them, a black current shimmered in the darkness. Everly dropped to her knees. With one hand gripping a plank, she splashed the hot water into her mouth. It tasted as eggy as it smelled, but the sulphur spring satisfied her thirst. Everly stole a few more gulps from the aquifer before pressing on.

Drinkable water, check.

Everly lost count of her steps somewhere in the mid two-hundreds. Backtracking for a recount was the smart move, but just as she was about to turn around, she heard a soft whistle coming from the wall. Her inner ears tingled as she strained to listen.

"Who's there?" Everly whispered. No response. Only the hiss and drip of the underground. Until something rustled directly behind her.

Everly froze, spine hunched, elbows tucked. The unseen form drew in a slow, ragged breath. Everly spun around and came face-to-face with the most sinister visage she'd ever seen. It had a large beak and two glazed eyes made of round, reflective lenses—a demonic crow made of leather and studs.

"Run," said the crow. "You should run."

The tunnel whirled past her as she sprinted, rolling her ankles on the uneven floor. A shriek was building inside her, but she held it in as she pushed through a cloud of steam. Something fleshy reached out from the darkness and hooked her elbow, dragging Everly sideways into a crack in the wall.

A soft, dirty hand covered her mouth. It was attached to a short, heavy-set girl with bloodshot eyes. She looked up at Everly with an animal intensity that willed her to be silent. The sound of footsteps neared. The stalker paused, listening, and moved past the crevasse.

The girl waited for silence before dropping her hand. "Did you just wake up here, too?" she whispered.

Everly nodded. She fought the urge to turn away from the girl's sour breath, painfully aware that her own mouth was likely just as foul. Her saviour's dark wavy hair was thick with frizz, her round face smeared with soot. Her white blouse and pleated skirt looked like they'd been dropped down a chimney.

"Who's out there?" Everly asked.

"*No sé*," the girl replied with unfamiliar words. "Were you in the room? The one with the boxes?"

"Yes. How'd you get here?"

"I have no idea."

"What's your name?"

The girl swallowed thickly. "Inés, you?"

"Everly. I don't know what happened. I was supposed to be—"

"Joining the rebellion?" Inés finished the thought. "Me, too."

"We have to get out of here. Can you run?" Everly asked, trying to ignore the quiver in her own legs.

Inés nodded, but she looked unsure. Was it bravery or shock keeping them both from falling apart? Staying close, the girls squeezed out of the crevasse and stepped into the tunnel. Everly's spine tingled. With each step, there was a chance an attacker would burst through the steam. Thankfully, after a few minutes of blind navigation, the tunnel loosened its grip and the air began to clear.

The ceiling lifted, replaced by a vast, towering column. Moonbeams spilled in from openings high above them. The air smelled of dead leaves and ozone. All around, the walls were illuminated by tiny mushrooms—specks of blue light against the black void. They crawled the walls in swirling patterns, like fireworks suspended in space.

"That's the surface," Everly said, pointing at the cracks above with vegetation crawling through.

Inés craned her neck so hard, she nearly toppled over. "We're under a tree," she said.

The girl was right. The hollow trunk boasted a two-hundred-foot vertical column, anchored by tentacled roots and ancient stone. Everly spun as she took in the sight.

A loud crash rang out from across the trunk. Everly strained, trying to locate the source, but she couldn't tell which of the eight tunnels it had come from.

"What was that?" Inés gasped.

Everly held up her hand. For a few seconds, all she could hear was her own panting, but then the trunk filled with a boy's desperate wails. The girls backtracked to the only tunnel they'd stepped foot in so far, the one with a Roman numeral II carved above it that led back to the coffins. Crouched in the shadows, they huddled together, sucking in wet air and blowing out steam like horrified dragons. They listened helplessly as the wailing grew louder.

"They're torturing someone," Inés whispered.

"That's not our problem," Everly stated.

From the far side of the trunk, through a tunnel marked with the number VI, a boy stumbled into the open space. Both hands cupped his nose; his t-shirt was caked in blood. Underneath the gore was a frame too massive for someone their age. He was tall, with angular copper features and a black ponytail sticking out the back of a baseball cap. The whites of his eyes flashed in her direction, and Everly knew his fear matched her own.

"He's one of us," she whispered.

"How do you know?"

"Look at him. He's beat up and terrified." Her gut, although cramped and knotted, was telling her to help him. Everly knew it was a risk, but there was strength in numbers. And they could use some muscle on their team. Without conferring with Inés, Everly grabbed a pebble from the tunnel floor and chucked it out into the open. It clipped along the boarded floor, giving away their position. The boy turned his bloodied face toward them.

Inés was crouched on her toes, ready to bolt. "What are you doing? You said—"

"There's a good chance we'll need to fight our way out of this," Everly whispered. "Can you throw a punch?"

The girl looked at her tiny hands.

"I didn't think so. We need him." Everly called to the boy with a whisper. "Over here…"

Exposed and vulnerable in the wide-open space, the boy hesitated. The sound of nearing footsteps in the tunnel behind him took away his options. He ran to the opening of tunnel II, and he would have sprinted right by the girls if Everly hadn't grabbed the hem of his t-shirt. He landed beside her with a thump.

"Who are you?" he gasped. "What is this place?"

Inés hushed him with her hands as shadowy figures filled the trunk. The darkness hid the details, but Everly could tell they wore the same heinous crow mask she'd encountered earlier. The crows searched the empty space, but a crashing sound sent them careening down another tunnel.

"Who are they?" Everly whispered once the trunk was clear.

"I don't know," said the boy. "I just know they were chasing us."

"Us?" Everly blinked.

He looked away, but she caught a glimpse of the anguish. "I was with another kid—Jessie. We were running together, but they were gaining on us, and Jessie just…stopped. Gave up or something. I lost him in the steam, and they must have grabbed him because he started screaming. There was nothing I could do, so I took off. I think I broke my nose on a boulder back there."

"Let me see," Everly said. He turned to her, looking impossibly young for someone so hulkingly big. There was a gash across the bridge of his nose, but it wasn't deep. "You'll live. What's your name?"

"Katak."

"What are you, twenty five?"

"Seventeen," he said.

Everly eyed the man-child suspiciously. "I'm Everly. This is Inés."

"You both wake up in boxes?"

"Maybe twenty minutes ago," Inés confirmed.

"I'm so stupid," Katak growled. "Some rebellion this is."

"We were all tricked," Everly admitted. "We have to get out of here. But we need supplies."

"I know where they keep the food," Katak stated, dwarfing them as he rose to his full height. "Come on."

The girls exchanged glances. The promise of food made it hard to think about anything else.

The trio scuttled along the concave wall of the trunk and ducked into tunnel III, which Katak said he was 'pretty sure' was the right one. Not far from the entrance was an opening covered by a beaded curtain. When he passed through it, the tinkling sound might as well have been a blow horn. Everly tried to be stealthy, but the wooden beads clinked their dangerous music as she parted the curtain. How far would the sound carry underground?

Stacks of wooden crates lined the walls of the small storeroom. They were labelled with runny brushstrokes: rice, sugar cane, honey. Everly was so focused on the food that she failed to notice the body hunched over in the middle of the room.

A girl with waist-length black hair turned around. She looked about sixteen. Her crimson sari was caked in mud. There was a smear of red paint on her forehead. A gold nose ring glinted in the darkness. She gripped a broken arrow shaft and growled. "Come at me and I'll gut you."

There was no reason to doubt the threat, based on her deadly expression. But she was the only thing standing between them and food. Everly stepped forward, her upturned palms pale against the darkness. "We woke up in boxes," she said. "Is that what happened to you?"

The girl zipped the bag at her feet. "Get out of my way."

"Whatever you say," said Katak. "But you might want a weapon for the road."

The girl glared at him through narrowed eyes.

Keeping his hands in full view, Katak crossed the small cave. He shifted a wooden slider on the wall and revealed a collection of hunting gear—crossbows and arrows with colourful fletches, jagged knives with carved bone handles, ropes, traps, hatchets, and old rifles beside tattered boxes of cartridge casings.

The girl in red tossed her broken arrow aside and went about selecting a knife.

"You got a name?" Everly asked.

"Vashti."

"How much food can you fit in that bag?"

"Enough," she said. "For one."

Looking up and down the wall, Katak selected an animal snare and a large switchblade. "We can hunt once we're above ground," he said with enough confidence that Everly believed him. She picked out an army knife and flipped out the blade. Without her permission, the image of the blade sinking deep into someone's abdomen flashed before her. It made her feel even sicker than she already did.

Inés grabbed a short, bulbous club. Vashti swung a machete like she'd held one before.

"I'll stay with you until we are above ground," Vashti said, like she was doing them a favour. "After that, you're on your own."

With that motivational message hanging in the air, the group left the storeroom. When they filed into the trunk, Everly looked from opening to opening, trying to decide on a strategy, but it was useless—any tunnel could lead them to freedom, or death, or back to this exact spot. She was about to say so when the air above her whirred and a bird appeared from the abyss. It whistled before swooping into a tunnel to the right of the group.

The cryptic words from the poem flashed in her mind: *The closer two birds of a feather…*

"Follow that bird," Everly yipped. The others looked at her like she was crazy. She didn't have time to explain about the grackle in the archive or the strange message in her dad's handwriting, so she went with a simpler explanation: "You look for birds when you're lost at sea. This isn't the same thing, but I think it might lead us out of here."

"Completely random theory," Katak noted. "But alright. Bird tunnel it is."

"Okay," said Inés.

Vashti looked sceptical, but she nodded her willingness to go along with the featherbrain scheme.

There was no time for second guessing. They stepped to the mouth of the tunnel marked VIII. But just as they were about to enter it, a young woman materialized from the darkness. She had piercing green eyes and pale lips. The grackle rested on her shoulder, with their horrified expressions reflected in its beady eyes.

In the space behind her, the tunnel filled up with human-sized crows. She took a step forward, saying: "And just where, exactly, do you think you're going?"

CHAPTER 4

"Go, go!" Everly yelled. The group scattered. Everly ran for the next tunnel over but was met with a wall of bodies. Using spears and clubs, a murder of crows, two-hundred strong, spilled into the trunk, herding terrorized teens in from all directions.

Back in the cave, Everly had counted thirty-two boxes. She didn't need a proper tally to know she was surrounded by the rest of the kidnapping victims. The crows forced them all into a tight cluster. Everly fumbled with the army knife. A screwdriver popped up, and she held it in front of her. From the other side of the shrinking circle, Katak brandished his serrated blade with a look that said he was ready to use it.

As if unaware of the scene, the young woman in black, who couldn't be much older than Shelby, drifted across the open space. The crows parted to let her into the middle of the fray. She was tall and lean; her sharp face was framed by blunt bangs and long curly locks. "Be still," she commanded. In unison, the crows dropped to their knees, creating an impenetrable barrier around the newcomers. "Lights," she barked. A whooshing sound filled the air and torches burst to life along the walls.

Everly felt her knees lock and her trachea spasm. Was it the paralysis of panic or something else entirely?

"Let us go!" Katak bellowed, seemingly unaffected by the peculiar girl's charm. "I'm warning you."

"Katak Atta of the Inuit," she said, using an illegal identifier. "The knife you are holding is made of rubber, as are all the other weapons. If you tried to fire one of the rifles, you would have discovered that the bullets are blanks."

Everly looked at the screwdriver and pressed into her hand—it bent. Her heart sank. It was a fake. They'd been set up. She tossed her useless weapon into the dirt and stepped forward, channelling as much courage as she could muster. "We want out of here," she demanded, hands clenched and trembling at her sides.

"If you want to leave the island, you have to go through me," replied the girl in black. "My name is Tazeen Salah Mahmoud, but you may call me Taz. We are standing beneath a rather large Bloodwood tree, in what is affectionately referred to as the Root. My friends here are called the Rooters, while I am the Umbo, the centre of the shield, the leader and protector of this island. As such, I am the only person who can help you get home. As we say on the island, one cannot move between moons, so I am afraid you're stuck here for a while."

Tazeen's voice was like the purr of a mountain lion; it made Everly feel sticky and vulnerable, like a newborn fawn. Despite her fear, Everly spoke out again above the murmur of the crowd. "Who are you people?"

Tazeen's gaze honed in on her. "We are the rumours. We are the hidden hope. We are the remaining freedom fighters, the last of the uprising."

"You're the Bloodwood Society," Everly stated, trying to sound calm with sweat beading down her back and nails carving crescents into the palms of her hands. Based on her dad's stories, Everly had imagined the counterforce to be a well-armed militia, not a colony of underground freaks. But the bird on Tazeen's shoulder looked exactly like the one from the archive and the illustration in her dad's book. *Grackles equal plague.* That couldn't be a coincidence.

"That we are, Everly Dahl," Tazeen replied. "You are not in Nova Scotia anymore."

Everly crossed her arms protectively over her chest. The leader knew some details about her life, so what? That didn't mean Tazeen could be trusted. "Is my sister alive?" Everly demanded with more strength than she felt.

Tazeen tilted her head and considered her, intently. "I don't know," she said.

Everly's skin prickled. She'd taken Micah at his word, perhaps making the single biggest mistake of her life. "Micah said you'd get her out!" she blared.

An expression Everly couldn't quite place flashed across Tazeen's face—was it recognition?—but the Umbo quickly covered it with resolve. "Recruitment is out of my scope," she stated.

Everly felt a black hole open inside her, drawing her into oblivion. She'd trusted a stranger and lost her sister in the process. The so-called rebels lived in a hole in the ground. They were mostly children. Shelby was either dead or imprisoned by the Dust. Both fates were the same—she was gone. And now, Everly could never go home.

Vashti shoved her way to the front of the group. "What do you want with us?" she growled, violence flashing in her eyes.

"That is the most pressing question," Tazeen responded. "Listen well, Hema Vashti Jahanara. As I've alluded to, you are here because you have been recruited. You happen to possess certain characteristics we find attractive—desperation, mostly, and a well-established hatred for the Dust. We all share a common goal, to be free from the shackles of dictatorship and to be the masters of our own destinies, which is why we have decided to invite you to the island for a tryout, of sorts."

"A tryout?" Vashti parroted. "For what?"

"Think of the one thing you want most in the world, beyond, even, a life free from the Dust. Maybe you want to undo a mistake, or negotiate a release, or find something or someone that has been lost. Whatever it is, we can make it happen," said the Umbo.

"You'll grant us a wish?" Everly gaped. The infinite compression of the black hole was instantly replaced with the opposite sensation, the expanse of possibility. There was only one thing in the world she wanted.

"Indeed," Tazeen confirmed. "Should you successfully complete the trials and join the Bloodwood Society, we shall grant you each one request. But first, you will have to prove your worth. Our trials are challenges designed to test your limits and weed out the weak. Should the Dust capture you, we have to know for certain that you will be loyal to the cause. That you will be willing to sacrifice everything, including your own life, for the greater good.

"Whether you can sense it or not, the Dust—the Union as you call it—still controls you. We have to tear you down and rebuild you, brick by brick. Adults require different reprogramming, which is why you won't find any here. We are dedicated, entirely, to the next generation of freedom fighters. Meaning you. What comes next will be the most physically strenuous, mentally taxing, and emotionally draining experience of your lives. Not all of you will make it. But those who do will be given the chance to fight for the only thing worth having."

Katak spat into the dirt. "And we're supposed to trust you? You're just a weird-ass cult leader."

Tazeen's eyelids narrowed into feline slits. "Do not mistake my kindness for weakness, Katak. One does not come to lead this island without toppling a few giants. Best keep that in mind when speaking to the Umbo. The Dust calls us the rebellion, but we are much more than that. We are the last remaining sovereign nation on the planet. Every one of us here has passed the trials and committed our lives to the Bloodwood Society. Unfortunately, one newcomer has already proven himself unworthy."

"What did you do to him?" Katak barked. "What did you do to Jessie?"

Taz flicked her wrist, and two crows entered from a tunnel, holding up a skinny boy with a powder white complexion. He was bound and gagged, with eyes as wide as teacups.

"Let him go!" Katak hollered. He took a lumbering step toward the Umbo, but her minions blocked his path.

The crows dragged Jessie across the trunk, through the barrier of bodies, and into the middle of the circle. They yanked a trap door from the floorboards. The water of the aquifer glistened.

"Sadly for Jessie, surrender is never an option," said Tazeen. With a slight lift of her chin, the Umbo gave the order. The crows hoisted Jessie off the ground and dropped him into the underwater current. His body barely made a splash.

"What the hell?!" Everly screamed. A collective wail rose from the crowd, horror and panic uniting them in a cacophonous cry.

"You killed him!" Katak roared above the crowd. "You're a bunch of psychopaths. Get me out of here, or I'll skin you all alive!"

"We have done him a favour," Tazeen said, grimly. "On this island, the weak do not survive."

All around her, people were shouting and shoving. Everly pushed back, trying to avoid being crushed. None of it made any sense. Waking up in a locked box and watching a boy get murdered wasn't freedom; it was a new form of tyranny.

Immune to their suffering, Tazeen moved through the group of wailing newcomers. She straddled the watery opening with one foot on each side. Tazeen reached into her pockets and tossed two fistfuls of powder into the aquifer. A blue cloud rose and luffed the dark fabric of her garb like a pirate sail. The water glowed with an eerie fluorescent blue light as a million tiny specs of algae reacted to the powder, flowing with a hypnotising swirl into the depths of the underground.

"On the island, there are three rules you must obey," she proclaimed. "Rule number one is simple; you have to earn your keep, meaning you are expected to work and train like the rest of us. Rule number two, you will be punished and rewarded as a team. The people you found in the tunnels are now your bandmates. I hope fate has chosen well for you. You're strangers now, but if you're going to survive, you're going to have to learn to trust each other."

Everly glanced sideways and met Vashti's incredulous gaze. The four of them, Everly, Vashti, Inés, and Katak, were in this thing together. Whether they liked it or not.

"Please," Inés cut in. Her voice quivered so much, Everly was surprised she could use it at all. "I just want to go home…"

"Trust me, Inés de la Rosa," Taz purred. "That is not in your best interest. We have arrived at rule number three. Should any of you fail a trial, or prove yourselves undeserving in any capacity, you'll be given a serum called Other Death to wipe your memory, and you will be sent home to face whatever fate you left behind. That is your only way off the island.

"You have until the Blood Moon to prove your worth. To honour the eight phases of the moon, you will be tested eight times. Unbeknownst to you, you have already completed your first trial, known as the Labyrinth. You needed to seek allies and band together. Aside from Jessie, you have all succeeded."

"You're saying, if we pass these challenges, you'll let us join the Bloodwood Society and you'll grant us some sort of special request," Everly summarized. "And we can ask for anything?"

"I'm not a magician," Tazeen replied. "But if it is possible, the Bloodwood Society will make it happen."

Everly could feel the weight of the newcomers' gaze upon her. She didn't want to speak for them, but another chance for questions might not come around. "How do we know you're telling the truth?" she asked.

"I am afraid you've got it backwards. It is you who must prove yourselves trustworthy. First, we must discover your innermost desire. The water will reveal it to me. This, my friends, is your second trial. We call it, the Wishing Well."

CHAPTER 5

A murmur swept across the newcomers like wind through tall grasses. Had they heard correctly? Everly wasn't worried about being outed as a Unionist; she hated the tyrants with every fibre of her being. But could Taz really see inside her mind and learn her deepest desires? The idea made her itch.

"We will start with the only band to successfully locate weapons," the Umbo announced. "Katak, Vashti, Everly, and Inés. Since you are already down a bandmate, with Jessie's untimely departure, I'll do my best to even the odds by assigning you a gifted mentor. Allow me to introduce Micah Kikwete."

Everly scanned the crowd, looking for the boy who'd gotten her into this mess. Slowly, a crow stood and removed his mask. Micah was wearing a beige shirt with a stretched out neck that revealed a band of shiny scar tissue arching over his shoulder. He looked confused at first, then thoroughly unimpressed. He opened his mouth to protest, but Tazeen cut him off. "We are certain you will make the Bloodwood Society proud."

Micah set his jaw. Everly scowled at him, sending invisible daggers. He spotted her amongst the crowd and smirked. The two of them had much to discuss.

"Katak Atta," summoned Taz. "Step forward, and I will tell you your wish."

The hulking boy hesitated, but what choice did he have? A head taller than anyone else in the crowd, he shuffled through the bodies until he was face-to-face with the Umbo. The water swirled between them. The algae glowed. He straightened his back and sniffed through blood-crusted nostrils. "This better be good."

Tazeen leaned forward, water droplets glistening in her thick, wavy hair. "Put your face in the water. You will know when to resurface."

Katak looked dubious. He glanced sideways at his newly named bandmates, but Everly and the others had nothing to offer. The room was silent as he dropped to his knees and braced his hands in the dirt on either side of the pool. He held his breath and dunked his head. The water exhaled a cloud of steam that obscured his outline. He stayed under for what felt like an eternity, until an invisible force flung the boy backward, sending him sprawling.

Taz crouched in front of him and put two fingers on each of his temples. She began to whisper. With each passing second, Katak's sturdy frame lost its rigidness. Finally, Taz dropped her hands. "Katak, is this your wish?"

"Yes," he whispered, with his chin on his chest.

"I give you my word," said the Umbo.

Katak looked at her with wide-open eyes. He moved to the edge of the crowd and sat with his cap pulled all the way down.

"Hema Vashti Jahanara," Tazeen summoned.

Vashti looked defiant as she walked over to Taz, pulling her long black hair into a braid before kneeling at the bubbling pool. She leaned forward and dipped her face in the water. Unlike Katak who'd stayed under for nearly a minute, Vashti sprang back within seconds. She scrambled away from Taz. "Stay away from me, witch!" she screamed.

Taz made a gentle wave-like motion with her hands, and the tension left Vashti's body. Whatever the Umbo said next made Vashti's head fall back; she stared into the towering pillar of the Bloodwood's trunk.

"Is this your wish?" Taz asked, calmly.

Vashti snapped back with a start, eyes boring into the Umbo's. "It is my wish," she said. "But it's impossible."

"I give you my word," said the Umbo.

Inés followed the same process and came out of it looking just as shocked and broken as the first two. Now, it was Everly's turn. She moved slowly to the shimmering pool, looking across at Tazeen. The mesmerizing light danced across the Umbo's brown skin.

"Everly Dahl, are you ready to learn what you want most in the world?" Taz whispered. The room and everyone else in it disappeared.

Everly swallowed hard. "I'm ready," she said. She dropped to her knees and submerged her face in the water. The feelings of alarm and doubt dissipated. Her mind cleared. She stepped inside of her own consciousness and was able to see thoughts and desires take shape.

Some were well known to her: to find out what happened to Shelby, to cure her sister, to rescue Jordan, to convince him to love her back. Then there were things that she longed for, that she knew could never be. Existing without the shackles of grief and the constant pain of loneliness. Growing up with a mom, instead of losing her to depression. Stopping the handlers when they came for her dad.

Everly wanted to stay within the moment of clarity, but she felt the Umbo's hands on her shoulders, pulling her back. With water dripping from her hair, she met Tazeen's gaze. From across the water, the Umbo leaned in and brushed her temples with calloused fingertips.

Her words hit like a freight train. If true, Tazeen's promise would unbreak the broken pieces of Everly's life. One solution would lead to many other solutions; one wish would grant many wishes. Tears swelled in Everly's eyes. Her sinuses burned.

"Is this your wish?" Taz asked.

She felt fractured in two. A voice inside was whispering, *this is a trap*. But Everly didn't care. She had nothing left to lose. "Yes, it's my wish," she said through a tight throat.

"I give you my word."

With that, Tazeen summoned Katak, Vashti, and Inés back to the pool. Their motions were slow, their eyes clouded. "There is one final step. Join hands around the water to receive the aquifer's blessing. In this way, you will become a band. In this way, you make a vow and commit to the trials."

Based on the day's events, Everly's decision was surprisingly easy—stay here and fight for her life, or return home and surrender it. But she couldn't do it alone. She needed her bandmates to come to the same conclusion. She reached out for Katak and felt his hand swallow hers. Her fingers interlocked with Inés's, their palms sealed with heat and sweat. Off to the side, Vashti scowled, the blue light flashing in her dark irises. She huffed, having made her decision, and grabbed Everly and Inés by the wrists.

Tazeen began to chant: "A Bloodwood promise is binding, may none put it asunder. The root of the root…"

"The salt of the earth," said the Rooters.

"Those who join will be rewarded, those who leave, forever lost. The root of the root…"

"The salt of the earth."

A drum began to thump. Then two. Then three. Their rhythms became interwoven; the sound of one drum with many hands. "This is our heartbeat," Taz called above the pounding noise. "Our heartbeats are one. Feel the driving force. Feel the darkness. Feel the heat. Hold onto it as your skin begins to glow. As we all ignite. The root of the root…"

"The salt of the earth!"

Everly's vision went black.

She was standing on the edge of the bluffs staring down at a blanket of fog.

"Be careful, Everly," a man's voice said. "Don't come too close."

She looked frenziedly from side to side, but Everly couldn't make anything out through the fog. "Where are you?" she called.

"Don't fall, sweet girl. Be careful," he said.

Everly looked to where her house should be but wasn't. In front of her, the fog cleared, revealing the jagged cliffs and her dad standing directly in front of her.

"Why'd you do it?" Everly cried. "How could you leave us behind?"

He met Everly's gaze with sorrowful eyes. He opened his arms, and Everly folded into them with a relief so dazzling it almost felt like death. Her dad pressed his warm lips against her forehead.

"Never forget how much I love you," he whispered. Twisting his body, Nathaniel threw his youngest daughter over the bluffs.

Everly watched, like a seagull floating on an updraft, as her body plummeted—down, down, down—into the grey foam of the angry sea. Before she was dragged beneath the waves, Everly heard the words Taz had spoken, as if they had come from the ocean itself: *Your sister is alive. We can get them both out.*

CHAPTER 6

Everly awakened with her head on a pile of dirt, which was never a good sign. Cracks in the ceiling let daylight through. The long, cramped cave was filled with thirty-something newcomers, hanging out in straw-lined nooks carved out of the walls. Katak was stuffed inside one of them, looking like an oversized rabbit in an undersized den. Further down, Vashti, who fit more comfortably in the carved out space, was busy picking dirt from her fingernails.

"Guys, she's awake," Inés said from her spot on the floor.

Everly tried to sit up in the nook, but immediately got a head rush.

"Here, drink this," Inés offered, handing her a metal canteen.

Everly drank her fill of the eggy water. "Where are we?" she asked, wiping her mouth with the collar of her shirt.

"In the burrow," Inés replied. "The newcomers all sleep together in one cave."

"Harder for us to escape," Vashti snarked, too preoccupied with her pruning to look up.

"What happened last night?" Everly asked. The fog in her brain was refusing to lift.

"Taz killed you," Vashti stated.

Inés scowled. "Clearly not."

From across the cave, Everly could feel Katak's eyes on her. "You fainted," he explained. "It was scary."

"Your eyes rolled back, and you started talking gibberish," Vashti elaborated.

"Taz said you were having a vision," added Katak. "Was she right?"

An uncomfortable heat flooded Everly's face. "I saw something," she admitted. "But I don't know what it was."

"What did it feel like?" he pressed.

"What's with the interrogation?" she bristled. Katak looked at the floor and nudged a glowing mushroom with his toe. Seeing as they'd stayed by her side all night long, she probably owed them some sort of an explanation, or maybe some reassurance that she wasn't completely unstable. Everly closed her eyes, trying to recall the sensations. Was it a vision, a hallucination, a dream, or maybe something else? "It was like being inside someone else's memory," she finally said.

Inés anxiously touched the crucifix that hung around her neck. Katak watched Everly closely. "But what did you see?"

Everly hesitated, struggling to come up with a safe answer. "I saw my dad."

"Could've been *Amaruq*," Katak said.

Everly rubbed her eyes. "*Ama* what?"

"A Trickster. The wolf spirit. Be careful. Sometimes they're helpers. Other times, they're just out to mess with you."

Be careful, Everly. Her dad's caution echoed through her bones. She tried to recall the sequence of events from the Wishing Well, but everything from before and after felt blurry. "We...we all agreed to stay here," Everly recalled.

"We *vowed* to stay," Vashti corrected. "Which means we're all trapped here until the imaginary Blood Moon arrives, or we die or get banished. Whichever comes first."

Everly remembered. Last night, in the steam and the darkness, the decision had been clear. But in the light of day, still kidnapped, still trapped underground, she wasn't so sure. She'd sold her life to the Bloodwood Society. There was no going back now.

"I know this sounds crazy," said Inés. "But Tazeen knew things about me she couldn't possibly know."

"Everything Taz said was complete bullshit," Vashti said. "She might as well have offered me a unicorn to fly away on."

"Unicorns don't fly," Inés pointed out. "That's Pegasus."

"What are you even talking about?" Vashti scoffed.

While the girls hashed out a useless argument over mythological creatures, Everly crammed her feet into her boots. Katak came over and leaned against the wall beside her. "You okay?"

"Never better."

"Do you think Taz is telling the truth? Can Bloodwood do the things she said?"

"No idea," Everly admitted. Since Katak was in a questioning mood, she decided to toss one back at him. "What did you wish for?"

"You first," he said.

Everly was still trying to wrap her mind around Tazeen's offer. If her sister had survived, she'd be locked away by now, to live out her limited days behind bars. Was the Bloodwood Society really capable of freeing people from the clutches of the Dust? Everly needed more than a unicorn. She needed a miracle. "The Dust has my dad," Everly said, keeping to the facts that she knew were true. "Tazeen says Bloodwood can get him out."

"I'm sorry," Katak said, solemnly. "I left someone behind, too. Her name is Napatsi."

Vashti abruptly exited her own conversation to ask, "Is she your girlfriend or something?"

"No, she's just a kid. But she doesn't have anyone else. Tazeen said they could help her."

The sound of someone clearing their throat drew the group's attention to the mouth of the cave. Their mentor was leaning against the wall, wearing camo shorts and an unbuttoned shirt. His muscles were not hard to look at, but Everly quickly dropped her gaze. Why did her stupid cheeks always have to give her away?

"Move your asses," he barked down the length of the burrow. "Taz has something special planned." Micah disappeared before anyone could argue.

Together, the newcomers made their way through the tunnel. Cracks in the ceiling let in slivers of sunlight that made the underground significantly less terrifying than the night before. Soon, they were standing, once again, beneath the hollow trunk. Birds swooped through sunbeams, swirling particles of dust onto cyclones.

The newcomers split into bands to meet with their newly-assigned mentors.

In the middle of the trunk, Micah stood with his hands on his hips looking supremely unimpressed. "I don't know how I got so lucky," he jeered when they were close enough to hear.

"What's your problem, man?" Katak sniffed.

"Oh, I've got bigger problems than you could ever imagine. And on top of them, Tazeen and the Lemurs, in all of their wisdom, are making me babysit."

"You want to go?" Katak asked, inviting Micah to brawl as if it were nothing. Katak probably had fifty pounds on him, but Micah's long, sinewy arms and legs suggested an agility that Katak couldn't match. It would be a good fight, but carnage wouldn't improve their situation.

"I would love to, Katak. That would be really fun for me, but it's not worth her majesty's wrath."

"I've got a question," Vashti swooped in with false sweetness. "Micah Kikwete. Is that an unusual name wherever you're from, or would it be fairly easy to track your family down?"

Their mentor's nostrils flared. "It's not a good idea to threaten me, little girl." He pulled a knife from his belt. Everly froze. He removed a stick of sugarcane from his waistband and carved off a sliver, chewing it while he spoke. "Stop wasting time and listen up. Don't bother running or trying to escape. As the Umbo said, you can't move between moons, so you're stuck here for a while. From now on, we're going to put you through hell to see if you're worth it, but my bet is at least one of you breaks before the end of the day. And I'd put money on that person being you."

Everly looked up. He was pointing a long finger directly at her. Her ears burned. Her hands clenched into fists. It was the arrogance that she couldn't stand, the same sense of impunity that the handlers had back home. "What makes you so sure?" her mouth said without permission.

Micah smirked. He motioned like he was fainting, the back of his hand pressed against his forehead. "Random unconsciousness is never a good sign. That, and I've read your file. You don't stand a chance."

Everly blushed with a mixture of rage and shame. Could he get inside her brain, too? Crack her open like an egg and peer at the yolk inside?

"I could have told you that," Vashti laughed. In a lightning-fast motion, Micah threw his knife into the dirt between her sandals. She yelped and jumped backwards.

"Not another word," Micah warned. Vashti pressed her hands into a prayer position and bowed her head. The next movement was practised and quick, but Everly caught it—Vashti used her foot to sweep the knife under her sari. Everly stared at the ground, waiting for Micah to notice and explode.

Instead, he turned and grabbed a hold of a rope that was camouflaged against the trunk. With a quick tug, his body snapped skyward and disappeared into the dark void above.

After several seconds of stunned silence, Katak took off his cap and slapped it against his thigh. "What the hell just happened?" he squawked.

Everly hushed him, straining to identify a sound far above. She looked into the dark hollow of the tree and could see a shapeless shifting, like carpenter ants on a black mound.

"This is bullshit!" Vashti shouted just as Everly recognized the sound. She lunged forward and covered Vashti's mouth with her hand. Vashti flipped her to the ground and leered over her, simmering. "Don't touch me," she glowered. Her eyes were serpentine.

Everly pointed upward. "Bats," she whispered.

Vashti looked up and listened, giving Everly a chance to roll out of her warpath. She was about to tell her to go dust herself, when a piece of wood the size of a chessboard landed in the dirt between them. It was attached to the rope, which Vashti snatched away.

"Careful, something might come down and crush you. Which would be devastating," Everly jeered.

"I'm not that easy to kill," Vashti smirked. She stepped onto the board, pulled down hard on the rope, and took off.

Everly followed the flash of red fabric as it skyrocketed up the trunk. The angry bats squeaked their displeasure at the intrusion as the board returned to the ground.

"That's intense," Katak said, craning his neck. "I hope nobody's afraid of heights."

The vision of her father flickered like static in the back of Everly's mind. Heights didn't scare her, but she respected what they stood for.

"We don't really have a choice," Inés pointed out.

Ignoring every instinct she possessed, Everly stepped onto the board and pulled down on the rope. A high-pitched whistle reverberated in her ears as she hurtled upwards. Before she could scream, she was thrown through a burlap cover and landed on her belly, cushioned slightly by a bed of moss. She rolled over onto her back and stared up from the foot of a giant.

Above her was the tallest tree she'd ever seen, stretching like an arrow pointing straight at the gods. Its layered bark melted from blood orange to burgundy, its trunk scarred with swirling knots. For two-thirds of its height, the tree was bare, a column of ancient wood so certain of its place in time and space that Everly was filled with the terrifying sense she was about to be stomped out of existence. When branches finally appeared, they cast an immense circular shadow around the base of the trunk.

The air above ground was thick with humidity. White moths fluttered by like pieces of confetti. A bright yellow slug smiled down at her. Between needled branches, she spotted a periwinkle sky. Rolling aerial roots spread out across a mossy clearing. Where they finally dived underground, a dense jungle sprung up, forming a green wall.

When her breath returned, Everly stood and brushed herself off. She teetered along an aerial root, following her curiosity halfway around the tree. Here, the earth fell away and the roots spread like tentacles, reaching down a jagged rock face. Blasting out from the cliff, a waterfall careened to the bottom of a rocky canyon. It reminded Everly of the aquifer, of the multiple holes covered by rickety planks. One wrong step was all it would take.

The mist from the falls drenched her face, and Everly licked the droplets on her lips. Back home, the Dust controlled the water and diverted it all to crops, frying everything else. But here, everything was emerald green and lush. Somehow this island had escaped the fate of the rest of the planet.

A sharp whistle sounded from the jungle's edge. Micah stood, waving his hand, beckoning, before ducking into the undergrowth. In a bolt of red, Vashti took off across the clearing.

Everly started to run. Newcomers shot out from several folds in the trunk, and she spotted Katak and Inés. "Move it!" she yelled. At the edge of the clearing, the jungle rose and blocked her path. She pushed through a small opening, revealing a red dirt trail through the underbrush. The foliage formed a low canopy, creating an iridescent tunnel.

Just ahead, Vashti was running with effortless strides. Even with yards of fabric gathered at her waist, she was making it look easy.

The path herded Everly back and forth; branches reached out and scratched her arms as she passed. After stumbling through a knee-deep mud puddle, Everly saw an opening that led to a beach. The sand was the colour of coffee grinds, and beyond it was a crystalline body of water. The sea back home was black in the sun and silver during storms. Aquamarine was for vintage postcards. Everly ran onto the beach, and her sense of awe was replaced by nausea. She bent forward and fought the urge to vomit.

When Katak and Inés caught up with her, they were both drenched in sweat and clearly suffering, which made her feel a bit better.

"So, they expect us all to be marathoners," Katak wheezed, flipping his cap around. "That's just great."

A handful of newcomers sprinted by them.

"Is everyone an athlete?" Inés coughed.

Halfway up the beach, Vashti was standing with her hands on her hips. The fabric of her sari luffed behind her. Further on, where the sand ran into rocky cliffs, the Rooters were gathered on makeshift bleachers, hollering and cheering as the newcomers approached.

Stretched out like a living nightmare along the shore was an obstacle course. "There it is," Everly said between gasps. "Micah promised us something special."

"*Ay Dios mio,*" Inés gasped. "How will we…"

"We're screwed," Katak stated.

Everly stood up, the nausea replaced by dread. Tazeen had warned them that only the strong would survive. And their third trial was about to tear them apart.

CHAPTER 7

The remaining newcomers spilled onto the beach from different paths, each realizing the enormity of the challenge in their own time. Some broke down in tears. Others collapsed into the sand. A few looked completely dumbfounded. Everly could relate—the missiles kept dropping, and before they could recover from one shockwave, another bomb detonated.

The ragged recruits moved down the beach and approached a set of rickety bleachers. The air was filled with raucous noise from drums, bells, and conchs. The bleachers bounced under the weight of two hundred Rooters, waving colourful flags with animals on them—fire ants, earthworms, bilbies, and more. Everly spotted a lemur flag and a piece of the puzzle clicked into place; the different bands were named after creatures that lived underground.

Everly scanned the crowd and spotted Tazeen standing on the top row. The Umbo whistled a deafening note. "Welcome to your third trial!" she shouted. The Rooters roared like scurvied pirates.

Beside her, a beefy boy with red scruff stood up. "Silence!" he bellowed. A hush spread through the spectators.

"Thank you, Andrew," said Tazeen. "My dear newcomers, we call this trial the Eliminator. You must make your way through each of the five obstacles, starting with the Wall of Shame, and finishing with The Last Resort. It's a race, of course, and the first across the finish line will be given a proper meal. Failure to complete the course will result in banishment from the island."

Everly's head moved on a swivel, taking in the layout of the course. The connective tissue that kept her guts in place had come undone during the run. She more-or-less understood the words coming out of Tazeen's mouth, but how was she supposed to compete with her organs already on the brink of failure?

"Newcomers, are you ready?!" the Umbo yelled.

"No!" Inés squeaked. The Rooters laughed at her, which made Everly's nostrils flare.

Tazeen grinned. "Min Jun, please do the honours. On your marks, get set…"

From high in the stands, a monkish-looking boy with a shaved head blew into a conch shell, starting the race with a long, low note.

The newcomers took off across the sand. Everly ran into the bedlam, trying to make a plan. Near the front, Vashti moved swiftly, shoving and tripping anyone within reach. The girl's actions were brutal, but Everly found herself committing the same acts whenever someone got too close. Somewhere beyond the finish line was Shelby. Coming in last was not an option.

Everly fought her way to the bottom of the Wall of Shame, a web made of knotted rope. She started to climb. About halfway up, Everly felt a hand wrapped around her ankle. Without even thinking, she kicked. Her foot connected with a girl's jaw, and she fell backwards onto the sand. Based on her shriek and the angle of her shinbone, the girl's leg had broken on impact. A boy with tight brown curls and thick forearms ran over to her and examined the damage. He looked up at Everly, eyes filled with rage.

"Jax, she's done for," another girl called from the wall.

"We're not leaving her!" the boy, Jax, barked back.

There was no stopping. No room for sympathies. Too much was on the line. Everly climbed to the top of the structure as Jax and his bandmate argued. The Wall of Shame was aptly named; Everly was disgusted with her own actions, but she didn't look back again.

"Nice one," Vashti said from the crossbar at the top. As she swung a leg over, her sari snagged. The harder she wrenched on it, the more hopelessly entangled she became. The Rooters mocked her from the stands as Vashti cursed vilely.

"Use the blade," Everly suggested, instantly regretting it.

Vashti scowled and flashed Micah's knife. "Mind your business," she warned.

"Be less obvious," Everly quipped before dropping down on the far side of the rope wall.

Katak was already halfway across the long stretch of monkey bars when Everly reached the next obstacle. Beside it was a wooden sign with painted lettering: Death Drop. Katak's toes dangled just inches above a gurgling mud pit that smelled putrid but didn't look all that deadly. A few newcomers were struggling to find a rhythm as they swung across the uneven gaps.

Too short to reach the first bar, Inés was stuck on the ground. "I need a boost," she said, looking around for help.

"Climb the post," Everly suggested. Without breaking stride, she jumped and caught the bar. Her elbows hyper-extended, and three bars in, she considered letting herself drop to the swampy pool below. But the surface of the mud started to bubble, and the back of something scaly and horrifying revealed itself one vertebrae at a time. Everly shrieked and pulled her knees up as a crocodile heaved its giant form from the mud and snapped its monstrous jaws. "Katak, look out!" she shrieked.

Two more reptiles reared, their attention shifting to the boy's low-hanging limbs. "Holy shit!" Katak hollered, struggling to catch a heel on the bar in front of him. A shadow moved across the muddy water, and Everly glanced up to see Vashti balancing on top of the bars. Stripped down to a cropped red blouse and black shorts, she strode directly over Everly without so much as a nod.

"Little help?!" Katak yelled as Vashti passed him over, too. She pretended not to notice his predicament. At the end of the bars, she hit the sand running, leaving her bandmates behind to deal with the monsters.

Crawling on her hands and knees, Inés appeared above Everly. "What do I—"

"Help Katak!" Everly shouted. He was the closest to being eaten, with three crocodiles now vying for his limbs.

Inés stretched herself across the bars and reached down to him.

"Grab my foot!" Katak yelled. He kicked hard, and Inés caught his heel, helping him to hook it in place. Now that he had some leverage, the boy hoisted himself away from danger. "You good?" he asked Everly over his shoulder.

With enough adrenaline in her blood to flip a small car, Everly lifted herself between the bars. The Rooters shouted and cheered as the crocodiles lunged from the water, and Everly did her best to ignore them—the crocs and the mob—as she bear-crawled across the structure.

Close behind her, a boy slipped from the bars; his body slapped the water. Everly's feet sunk into the black sand as she ran with her head down. She couldn't bear to watch.

The next obstacle shimmered like a desert mirage; a bed of red-hot coals covered a twenty-foot stretch of sand dubbed the Brimstone Block. It was outfitted with poles spread out like pegs on a cribbage board. Half the newcomers had already made it to the far side. Vashti was balanced on top of a pole around the halfway point. Having learned from the monkey bars, Inés scurried up the nearest pole and leapt with impressive agility to the next one.

Fully intending to duplicate her bandmate's execution, Everly scrambled up the pole and leaped to the next, but she misjudged the distance and sprawled painfully across the top. Had it been any sharper, she would have been skewered. The structure shook as Katak appeared below her, clinging to the side. Everly watched as he propelled himself from pole to pole, keeping low and overtaking Vashti and Inés.

"Katak!" Inés called out near the end of the coal pit. "The last gap is too big. I'll never make it."

Hanging off the final pole, Katak turned around and reached for her. Without hesitation, Inés jumped and caught his hand. He swung her into place. Sparks flew up behind them as they hit the ground in tandem.

Vashti tisked. "If she didn't have a pet giant, she'd be screwed."

"Jealous?" Everly panted.

"Devastatingly," Vashti chafed. With one last powerful leap, she completed the obstacle. If the coals were roasting her uncovered toes as she sprinted, the girl didn't let on.

Smoke burned Everly's eyes as she stuck the final jump and slid to the ground, never more grateful for her heavy Union-issued combat boots. Only two challenges remained. The finish line at the base of the bleachers was in sight.

The bamboo quarter pipe stopped the newcomers in their tracks. They were stuck at the bottom of a 30-foot vertical ramp, trying to figure a way to the top. The Pipe Dream extended halfway into the water with waves crashing against its supports.

With a powerful surge, Katak ran up the ramp and caught the lip, pulling himself onto the platform. "Come on, come on," he pleaded, motioning to the girls.

A whistle sounded, and Everly looked over to see Tazeen with her thumb and finger pressed between her lips. From the jungle fringe, a pack of orange and black wild dogs came tearing across the beach, red-eyed and bone thin. Panic swept through the newcomers who began clamoring and pushing at random.

Skirting the crowd, Inés ran hard at the pipe, stretching to reach Katak's outstretched hand. Not one to waste an opportunity, Vashti followed suit and wrapped her arms around Inés's torso. Everly joined the chain at the bottom.

"Get off me!" Vashti glowered.

"You get off me!" Inés cried.

Katak grunted as he heaved his bandmates onto the platform. Without thanks or even acknowledgement, Vashti plugged her nose and jumped off the far side, disappearing into the waves below.

Katak looked back down at the newcomers who were now trying to form a human ladder. Everly could sense his despair as the wild dogs drew closer. "It's an elimination race, Katak," she reminded him, and then felt the guilt rush in. Was she really okay with feeding a bunch of helpless kids to the dogs?

Everly spotted a rope dangling over the far edge. "Help me," she said, and together, she and Katak hauled the rope from the water and dropped it down the quarter pipe. At least now, the others stood a chance.

With no other way off the platform, Everly careened into the

47

cloudy sea with Katak and Inés at her side. As she fell, Everly saw the black waters of the bluffs from back home. She screamed, but was silenced by salt water. A current swept her parallel to the beach, until a wave tumbled her like wet laundry and dumped her on the sandy shore.

The final challenge loomed—bamboo rods formed a tunnel with leafy branches hanging down like curtains. Her bandmates disappeared through the foliage. Everly was hot on their heels and didn't have time to process their screams. The instant the first leaf brushed her skin, she knew it was suicide nettle.

The pain zipped along her flesh like an electric shock. A branch slapped her across the cheek, and the pain was so severe it knocked her to her knees. In the unseeable distance, Rooters cheered; someone must have crossed the finish line.

Everly sacrificed her hands and parted the branches as she stumbled forward, but she tripped over a body at her feet. Inés's face and arms were covered in egg-sized blisters. "We have to keep going," Everly insisted. "When I say go, run as hard as you can."

Dead-eyed and convulsing from the pain, Inés clambered to her feet.

Everly crossed her forearms in front of her. "Go!" she shouted. She busted through the end of the tunnel and limped across the finish line. She dropped to her knees and vomited salt water in front of a jeering crowd. Her flesh was burned and blistered, and her pelvis felt like she'd been beaten with a bat. Everly wanted to cry, but she couldn't give the Rooters the satisfaction. She hated them all so much.

An eternity later, when the last kid crawled across the finish line, a lanky boy with dog bites on his shins, the Rooters booed. Tazeen clapped her hands in a slow applause as she climbed down from the bleachers. "Congratulations to our trial winner, Vashti Jahanara!"

Sitting nearby, Vashti spat into the sand. "I kicked your asses," she grinned, panting. Even though she looked just as war-torn as the rest of them, and her feet were black and shiny in a way they shouldn't be, her smug expression was enough to make Everly want to throw up again.

A Rooter presented Vashti with a new set of clothing—royal blue trousers and an orange tunic. Back at the rope wall, her red sari fluttered in the wind. She'd shed it like a snake sheds its skin.

"Now, Vashti, if only you had remembered rule number two," continued the Umbo, "your band would be feasting tonight. But because you opted to go it alone, you and your friends will subsist on rice and rice alone."

Vashti's eyes darkened. "They're not my friends."

"Allies, then," Tazeen countered. "Speaking of rules, I am afraid one band has made a fatal miscalculation." She motioned to the last newcomer to cross the finish line; he was lying cheek-down in the sand, barely conscious. "Akimitsu lost the race, but his band lost much more. You succeed as a team; you fail as a team. You are all banished."

As the news set in, Akimitsu's four bandmates began to protest. A group of Tazeen's enforcers climbed down from the bleachers and corralled them. The failed recruits cursed, cried, and begged as they were dragged down the beach and into the jungle.

"The rest of you have passed the Eliminator," the Umbo concluded. "You should be very proud."

Weak and in agony, Everly surveyed the carnage. She spotted a newcomer, fully caked in mud. It was the boy from the croc pit; someone must have dragged him to safety. The girl with the broken leg had also made it across the finish line. Carried, most likely. The rest of her band, Jax and two others, were huddled together. If the injured girl hadn't finished, all four would have been banished. Based on their furious expressions, Everly was to blame. Perfect.

The spectacle was over, so the Rooters climbed down from the bleachers and made their way to the footpaths. Micah strolled by, his arm draped lazily over the neck of a dazzling blonde girl.

"These ones yours?" the girl asked with a giggle. "They'll never make the cut. Mine, however, showed some promise."

Micah looked over his recruits. "You've always had a nose for these things, Nikol." Hand-in-hand, the two walked down the shore.

Vashti jogged after them. Either she was numb with shock, or she enjoyed the pain.

"We're screwed," Katak huffed, watching the Rooters grow small in the distance. "We signed up for a rebellion, but the Bloodwood Society is just as bad as the Dust."

Beside him, Inés was sobbing into her hands, which were covered in oozing welts from the suicide nettle. "I wish I'd never come here," she cried.

Everly pictured Shelby's face, tear-streaked and bloodied, with a renewed bout of nausea twisting her gut. Her sister wouldn't last long in prison, and there were still five trials left.

CHAPTER 8

It took a week for most of the newcomers to recover from their injuries. The days were long and boring, filled with menial tasks like washing dishes and scrubbing laundry. The Rooters barely paid attention to the ragtag crew. Except for Maria Jose.

She was part of Tazeen's band, the Lemurs, and she came to the burrow every night to ply her patients with medicinal herbs, serums, and balms. The dark-skinned girl with a mane of curly brown hair had proven herself a skillful healer. She was useful in other ways, too, having procured running shoes, changes of clothes, toothbrushes, and rubber menstrual cups. Everly had been worried she'd busted an ovary during the obstacle course, so it was a relief when her period finally arrived.

Right on schedule, Maria Jose appeared in the entrance to the burrow with a mortar and pestle in hand. Like toddlers drawn to the only adult in the room, the newcomers crowded around her. So far, the Lemur was their only window into the inner workings of the Root. Everly hung back, taking mental notes.

Maria Jose doled out greetings before getting down to business. She pointed at Vashti, who was lounging in a nook. "You. Feet. Now."

Vashti rolled her eyes, but complied. The newcomers with the closest view gasped when she removed her bandages. Her toes were grisly—black in some spots, bright red in others, and peeling all over. Maria Jose spread a sweet-smelling cream on the burn sites while Vashti looked away, pretending her feet weren't in agony.

"What is that?" Inés asked from her front row seat.

"Aloe vera, honey, willow, and calendula," Maria Jose replied, listing off the ingredients.

"Where did you learn all of this?" Inés pressed.

"From watching older rebels," Maria Jose replied. "Most of them have moved on now. There are endless treatments on the island, you just have to know where to look."

Everly perked up in her nook. There was no question Maria Jose's homeopathic remedies were effective for injuries, but what about illnesses? Shelby didn't have a formal diagnosis, since the Union wouldn't let a potential traitor near the fancy equipment. But maybe there was something on the island that could help her sister. Everly didn't want to ask in front of an audience, so for now, the question would have to wait.

"How old is everybody here?" she queried instead.

"Tazeen is the oldest. She's twenty. The rest of the Lemurs are nineteen. The Fire Ants, that's Micah's band, are eighteen. The rest are a mix. People get recruited at different ages. Inés, you're what, fourteen?"

"Sixteen," she said with a slump.

"Looking young might come in handy. Don't stress it," the healer rebounded.

Inés sighed and moved on, saying, "So, you run the infirmary, and the big, scary *pelirojo* runs the galley."

Maria Jose chuckled. "Andrew is big and loud, but he's not scary. He's a redheaded teddy bear. And he makes a delicious *paella*."

"That I do not believe," Inés said with her nose in the air.

Maria Jose finished replacing Vashti's bandages and got to work removing infected stitches from Jax's forearm. He caught Everly staring and glared back at her. A week of recovery hadn't eased any of the tensions. It had taken four Rooters to hold his bandmate steady while Maria Jose reset the bone in her leg. The girl would live, thankfully, and Everly couldn't really blame Jax and the rest of his bandmates for hating her. She had caused the injury, after all.

"What do the other Lemurs do?" Jax asked, watching as Maria Jose pulled pus-covered threads from his arm.

Tazeen is the Umbo, so she's in charge," the Lemur chatted. "Min Jun grows our food. And Ebimi is the groundskeeper.

Sometimes she and her crew go hunting, if it's a special occasion. Your job as recruits is to find your strength and lean into it, so that when you leave, you have something to offer in the fight against the Dust."

"Who decides what happens to us?" Everly asked. "After we leave?" They'd been so busy surviving, there hadn't been many opportunities to think about a future away from the island, one where they left with their brains intact and joined the rebellion.

Maria Jose used a stethoscope to listen to a girl's lungs. "Our people on the outside, the Spearheads," said the Lemur.

"Who are they?" Everly pressed.

"Senior leadership," she said with a shrug. "You have to understand. Secrecy is security. We follow the Umbo, and she follows the Spearheads. That's all you need to know."

"I know you trust Tazeen," Everly said, careful in her approach. "But we watched Jessie die." The sounds in the burrow shuffled into an expectant silence. The rest of the newcomers wanted answers just as much as she did.

"The Dust has killed millions. Hundreds of millions. And they'll stop at nothing to end the rebellion. We are only as strong as our weakest link. I know it seems harsh and heartless. But sometimes, for the greater good, you have to sacrifice the few for the sake of the many. Now, I have to go," Maria Jose said, packing her supplies.

"What's the hurry?" Katak asked, peering out of his nook.

"Council meeting," she replied.

"Can we come?" he asked.

Her bangs bounced as Maria Jose shook her head. "Initiated rebels only, I'm afraid. And it's after curfew. Get some sleep. Tomorrow, your training starts again."

Learning that their convalescence was over sent a nervous wave through the burrow. The newcomers mingled for a while before turning in for the night. Soon the cave was filled with the sound of snoring. Everly stared at the dirt ceiling of her nook, the cogs in her mind spinning. The Rooters would be distracted with the Council meeting. And Everly had an itch she was dying to scratch—Micah said they had files, and she had an idea where they might be kept.

Moving slowly, Everly climbed from her nook. The mossy floor muted her footsteps as she entered the tunnel. Going alone wasn't the safest strategy, since one wrong step could send her into the aquifer without help or a witness. But who could she really trust?

The darkness was so thick, it felt like she was sleepwalking. When Everly reached the trunk, she was relieved to find it empty; the Council meeting was happening elsewhere, offering her a clear path to her intended destination. She scuttled across the open space and entered tunnel III. As soundlessly as she could manage, Everly slipped through the beaded curtain.

The storeroom looked the same, with crates stacked along the walls and burlap sacks heaped on the floor. She crept to the back of the cave and lifted a lid from one of the crates. Honey jars. The next crates contained rice, beans, dried coconut, and sugar cane. Dammit. If the entire room was stocked with food, the late-night excursion would prove to be a complete waste of time.

Everly was about to give up when a blue glow in the farthest corner of the cave caught her eye. A pixie ring of glowing mushrooms offered enough light for her to make out the markings on the crates. The first one read "Aa-Br."

Jackpot.

Inside was a treasure trove—hundreds of leather-bound journals, each with a name etched on the front cover. Everly shuffled the pile and found one she recognized: "Atta, Katak."

Micah hadn't been lying. Each kid came with an instruction manual.

Everly sat down beside the pixie ring and flipped open the journal:

Atta, Katak
D.O.B. 21.12.2058
Union Territory IQ107
Mother: Ilupaalik, Maya (deceased)
Father: Atta, Yuka (deceased)

Katak Atta was orphaned in 2068 when the family's snowcycle went through thin ice. He was thrown from the vehicle and suffered minor injuries. Since his parents' death, Katak has been a ward of the Union Territory. He has run away from multiple foster placements. In January 2075, Saanvi Kumar was given temporary custody of Katak. Katak joined two other foster children at Ms. Kumar's home, Napatsi Neevee (6) and David Johnson (17).

On Friday, June 14, 2075, Katak's school records show he was present. According to the neighbours, Katak arrived at their house at 3:45PM to collect Napatsi, who often played at their house after school. Katak was informed that Napatsi had been picked up by David half an hour earlier. Katak returned to Ms. Kumar's house and followed the sound of a television to an upstairs bedroom. There, he discovered that David was sexually assaulting Napatsi.

Based on interviews with Napatsi, Katak attacked David and beat him with his bare hands. After David became unconscious, Katak took the neighbour's snowcycle and drove Napatsi to the nearest Union hospital, which was two hours away. They waited for another two hours in the ER for Napatsi to be treated by medical personnel. Posing as a doctor, our recruiter extracted Katak from the hospital and transported him to the island.

Katak's physical size and strength make him an asset to the Bloodwood Society. His protective instincts will also be of value. However, Katak's mistrust of all authority figures, along with his dislike of rules and structure, will be difficult to overcome. He will likely always be a flight risk.

Estimated odds of successful initiation: 5/10

Everly's eyes were dry and burning. She tried to focus on the discomfort so she wouldn't have to think about what Katak had seen, what Napatsi had suffered. Both Katak and Everly had people at home who depended on them, whose lives would be worse without them around. The knot in her throat kept twisting tighter, but she couldn't stop reading now. The more she knew about her bandmate, the better her chances of survival.

The remaining pages were filled with hand-written notes from the recruiter. They'd been watching Katak for over a year, a detail that made Everly's skin crawl. Her recruitment had felt like a smash and grab, but had Micah actually been stalking her for months? Were her secrets scribbled in one of these notebooks for anyone to come across?

Everly sensed she'd been away from the burrow for too long. Someone was bound to notice. But a nearby crate labelled, "Ja-Ko," was too tempting to ignore. The story of Vashti Jahanara was right there for the taking. Aware of the gushing sound of blood in her ears, Everly lifted the lid. She'd expected Vashti's journal to be sitting on top. Instead, "Kikwete, Micah" was staring right at her. She picked it up. The soft glow of the mushrooms illuminated the lettering.

Before she cracked the binding, footsteps echoed through the tunnel. Everly squeezed herself between two crates, holding Micah's journal against her chest. A pair of Rooters stopped beside the entrance to the storeroom. She held her breath. What would the punishment be if someone caught her snooping around?

"We have to tell them the truth, Min Jun," a voice said from just outside the beaded curtain. It was Tazeen.

"Are you sure now is the right time?" The voice belonged to the Lemur with a shaved head.

"I'm sure," said the Umbo. "If there really is a spy on the island, I'm going to smoke them out."

CHAPTER 9

The Lemurs moved further down the tunnel, their conversation muffled by the hiss of steam. Leaving behind the leather journal was the smartest move, but based on Tazeen's revelation, security was about to get a lot tighter. Everly tucked the book into the waistband of her pants and closed the crate. She stole one last look around. Was the storeroom hiding books about medicine? Now she might never find out.

Back in the tunnel, the steam hid her silhouette as she followed Tazeen's voice. Everly moved quickly, trying to keep track of the twists and turns in the subterranean pathway. She paused, straining to listen. The voices were gone. The tunnel was completely unfamiliar, and now, somehow, she had to find her way back to the trunk. Or die trying.

A trill sounded behind her. Everly spun to see Tazeen's grackle perched on a tuber. The bird twittered before disappearing into the wall. *Icterids* were smart; they could solve puzzles and pick locks. Were they smart enough to lure someone into a trap? The grackle had, in a way, already lured her to the island. Everly decided to risk it.

She traced her hand along the wall and felt a puff of cool air coming from a crevasse just wide enough to pass through. As she wedged herself into the space, she tried not to imagine getting stuck, pressed forever like a flower between the pages of a book. Just as she was about to abandon the idea, a ladder appeared. The grackle was perched on the upper rung. It whistled before taking off.

Above her, she could hear voices. She'd found the Council meeting. So much for members only. Moving slowly, Everly climbed to a slender outcropping. She inched her way forward, mindful of the rock shelf just above her, and peered over the edge. The hidden perch overlooked a smaller cave with a circular hole in the ceiling. Through the opening, Everly could make out the waning moon. The Rooters were seated in concentric circles, and in the centre stood the Umbo with the rest of the Lemurs. An exhilarated chill swept up Everly's spine. She shuffled back; if she could see them, they could see her.

"I know you have a lot of questions," Tazeen called over the scattered conversations. "But I can only tell you what I know. The Spearheads would not have risked contacting me unless they had compelling evidence."

"There's a traitor among us," a Rooter shouted.

"A spy for the Dust!" cried another.

Taz calmed the crowd with her hands. "All we know is the Spearheads are concerned that a Rooter may have been turned. For the moment, this is the only information we have."

"Can't we use the Wishing Well?" a voice called out.

"The Wishing Well only works the first time," Tazeen explained, "when newcomers are open and vulnerable to its effects. Once a mind is closed off, the water cannot access it."

"It must be a newcomer," said the Lemur named Ebimi. She had a midnight black complexion and thick, beaded locs. "We know everyone else here. They are strangers to us."

"Think logically, Ebimi," Tazeen cut in before the mob could latch on to the idea. "For it to be a newcomer, the Dust would have needed to know our recruitment plans beforehand, plans that not even I was privy to. Which would require a Dust spy at the level of the Spearheads. Our leadership has not been compromised. The newcomers are the least likely suspects."

Andrew clapped his enormous hands. "We will find the traitor, through whatever means necessary!" he boomed.

"That's enough," the Umbo snapped. Her intensity silenced the room. "We are not going to panic. We are not going to overreact. We are going to think and watch and wait for further truth to reveal itself. For now, I will say this—if you are in trouble, we can help you. If you are in danger, we can protect you. Whatever they have offered you, whatever they have promised, the Dust cannot be trusted. Your family and your home is right here. Come forward, and there will be no punishment—"

"Like hell!" Andrew shouted, his thunderous voice bouncing off the stone walls.

"I am the Umbo!" Taz exploded. "You will not interrupt me again." Her voice had an edge like a boning knife, and no one, not even the birds or the bats, dared to make a sound. Andrew's face turned bright red as he backed down.

"Hear me now," Tazeen said. "I will give this person, this alleged spy, until sundown tomorrow to approach any one of the Lemurs. We, the Council, will issue no punishment. Nothing that has been done is undoable. Not yet. We all understand the Blood Oath that we have taken, and the lifelong commitment that comes with it. Blood-wood is your greatest asset and your greatest ally, but should you turn your back on your family, the consequences will be far-reaching and dire. The same goes for anyone found to be withholding information. The simple act of keeping a secret can be an act of treason."

The Umbo waited, holding everyone captive. When she finally sighed, releasing them from her invisible grasp, the Rooters exhaled as well. "Now, if there are no more questions…"

The trunk exploded with a chorus of Rooters all shouting out at once. Using the noise as cover, Everly climbed back down the ladder. Micah's file was still tucked into her waistband. With everyone on high alert, getting caught out after curfew with stolen property wasn't going to end well. There was just enough space behind the first rung of the ladder to tuck the book away for safekeeping. Micah Kikwete's life story would have to wait for another night.

As she scuttled across the empty trunk, Everly tried to wrap her mind around what she'd just overheard. With a single nuclear blast, the Dust could sink the island to the bottom of the sea; but, if they knew where the rebels were hiding, it made sense to send a spy first. That way, they could collect intel on the Rooters and go after everyone they'd ever known or loved. Public executions. Mass graves. The same things happened during the War, according to her dad's retellings.

Tazeen believed the spy wasn't a newcomer, but was that a safe assumption? If the Dust had made it to the island, how much harder would it be to infiltrate the Spearheads? The entire rebellion depended on the mysterious leaders, but how much did Tazeen, the all-powerful Umbo, even know about them?

As for Everly's own band, having read Katak's file was enough for her to trust him. Someone that loyal and protective wouldn't flip. Vashti, on the other hand? Everly would rather put her faith in a pit viper. And what about Inés? Everly wanted to trust her, but it was tough to know for sure. After all, a spy's best talent was hiding in plain sight.

Everly turned down the low tunnel that led to the burrow, so lost in her own thoughts she didn't notice that the shadow in front of her had fortified. The silhouette shifted, blocking her path. Instinctively, Everly threw an elbow and connected with the shadow's floating rib.

They folded over. A glowing mushroom on the floor illuminated Jax's features. His blue eyes were raging. The muscles in his sizable jaw were flexed. Everly tried to step around him, but Jax pounced, grabbing her by the shoulders and slamming her against the cave wall.

"Get your hands off me," she demanded, fear rippling through her.

"Or what?" he simmered.

"I'll scream."

"What will you tell them? You're out snooping after curfew."

"So are you," Everly growled. "What do you want?"

Jax scowled, tightening his grip. "Your stunt at the obstacle course nearly got me and my band kicked off the island."

Jax wasn't wrong that Everly had caused his bandmate's fall, but that didn't make her responsible. The race had been a free-for-all. She couldn't have known that one newcomer left behind would mean banishment for an entire band. Taz hadn't mentioned that vital piece of information. Everly's sole focus had been surviving the trial. But every choice had a boomerang effect, and this one had come back to haunt her.

"That girl grabbed me," Everly stated. "She was trying to drag me down."

"That girl has a name. It's Jolene."

Everly tried to break free, but Jax clamped down even harder. "What are you, her saviour?" she scowled.

"I'm her twin brother."

Jax's words hit like a hammer. Unlike everyone else, Jax hadn't come to the island alone. If the island accepted siblings, why the hell wasn't Shelby here with her? With a growing sense of despondence, Everly realised she already knew the answer. The Umbo had presented it within hours of their arrival—*On this island, the weak do not survive.*

"You were recruited together..." Everly stated, voice catching on its way out.

"That's right," Jax snarled. "My sister is in the middle of nowhere with a busted leg and no real doctors in sight. All thanks to you."

Everly met his eyes. They were focused. Formidable. But there was something else she recognized, too. Dread, paired with the inescapable knowledge that you have something to lose, something you can't live without. Jax didn't know a thing about Everly, but maybe if he knew what she was fighting for, he'd stop breaking the blood vessels under her skin. "Listen, Jax—"

"No, you listen," he said, pushing her harder into the stone wall. "We're getting our wishes, and Jolene and I are getting out of here. I'll burn the whole island down if I have to. And if you get in my way again, I will end you."

The threat hung in the air between them. Finally, Jax let go of her. Everly ducked under his arm and fled into the mist, the slap of her footfall echoing in her wake.

She ran all the way back to the burrow and paused at the entrance to steady her breath. All was quiet. Katak and Vashti were asleep in their ground-level nooks. Everly crept to her place along the wall and laid back. She sucked air through an invisible straw, trying to slow her jackrabbit pulse. In the darkness, she clasped her hands together and willed them to stop quaking.

Inés's face appeared, hanging upside-down from the nook above hers. "How was the Council meeting?" her bandmate asked in a whisper.

Despite the shock that currently held her captive, Everly could recognize the farce. Apparently, she had the stealth of a bulldozer. Two newcomers and a bird knew she'd snuck out, and it wasn't even daylight yet.

"It was boring," Everly lied through chattering teeth.

"Then why are you shaking?"

Without an invitation, Inés climbed down the wall and shimmied into Everly's nook. She lay on her side, breathing softly through her nose and watching Everly's profile.

"I saw Jax leave," Inés whispered. "Did something happen?"

Everly blinked, livid at the tears about to form. Maybe Jax would get caught by the Rooters. Maybe they'd call him a spy, force Other Death down his throat, and ship him off in a box. More likely, he'd be back any minute, and she'd have to share a room with someone who'd left unwelcome impressions on her skin.

Everly rolled onto her side so the girls were face-to-face. "Jax is dangerous," she whispered.

"Did he hurt you?"

"Not yet," Everly said.

Inés's eyes were wide and glossy. "What are we going to do? We can't leave, but…"

"We're going to fight for our wishes. And try not to get killed in the process."

"Okay," Inés agreed. "Everly, is it okay if I stay here tonight?"

Everly sighed as the shock loosened its grip. She wasn't about to admit it, but back at home, she and Shelby shared their mom and dad's old spring mattress. Her sister's warmth was comforting and helped ward off the constant anxiety that the house was about to collapse on top of them. But that wasn't the only reason. Sharing a bed was the only way Everly could make sure that, if her sister's body failed in the night, Shelby wouldn't die alone. Her sister, who was too weak for the island. Her sister, who had been left behind on purpose. Failed by the Bloodwood Society.

"You can stay," Everly whispered. "I don't mind."

CHAPTER 10

Shortly after sunrise, Everly sat with her back resting against the bark of the Bloodwood tree. The combination of her midnight escapades and the unexpected bedfellow had left her feeling sapped. She longed for sleep. And calories. Resting beside her, Inés looked just as exhausted. And even though they'd competed in a snoring contest for most of the night, Vashti and Katak were both draped across aerial roots like they had no bones.

Across the way, Everly spotted Micah where the red dirt trail spilled onto the mossy clearing. Their mentor was shirtless, his chest lined with streams of sweat, his body long and lean. Were all boys from the Afro-Continent built like him? Did they all speak in the same deep, rounded tones? His raised scar was bigger than she'd realized; it started at his shoulder blade and came down past his clavicle, like someone with an axe had mistaken him for firewood. The scar made him look tough. If it weren't for his perma-scowl and overall demeanor, a pathetic version of herself could imagine climbing Micah like a tree. Everly almost laughed.

Suddenly, Micah was standing over them. "On your feet," he ordered. "All of you."

"Nice of you to show up," Vashti yawned. "Sunrise was half an hour ago."

"I ran six miles this morning, princess. What have you accomplished?"

"I avoided contracting lice in that cesspool of a burrow," Vashti replied.

"It is pretty awful down there," Katak agreed. "Where do the Rooters sleep?"

"Go get your stuff and I'll show you," Micah offered.

Katak perked up. "Really?"

Micah rolled his eyes. "No Katak, not really." Their mentor walked around the tree, following the curvature of the trunk, failing to mention if he wanted them to follow.

Everly scowled at Micah's back until he disappeared.

"I don't know what it is about that guy," said Katak, "but I hate him."

Inés snorted.

"Does he expect us to tag along?" Everly wondered aloud.

"I didn't receive a formal invitation," Vashti said, clucking her tongue.

Micah's head popped out from around the tree. "Move your lazy asses!" he boomed.

Completely devoid of enthusiasm, his charges obliged. They walked to the far side of the Bloodwood tree and gathered near the edge of the cliff. Micah stood with his back to the waterfall, mist collecting in his hair.

"We're here," their mentor announced.

Everly looked around, still half asleep. Unless swan-diving was on the agenda, there weren't a ton of options for whatever Micah had planned. She crept to the edge, and the view made her shiver. How deep was the river below? How sharp were the boulders?

Vashti sucked her teeth, impatiently. "Here, where?"

Micah smirked—always with the smirking—and pointed up.

It was hard to see anything through the thick branches, but deep in the crown of the Bloodwood, Everly spotted a small structure. The air rushed from her diaphragm with an audible, "Woah."

"That," he said, craning his neck, "is the Crow's Nest."

"You've got to be kidding me," Vashti spat. "We're going up there?"

"Don't worry," Micah grinned. "The climb won't kill you. But the fall might."

Everly wanted to slap the smug expression right off his face. "You can't be serious," she sputtered. "That treehouse is a mile high."

"Slightly under five hundred feet, actually," Micah corrected, as if the exact measurement of what surely must be the largest living tree on the planet would somehow assuage her fears.

"You want us to free climb the height of a skyscraper?" Everly gawked.

"That's correct."

She glared at him, pulse quickening. "Without ropes?"

"That's the definition of free climbing, no? Pro tip, always keep three points of contact. Test each hand and foothold before you trust it. And this goes without saying, but I'll say it anyway—don't look down. I'll see you at the top of the Bloodwood tree."

Everly and the others watched in stunned silence as Micah began his ascent. He made it look easy, like climbing an unfathomably tall ladder. But one slip was all it would take.

"Are we doing this?" Katak asked. He was rubbernecking so hard, Everly worried he might stumble backward and fall from the cliff. So many ways to die.

Inés looked around, wringing her hands. "If we fall…"

"We'll be eviscerated," Everly concluded.

The early sunlight stretched Micah's profile into an elongated shadow—a hunched panther navigating a vertical expanse. His voice called down to them. "Did I mention this is your fourth trial?"

"I wasn't planning on dying today," Katak said to himself.

"As if anyone would notice," Vashti quipped.

"I would," Inés countered.

Vashti looked back and forth between them. "Barf," was all she said. Even though there was more than enough space to move around him, Vashti elbowed past Katak and used the first few grooves in the bark to hoist herself up.

Katak waited in silence, putting some distance between them before he started his climb.

"Did I say the wrong thing?" Inés whispered.

"No," Everly said, trying to reassure her. "Maybe Katak isn't used to hearing nice things."

"I don't think Vashti is either," Inés pointed out, showing more empathy for their bandmate than Everly could muster.

"Probably not."

Inés bowed her head and muttered a prayer. She touched the metal cross that rested at her collarbone. "I put in a good word for you," she said before leaving the ground.

Everly blushed, unsure of the proper response. She doubted the gods thought much about non-believers, but she appreciated the gesture. Before she began the death-defying climb, Everly tried to empty her mind and focus only on the placement of her hands and feet. Three points of contact. Test the hold. Don't look down. Simple enough.

Halfway up the Bloodwood tree, her foot slipped. For a few delirious seconds, Everly clung to the bark with just her hands. Vertigo swept through her like ice water. A scream formed on her lips, but there was no one close enough to help. Frightened and exhausted, her focus fell to where the Bloodwood tapered to a point and pierced the earth.

"Not today," Everly growled. She kicked hard and felt her toe sink into the tree. A lifesaving foothold. The tendons between her shoulders popped and spasmed as she heaved herself to the next groove.

Moments passed like eons, and just when Everly worried her grip might fail, she looked up and saw the underbelly of the Crow's Nest. Katak and Inés were waiting, stretched out on their stomachs, reaching for her, cheering her on. The relief was dazzling. She blinked sweat from her eyes and climbed the final stretch.

When Everly was finally close enough, her bandmates grabbed her by the wrists and dragged her onto a platform, where she lay, muscles cramping, heart fluttering. A few minutes later, finally able to stand, Everly looked beyond the railing and stood in awe of the view from the top of the world.

The panorama was so vast and sprawling, Everly could sense the weight of the sky. Far below, the jungle floor shimmered beneath a layer of heat and humidity. The river snaked across the landscape, pouring into countless tributaries and velvety lakes. In the distance, Everly spotted the coffee-coloured beach and weather-beaten obstacle course. Everywhere else, the curvature of the island, rocky and overgrown, met with a dark blue band of ocean that melted into the horizon.

The Crow's Nest was a treetop gazebo, octagonal in shape with planked floors, rough railings, and a thatched roof. It balanced across massive branches and was anchored directly into the bark of the Bloodwood tree. Hanging on the back wall, where the bark had been stripped, was a row of hooks, each weighted down by a wooden tile the size of a playing card. The tiles spelled out a pair of words that didn't belong together:

SKELETON DRAMA

"Welcome to the Crow's Nest," Micah said from his perch on one of the upper branches. "Congratulations on not dying."

Katak coughed, asthmatically. "Thank you," he wheezed.

Micah moved on before Katak's lungs had settled. "I have a question for you all. So far, what have your trials had in common?"

Everly sat down to give herself a few more minutes to recover. She considered the perilous climb they'd just completed; she recalled how the Eliminator had ravaged them on the beach in the distance. "Strength," she said.

"Makes sense," Micah agreed. "Rebels need to be tough."

"The Labyrinth wasn't about strength, though. More like survival strategy," Vashti pointed out. "As for the Wishing Well, who knows what that was about."

"It was about honesty," Inés said, quietly.

Micah pursed his lips, like he enjoyed watching them struggle.

All four challenges were so drastically different, Everly was finding it difficult to draw an invisible line between them. Were they testing their character? Or valour?

"Teamwork," Inés finally said. "To survive the tunnels, to become a band at the Wishing Well, to complete the obstacle course. So far, it's been about working together."

"That's correct, Inés," their mentor said. "But today's climb was merely a warmup. To complete your fourth trial, you'll need to make your way back down, without retracing your steps."

Micah opened his backpack and laid out four canteens and a bag of shelled almonds. "I suggest you ration wisely. The other Fire Ants and I were stuck here for three days, back when we were recruits."

"Doing what?" Everly asked.

"Cracking codes. The Dust controls the airwaves and all the networks. So, we've had to get creative and disguise our communications. Decoding is a vital skill as a rebel. And today, the stakes could not be higher." He chuckled at his own joke.

"What's this trial called?" Everly asked, hoping for more insights.

Micah strolled out onto a branch that jutted away from the trunk. Flashing an impish grin, he replied: "Skydive."

With that, their mentor flipped backward off the limb and yipped, gleefully, as gravity took hold.

CHAPTER 11

Micah's charges scrambled to the railing. Everly expected to witness the boy's final seconds alive as he plummeted into the mist of the distant falls. Instead, their mentor was crouched on a lower branch. Smirking.

"Good luck," he called up to them. Micah leapt from branch to branch, and when they ran out, he began the long descent down from the treetop.

Everly couldn't help but wonder, if he slipped, would Tazeen give them a new mentor? One could only hope.

Inés dropped to the floorboards and undid the top button on her blouse. "I thought he actually jumped. *Está loco*."

"Dude is a maniac," Katak agreed.

"He's a waste of space," Everly stated. "Let's find a way out of this tree and be done with it."

Vashti had already helped herself to a canteen and a handful of nuts. She moseyed over to the rear of the gazebo and read the tiles aloud. "Skeleton drama. What does that even mean?"

"Nothing," Everly replied. "It's gibberish."

"It's not nothing. It must be a riddle. Maybe it's an anagram?" suggested Inés.

Katak raised his eyebrows. "What?"

"A word you can rearrange to make a new word," she explained.

Everly lifted the letter A. As the hook raised to an unweighted position, she heard a muffled metallic grind from deep within the tree. "There are gears or something behind the hooks," she noted.

"A trap door, probably," Vashti guessed.

Everly pressed her cheek against the bark, looking for a seam, a hinge, something. But the Crow's Nest appeared to have been abandoned a while ago, and whatever clues there might have been were long since overgrown.

"I'll bet if we figure out the right word—" Inés started.

"We'll figure out a way down from here," Everly finished the thought. "It's worth a try."

Katak joined the girls at the back wall. "It's only thirteen letters," he said. "How hard could it be?"

They started arranging the tiles purposefully on the hooks to make simple words like tree, deer, and elm. The hardest part was messing around with the remaining letters, trying to use them all. Inés impressed with a college-level vocabulary—lemonade, enamored, mandrake. It took a few hours to find an answer that used all 13 letters: OARSMAN TALKED

The Crow's Nest remained unchanged.

An hour later, Inés used the hooks to spell out, SANDLOT REMAKE. Again, nothing happened. Some time later, Everly's attempt, ALAMO TREKS END, which admittedly made zero sense, put them nowhere closer to a solution.

Everly's enthusiasm for the riddle had run out completely. There must be thousands of potential words and phrases. What if they never solved it? The supply of water and nuts would barely last to the end of the day. With the afternoon heat settling in, other concerns made their way into Everly's mind. Every second they wasted, Shelby grew sicker. Each failed attempt increased the likelihood that her sister would die in a Dust prison before Everly could devise a way to get to her. The realization filled her with scorpions.

Katak broke the frustrated silence with a loud clap. "I think I've got it!" He moved the letters around on the hooks and spelled, OLD MENS KARATE.

Nothing.

"This is impossible," Everly groaned.

"Out of my way." Vashti hip-checked Katak to take his place in front of the tiles. She spent several minutes shuffling letters and threw up her hands when SALAD TREE MONK also failed.

Inés squinted at the letters. "It would be so much easier if we knew what kind of words we were looking for."

Katak fanned himself with his cap. "My brain hurts," he whined.

"What brain?" Vashti snarked.

"If you want out of this tree, I can think of one way down," Katak sniffed.

"Try it," Vashti said with fake sweetness.

In her current state of mind, Everly wasn't entirely against getting rid of Vashti. But a small, more rational part of her knew it wouldn't help their cause. Four heads were better than three. But they were going about their task the wrong way. Random phrases weren't going to crack the code. They needed more insight to help them connect the dots. Everly thought back to the notebooks in the storeroom, and they gave her an idea.

"What if the clue has something to do with us?" Everly called above the squabble.

The other two stopped swapping insults and looked at her, expectantly.

"What do you mean?" Inés asked.

Everly rubbed her temples; a tension headache was setting in. "What if the whole point of the trial is for us to talk about our pasts. Skeleton drama, as in, the skeletons in our closets."

The other three were silent for a beat. Abruptly asking people to reveal their personal traumas wasn't particularly discrete, but Everly was running out of time. For tact. For riddles. For Shelby.

Katak said nothing as he moved to the railing and sat with his feet dangling over the edge. He thought his secrets were his and his alone, but Everly had uncovered them just hours before. She felt a pang of guilt for being in possession of such intimate knowledge. But she would read ten thousand journals if it meant getting one step closer to helping her sister.

Since she was the one who'd made the suggestion, Everly decided to kick off the conversation that none of them wanted to have. "My life back home was a classic fairytale," Everly started. "My mom is dead—"

"Killed by the Union?" Vashti assumed.

"Actually, my mom killed herself," Everly admitted, tasting the bitterness of the words on her tongue.

"That was pretty common, after the War," Inés offered, gently.

It was true. After the Union's takeover, everyone from that generation had their own reason to put a gun in their mouth or tie a homemade noose around their neck. But death was the ultimate defeat; living was the bravest act of defiance. At least, that was what Everly's dad had told his young daughters, seven and nine at the time, as Union divers searched the waters off the coastline for their mom's body.

"How'd she do it?" Vashti prodded.

"She jumped," Everly stated, the word falling from her mouth like a broken tooth.

Vashti's expression remained unchanged. "And your dad?"

"Arrested for treason. Two years ago. It's just me and my sister now. But the Dust has her, too." Everly looked at her hands and picked at a blood blister. The admission left her feeling exposed, like she'd covered herself in peppermint oil and all her pores were open to the elements.

"I'm sorry, Everly," Katak said from the railing. "I hope your sister is alright."

Everly nodded, feeling an unexpected rush of gratitude. Back home, sympathy was hard to come by. Bad things only happened to bad citizens, according to her neighbours and classmates. The Dahl family got what was coming to them.

"My parents are alive," Inés said, mercifully shifting the focus. "They run a small agave farm that the Dust now controls. But my dad grows other stuff, too. In the storm shelter, with hydroponics."

"Seriously?" Katak said with a chuckle. "That's sweet."

"Not enough that anyone would notice. I'm not supposed to go anywhere near it. But I was going away for school, and I thought it might help me."

"Help you what?" Everly asked.

"Make friends," Inés admitted, bashfully. "And, I mean, look at me—would you ever think I was the one supplying the whole school with *la mota*?"

"Nope," Vashti agreed.

"Anyway," Inés continued, "my plan worked. I was popular, which was a new experience for me."

"That sounds decent," Katak smiled.

"It was. Until Sister Antoinette figured out what I was doing."

"Crap," Everly sighed. "How big was *that* fine?"

"Not a fine. Sister Antoinette threatened to send handlers to my family's farm. When I begged her not to, she demanded payment."

"How much did she want?" Vashti asked.

"She didn't want money."

The Crow's Nest fell silent. The gnawing tension in Everly's skull was made worse by the combination of dehydration and all the sordid details Inés was leaving out. The unspoken truth hung like smoke in the treetops.

The back of Katak's shirt was drenched in sweat. He kept rapping his knuckles against the railing. The connection between Inés and little Napatsi was impossible to ignore. Was Katak thinking the same thing?

Inés pushed her thick bangs to the side before continuing. "But that wasn't the worst thing that happened. And please, don't interrupt me, or I won't be able to say it. And I want you to know, so we can maybe get out of this tree.

"The night I was recruited, I stopped by the chapel to pray. It was late. I must have fallen asleep. Sister Antoinette found me in the pews. I tried to get away, but I knocked over a table that was covered in candles. In a matter of seconds, everything was on fire. The sanctuary filled with black smoke. I couldn't see anything. I couldn't breathe. I could barely move.

"In the aisle, I tripped over Sister Antoinette. She must have passed out. I tried to drag her to safety, but she was so heavy, and the smoke was so thick. I remember watching the fire crawl up the walls of the nave, around a stained-glass window. It was full of angels. I saw the priest come through a side door. He ran over to me, screaming. But I was coughing so hard, I couldn't understand him. I just wanted him to leave me there."

Inés paused.

"Why, Inés?" Everly asked, softly.

Her bandmate's eyes were glassy. "I put my family in danger. And they'd never forgive me if they found out the truth. At least, if I died in a fire, they'd remember me as a good daughter. Not someone...someone ruined."

"You're not ruined." Everly didn't need to know the whole story to be sure.

"Everly's right," Katak comforted. "We've all done things. It doesn't mean we're ruined. You...you're good, Inés."

"You're good," Everly repeated. She'd only known the girl for a week, but Inés's goodness was undeniable, her kindness unmatched. The cuts were deep, though. Their words wouldn't be enough. But they were something.

Vashti stood up and moved over to the hooks, putting as much physical distance as possible between herself and Inés. Everly scowled at her. People always turned away when they saw scars, as if suffering were contagious and the simple act of witnessing another person's pain put the viewer at risk.

"Inés, you said all of this happened just before you were recruited?" Everly prompted, cautiously.

"Yes," Inés replied. "The priest dragged me outside. He told me the nun had confessed her sins to the Dust, and the handlers knew about my family's farm. The priest said, if I agreed to go along with his plan, he'd make sure my parents had some warning. What was I supposed to do? He stuck a needle in my neck, and I woke up... here."

Everly recalled her memory of Inés from their first encounter— hiding in a stone crevasse, covered head-to-toe in soot and ash that Everly had mistaken for dirt. The poor girl had fallen out of the fire and into the hell hole.

Leaving the railing, Katak shuffled over to Inés and sat with their bent knees touching. "I think I know why Bloodwood recruited you," he said.

"Oh yeah, why's that?" she asked.

"Only a rebel would light up a church." Katak said, playfully placing his cap on her head.

"And, on the bright side," Everly added, "whatever we've all done, Vashti's done way worse."

"True story," Vashti said from the hooks, flipping her long black mane.

"How about it, Vashti Jahanara? Ever kill anybody?" Katak asked.

"I hire hitmen for my kills."

Katak sucked his teeth. "Seriously, what's your story?"

"My life was perfect, and then I was kidnapped. The end."

"I'm sure," Everly frowned.

"It's the truth. My uncle is high up in the Dust. I live with my mom and two sisters in a beautiful hotel. We have cleaners, cooks, chauffeurs…" An unfortunate mosquito flew in front of her, and Vashti squished it mid-air. "Bloodwood picked wrong when they recruited me. Dust is my bread and butter. Why would I want to rebel?"

"That's garbage," Everly scoffed. "We all saw you at the Wishing Well. There's something you want, and you want it bad enough not to get yourself banished. There's no such thing as a perfect life. The War took something from everyone."

"You can think whatever you want," Vashti shrugged. "Some people are trash and some people are treasure."

"*Cygnus inter anates,*" Inés mused.

"Enough with the Spanish," Vashti barked.

"It's Latin, actually," Inés pushed back. "It's my school's motto. 'Swan among ducks.'"

"I like that," Vashti simpered.

Inés frowned. "You would."

The Latin phrase swirled around inside Everly's throbbing brain and mixed with the words from her dad's textbook. Swans and ducks. Grackles and ravens. Lemurs and earthworms. "That's it!" Everly shouted.

Inés flinched. "What, what?!"

Everly stood and began sorting the tiles on hooks.

As the words took form, Katak blew a raspberry with his lips. "You're messing with us."

"I'm not, just wait." Everly paused, holding the final letter, S, in her hands. "Here goes nothing."

The weight of the tile lowered the final hook. From deep in the wall came a click, before the trunk behind the hooks fell away, revealing a trap door. For a second, the newcomers stared blankly at the void. Then a thundercloud of bats poured from the opening, and thousands of translucent wings and fangs filled the Crow's Nest.

Everly fell to her knees and wrapped her arms around her head. The creatures flew chaotically, swerving away from her at the last second. All Everly could do was wait for the high-pitched squeaking to stop.

Finally, the last of the bats dispersed into the blushing sky. Everly looked up from the crook of her elbow. Vashti was hanging precariously off the far side of the railing. Katak was braced above Inés, who was curled into a tiny ball.

"It's okay," he said, rolling away from her. "They're gone."

"All of them?" she hiccupped.

"I promise. Everly solved the riddle. We're getting out of here." Katak gestured to the hooks where the words NAKED MOLE RATS hung above the trap door.

"Are you kidding me?" Vashti barked as she climbed back to safety. "What does that even mean?"

Everly sat up. She couldn't believe it had worked. "All the bands are named after animals that live underground," she explained.

"So?" Vashti asked.

"So, that's our band name. Naked Mole Rats." There was a beat of shocked silence before Everly burst out laughing.

Vashti blinked as the news set it. "But that's the worst name ever!"

Katak's guffaw shook the whole gazebo. "That's awesome! Naked Mole Rats is a totally badass name."

"Do they have to be naked?" Inés squeaked. She sounded genuinely concerned, which made Everly laugh even harder.

In the corner of her eye, Everly noticed a black cord dangling just inside the trap door. She walked over and yanked on it. The gazebo rattled as two contraptions slid along the roof on hidden tracks. The thatched ceiling was blocked by brightly coloured fabric that luffed in the gentle breeze.

"What are we dealing with here?" Katak asked, climbing to his feet.

Vashti hadn't even noticed the new equipment. "Seriously, I'm going to talk to Taz because I am simply not going to be associated with a pink, hairless sausage."

"Vashti, get over it," Everly said. "I think we found our way down."

Vashti stopped her rant and stood tiptoe to touch the fabric. "What are these things?"

"Oh no." Inés clapped her hands over her mouth.

"What is it?" Everly asked.

"It's a sail," she whispered.

"A what?" Vashti asked with a sideways glare.

Inés clasped her crucifix. "They're hang-gliders. They want us to fly."

CHAPTER 12

Everly's stomach dropped, anticipating the fall. She grabbed a hold of the railing to steady herself. Their fourth trial meant hurling themselves from the top of the Bloodwood tree. But it was a death drop.

"They actually want us to make like flying squirrels and just go for it?" Katak balked, slack-jawed.

"Looks like it," Vashti said, as if the news were more annoying than horrifying.

Katak reached up and grabbed the metal frame on the first hang-glider. The whole apparatus dropped to floor level, held in position by a series of ropes and pulleys. He spun around with a goofy smile on his face, saying, "I've always wanted to try this."

"You can't be serious," Everly almost shouted. "This equipment is a thousand years old. We can't just throw ourselves out of a five-hundred-foot tree and hope for the best."

Katak waved her off. "You worry too much."

While the others examined the hang-gliders, Everly did her best to hide her shaking hands as she drank from a canteen. Beyond the alarm bells going off in her head, something deep in the recesses of her mind was trying to make its way forward, like a dream that vanished the second she tried to remember it. She recalled her dad's ghostly words: *Don't fall, sweet girl. Be careful.*

"There are only two gliders, so it looks like we're flying in pairs. Inés, would you do me the honour?" Katak asked.

"Surprise, surprise," Vashti said.

He raised an eyebrow. "Jealous?"

"Only that she'll get to use you as a crash pad."

Inés giggled and then looked at Katak apologetically.

While they wiggled into the harnesses, Vashti made herself useful, for once, by locking old carabiners in place. Everly tried to distract herself by sorting out the mechanics of the glider. From the upper section, the hammock-sized harnesses were supported by straps, one slightly higher than the other. The wings were folded like an accordion, with a rope attached that, once tugged, would snap them into position. There was no landing gear, so the Naked Mole Rats would have to land on their feet. Somehow.

"How do I look?" Katak asked, striking a pose. The harness covered his chest, and there were holes for his legs. The rest of the harness stuck out the back, with room for his feet to tuck in.

"Like a grasshopper," Inés snorted.

He looked over his shoulder at his extended bottom. "You're not wrong."

Vashti climbed on top of the rusty frame and double-checked the apparatus. "I've done all I can do here," she announced. "If you crash and die, it's not on me."

"You do realize she's just using you as guinea pigs," Everly noted.

"I'm no guinea pig," Katak said. "I'm a Naked Mole Rat."

"Worst," Vashti snarked.

With the sun now low in the sky, they were almost ready to test the laws of aerodynamics. The wind picked up and rustled the folded sails; they were thin and synthetic. Everly sent out a directionless prayer that the sails wouldn't shred mid-air.

Seeming more excited than nervous, Katak lay belly-down on the platform, suspended just above the wooden boards. He shifted his weight from side to side; the harness swayed. "Flying will be a cinch, but how do we land this thing?"

"I appreciate your confidence," Everly said, even though she didn't share it. "I think if you push forward on this bar in the front, it'll send the nose up, which should slow you down. Just don't push too hard…"

"Okay," Inés jittered. She quivered and gripped the crossbar with white knuckles. "Trial number four," she whispered to herself.

"That's right," Everly confirmed. "Once we've passed it, we're halfway there."

Inés drew in a shaky breath and nodded.

Together, Everly and Vashti dragged the hang-glider to the edge of the gazebo. It creaked and moaned as they pulled it along. Katak and Inés whooped and whimpered as the jungle floor came into view. One shove was all it would take.

"This is going to be awesome!" Katak yipped.

Inés clamped her eyes shut and mouthed a prayer.

Vashti released the metal clip that moored the hang-glider to the Crow's Nest. "Everly, do you want to do the honours?"

Everly touched the rope that controlled the sails. "Are you ready?" she asked her bandmates, feeling anxious enough to vomit a mixture of water and mashed almonds.

"Ready!" Katak yelled.

"Ready," Inés said, barely above a hush.

Everly yanked on the rope. The sails snapped open, and with nothing left to stop it, the hang-glider rolled forward and unceremoniously tipped from its perch.

Gripped with horror, Everly could only watch as her bandmates plummeted headfirst toward the earth. Just before crashing through the lower canopy, the nose of the glider turned upward, and the duo blazed into the sky. They steadied their aircraft and glided above the treetops, soaring in the direction of the beach, their triumphant shrieks and cheers carried on the breeze.

Vashti hummed. "They survived."

"Disappointed?"

"Surprised. You ready?"

Everly gripped the railing and looked out across the expanse. The sun was close to the horizon. The dazzling brightness burned a perfect circle into her retinas. Dusk was spreading quickly across the island. Everly allowed herself one final chance to look down at the jungle floor. Along a path leading away from the clearing, a half dozen pin pricks of light appeared. A group of miniature Rooters were moving through the jungle, using torches to find their way.

"What are they up to?" she wondered aloud.

"Who?" Vashti joined her at the railing.

Everly pointed to the line of flickering lights. At the front, she could make out Tazeen's black garb. Andrew's bright orange hair bobbed beside Min Jun's shaved head, with something being carried between them. "It's the Lemurs," she said.

"They're moving something."

Further back on the trail, Everly spotted another figure. They were keeping pace with the Lemurs, but staying back, which felt off. Why wouldn't they try to catch up? A chill swept through Everly as she realized what she was seeing. "They're being followed," she gasped.

Vashti tranced a finger along the path until it landed on the hooded figure. In the low light, it was impossible to tell who they were. "They're probably just out for a walk," Vashti clucked. "Don't be so dramatic."

Everly's mind raced. With an alleged spy on the island, she needed to alert Tazeen, but she couldn't do it without revealing valuable information to Vashti. Then again, if the shadowy figure really was the spy, that meant Vashti was one of a handful of people who Everly could cross off the list of suspects.

"Can you keep a secret?"

"When it suits me."

"I mean it, Vashti."

"Try me."

Everly hesitated, but the sun had almost set; they needed to act, now. "Someone on the island is working for the Dust."

Vashti's nostrils flared. Her gaze traced the movements of the shadowy figure, scoping them out like a sniper. "How do you know?"

"I heard Tazeen talking."

"When?"

Everly paused. "At the Council meeting."

Vashti's eyes flicked sideways at her. Appraising. Reconfiguring. Out of nowhere, she started to scream: "Tazeen! Umbo! Up here!"

Everly's muscles twitched in surprise. "What are you doing?!"

"Warning them. Tazeen! Look up here!"

"They probably won't hear us," Everly noted.

"You got any better ideas?"

Everly looked around, but couldn't come up with an alternative approach. She put her hands together and made a loon call the way her dad had taught her years before. With any luck, the vibrations would find their way to the jungle floor.

Far below, the torches stopped moving. Seconds later, the air whistled as a black form cut through it. The grackle stopped in front of them, floating on an updraft.

Vashti stumbled backward and landed hard on the gazebo floor. "What the hell?!"

Everly hushed her with her hands. "You'll scare it away. It's Tazeen's bird."

"What does it want?" Vashti grumbled, massaging her hip.

Everly stared at the bird. The grackle landed on the railing and stared back. "We can use it to send a message," she realized. Everly looked around the Crow's Nest. There was nothing to write on, not even a leaf, since the Bloodwood tree grew flat, waxy needles.

"The tiles," Everly said, snapping her fingers. "Here, give me a boost."

Clearly unimpressed with the plan, Vashti allowed Everly to climb onto her shoulders so she could pluck the tiles from their new position above the trap door. It was unsteady and risky; falling inside the tree would be just as deadly as falling outside of it. Once safely back on the platform, Everly selected seven tiles and spread them out on the floor.

"That might work," Vashti admitted through pinched lips. "But are you sure?"

"Sure of what?"

"Do you really want to tell the Umbo what you know?"

Everly chewed her bottom lip, thinking. Vashti was right. By alerting Tazeen to one shady action, she was admitting to another. But if there really was a Dust spy down there, the less they knew about the island, the safer everyone on it would be.

Sacrificing a sock, Everly shoved the tiles inside and tied a knot to secure them. Slowly, she approached the grackle on the railing with an outstretched hand. The bird pinched the welt of the sock in its beak and took off.

They watched the grackle's black body disappear into the darkening canopy. A few minutes later, one by one, the torches went out.

"I guess Tazeen got the message," Vashti said. "Using the tiles wasn't the stupidest idea you've ever had."

Everly ignored her, already planning their next steps. "What are we going to tell Katak and Inés when we get down?"

Vashti frowned, incredulously. "You really don't get it, do you? Secrets are currency. We're not going to tell anybody what we just saw. If you want to stay alive on this island, you shouldn't trust a soul. Not even me."

"I don't trust you," Everly stated.

"Good."

Moving in silence, the girls climbed into the harnesses and secured themselves to the hang-glider. Vashti insisted on steering, so Everly assumed the upper position. If Vashti wanted to be the crash mat, so be it. Vashti unclipped the glider from the wall. Using their hands, the girls clawed their way to the edge of the platform, where the canopy spread out before them. Dangling facedown over the abyss, Everly clamped her eyes shut.

Everly must have been shaking, because Vashti broke character long enough to say, "Don't sweat it. We're not dying today."

Vashti wasn't a fortune teller. This could very easily be the last stupid decision either of them ever made. Everly began to hyperventilate as a distant memory gnawed at her like déjà vu. Through a kaleidoscopic lens, she could almost make out its shape.

Don't fall...Don't fall.

The wind swept up the height of the tree and ruffled Everly's hair. "Now!" Vashti shouted.

Everly pulled the rope, freeing the wings. The girls leaned forward as the wind filled the sails. They rolled from the platform, and their bodies became weightless, soaring high above the treetops. Everly laughed with overwhelming relief. She'd never been off the ground before. She wished Shelby could have seen it, could have felt it. Her sister deserved the chance to take flight.

Somewhere far below them, the jungle concealed the Lemurs. And the spy. As Everly and Vashti floated through the hot night air—to where they would soon crash into the shallow surf and be rescued by their bandmates—Everly envisioned the tiles fanned out between Tazeen's thin palms:

SEE A RAT

CHAPTER 13

Without any tree coverage, the air in the meadow was unsympathetically hot. Nearby, a stream trickled below a short bridge, but the newcomers had been warned not to drink from it. Parasites, allegedly. Everly didn't care that the meadow was beautiful, covered in blue and green mosses, perfumed with pink ginger blossoms. After four weeks on the island, she still had nothing to show for it. And she wasn't in the mood for a botany lesson.

Min Jun was in the midst of explaining the relationship between bees and the island's ecological survival. The meadow was home to a dozen wooden boxes that had been transformed by the eager colonies. Min Jun moved slowly as he removed a slide from one of the hives. The square was covered in bees, who barely registered his presence. He held it out for the bands of newcomers to examine.

Everly moved closer, but kept her neck low in her collar. What if the bees changed their minds and decided to punish everyone for the unwelcome invasion?

"We have to check the hives every few days to make sure they haven't been knocked over or disturbed," Min Jun explained.

"What kind of animal would take on a beehive?" Katak asked.

"Sloth bears, kinkajous, coatis…they all love honey," replied the Lemur. "And can you blame them? It's a miraculous substance, especially honey produced on this island. It's antibacterial, antifungal, antiviral. Not to mention it's just about the sweetest thing on earth."

Everly's ears perked up a bit. She and Shelby spent any extra money they had on home remedies, mystery capsules, and so-called miracle teas and oils. Nothing worked. "Would honey help if you were really sick?" she asked.

"That depends. What kind of sickness are we talking about?"

"I don't know." Everly hesitated, considering how much she wanted to reveal in front of the crowd. "Tumours, maybe?"

"Complex diseases require complex treatments," he replied. "But honey certainly wouldn't hurt."

"How come I've never seen a bee before?" asked a girl from the back of the group.

"Bees vanished from many places around the world because of the drought," Min Jun explained. "It was part of the ecological collapse that happened just before the War."

Everly's focus drifted to the edge of the meadow, where the six mentors were relaxing in the shade. Micah and Nikol were among them, canoodling like they were the only two people alive. Everly hadn't compared notes with the other newcomers, but she was sure Micah was the worst mentor of the bunch. At least he'd bothered to show up today, but he was clearly distracted. She couldn't really blame him; Nikol was a knockout.

Without her permission, an image of Jordan appeared in her mind's eye. His easy smile, his lingering gaze. How would it feel to share the island with someone who already knew so much about her? Someone who never let her down?

Moving carefully, Min Jun placed the slide gently on the mossy ground. Unbothered, the bees performed their zig-zagging dance across a yellow sheet of wax. The Lemur explained that the movements were actually instructions for where to find pollen. From the ash of a campfire pit, Min Jun removed a knife by its wooden handle; its iron blade glowed red.

"We use a hot blade to uncap the honeycomb," he said, demonstrating the technique. The process, which reminded Everly of scraping icing from a cake, revealed the intricate honeycomb pattern hidden beneath the clumpy beeswax. She could barely fathom the mathematical precision of it, how a hive could replicate the same shape, over and over, turning the simple wooden frame into a geometric masterpiece.

"That's wild," Katak exclaimed.

"It's the opposite of wild," Everly countered. "It's *civilized*."

Inés took in the elegant design. "The bees built a beautiful city by working together."

Seated off to the side, Jax laughed, coldly. His band was newly dubbed the Ghost Shrimp, which was fitting—the sound of his voice gave Everly chills. "Please," he scoffed. "The bees are slaves. The queen is their ruler."

"She's not controlling them," Inés disagreed. "They're acting on instinct."

"Wrong," Jax said. "She's using pheromones. The workers are all doped up. We're just like the bees, if you think about it. The Dust built a global empire on the backs of the people. And most of them didn't fight back."

"That's because they didn't have a choice," Everly snarled. "It would be different if everyone knew the rebellion was real. If they knew they had a real chance to fight for something better."

"Not everyone's built to be a rebel," Jax stated, looking her over. "Obviously."

Min Jun raised a hand to pause the debate. "We can learn a lot from the bees. About organization and discipline. About small roles that have an immeasurable impact. In a hive, no one is fighting for power. Humans are different. We all want control. It is an instinct we must learn to suppress in ourselves, so we can fight for one cause."

The sun beat down and the low buzz of the bees tickled the inside of Everly's ears. Did cooperation always mean relenting power? Back at home, she'd never once felt in control of her own life. She couldn't surrender something she'd never had.

Min Jun finished the lesson with some final instructions: "Each band is going to harvest a slide from one hive. If you stay calm and keep the fires smoking, the bees will leave you alone. Put the wax and honey in the buckets and carry them back to the Root when you're finished. There is a special surprise waiting for you there, in honour of the full moon."

"What kind of surprise?" Vashti asked.

Min Jun shrugged. He packed his satchel and waved from the bridge. "Happy harvesting, my friends."

The other bands spread out across the meadow to where their mentors were waiting. Everly scanned the clearing. Micah was nowhere to be found.

"Micah seriously ditched us again?" Katak scoffed.

Everly huffed. "I think he wants us to fail."

Armed with the only guidance they were going to receive, the Naked Mole Rats settled around a hive near the jungle's edge. The other mentors had taken the time to start fires and pre-heat their blades. Everly looked down; their firepit, a mossy circle of rocks with a mushroom troop sprouting in the middle, was untouched.

Katak collected a small pile of pinecones. "Anybody bring matches?" he asked, hopefully.

"Of course not," Vashti clucked.

Out of habit, Everly searched her pockets, expecting to come up empty-handed. Instead, deep in the back pocket of her cargo pants, she felt the outline of something solid. She'd left the archive in such a frantic state, she didn't even remember taking it. Her father's Union badge felt warm in the palm of her hand. Its glass centre bounced the sunlight; she squinted and looked away.

"What's that?" Vashti asked, nosily.

"Our firestarter," Everly replied. She crouched down and angled the glass into the sun. Instantly, a thin beam pierced the pinecones, sending up a spiral of blue smoke.

Katak clapped his hands. "Yes, Everly!"

"That's awesome." Inés grinned.

Everly's cheeks flushed. It felt good to be able to offer something for once. They fed dried leaves and twigs to the fire. When the flames were stable, they added damp moss, filling their site with a smoky haze that burned in the back of Everly's throat.

"Now the only problem is we don't have a blade," Inés pointed out.

Everly looked at Vashti, expectantly.

"What?"

"Seriously, Vashti?"

Reluctantly, and with a scowl, Vashti took Micah's knife out of her pocket and tossed it into the embers. "You should shut your mouth before I shut it for you," she grumbled so only Everly could hear.

"Micah left us here without a blade because he knew you already had one," Everly countered. It wasn't necessarily true, but the logic was sound.

"Micah knew about his own knife. That's one thing. But he also knew what was in your pants. That's another thing altogether." The comment made Everly feel uneasy, like she was at the centre of a salacious rumour. No one could have known about the badge; Everly didn't even know she had it. She slipped it into her front pocket for safekeeping.

Once the blade was hot, Inés got to work uncapping the honeycombs. The wax sat in a golden mound with honey pooling at the bottom of the bucket.

"I'm starving," Vashti wined. She picked up a chunk of honeycomb. "Let's try some."

"Don't even think about it," Katak warned. "You get caught stealing food, my bet is we all take a beating."

"For a big boy, you're kind of a wuss, you know that?"

"I'm a wuss?"

"Yup."

"Think I won't hit a girl?"

"Think I won't pull a knife?"

"Keep talking." Katak clucked with a wave of his hand.

Vashti walked over to the campfire. She kicked a sandalled foot against a smouldering stick and sent it flying into Katak's lap. He squawked, brushing away live sparks. "Are you insane?" he bellowed.

"Knock it off, you two," Everly warned. "You're pissing off the bees."

"You're a special kind of psycho, you know that?" Katak snapped.

Vashti bared her teeth. "You have no idea."

It happened so quickly. A whistle through the air. A thunk against the wooden box. The chainsaw-like roar as the bees responded to the red-feathered arrow that had just pierced through the Naked

Mole Rat's hive.

"Move!" Everly cried as the angry bees rose into the air.

The Naked Mole Rats sprawled in different directions. Vashti ducked into the jungle, the sound of breaking branches and violent curses trailing behind her. Inés and Everly ran for the bridge. Before crossing, Everly glanced over her shoulder.

The meadow was in a state of chaos. Their hive had triggered a chain reaction, and now all the hives were swarming. Newcomers and mentors ran for cover, sprinting into the jungle or diving into the shallow stream. In the middle of the clearing, Katak was under attack. With only one victim left to focus on, the bees descended.

"Katak!" Everly screamed.

Inés whipped around. She saw Katak's predicament and froze, face marred with horror.

"We have to help him," Everly shouted.

The two girls ran back into the fray and dragged Katak to his feet. He moaned and stumbled, but managed to stand.

"Get to the water!" Everly yelled. She ran hard, but that didn't stop the bees from stinging her arms and legs so many times she lost count.

The trio slid down the muddy bank and into the stream. Together, they kicked and pulled through the shallows, using the slippery river bottom to claw their way along. After a short distance, the stream widened into a pool. Everly peered above the water. The swarm had stopped at the bridge.

They waited a few more minutes to make sure the coast was clear before they crawled from the water and collapsed onto the muddy bank like beached whales. Everly's skin burned with a foul heat. She pulled up her shirt and found a bee still attached to her, hanging on by its stinger. She tossed it into the stream.

To her left, Katak was in a bad state. The welts on his cheeks were joined into pumpkin-like ridges. "I'll never eat honey again," he coughed, checking to make sure his cap was still in place.

Inés dug her fingers into the red clay and spread it across her legs. "This helps," she whimpered. Everly smeared a handful all over.

The red earth felt cool and soothing.

"We have to find Vashti," Katak groaned, smearing clay along his jaw.

"Do we?" Inés scowled.

"It wasn't her arrow," he pointed out.

"Inés, you stay with Katak," Everly instructed. "I'll go find her."

"Be careful," Inés said.

Everly climbed the slippery bank and kept close to the shore as she made her way back to the meadow. Thankfully, the bees didn't hold a grudge and had shifted their focus back to their hives. Everly entered the bush where she'd last seen Vashti.

The jungle was littered with newcomers, each emerging from their hiding spots. As Everly jogged by, she saw Jax crawl out from between two logs. He reached back to help Jolene, whose leg was still wrapped in a plaster cast.

"Vashti!" Everly hollered. "Vashti, where are you?"

"I'm up here!"

Everly followed the sound to the base of a mango tree and found Vashti swinging by a thin branch near the top.

"Is it over?" Vashti asked.

"Yes," Everly confirmed.

Vashti shimmied through the branches and climbed down the trunk. She sank to the jungle floor, panting. She'd escaped the bees, except for a pair of stings on her right hand that were growing by the second.

"Are you okay?" Everly asked. "You don't look so good."

"You're no beauty queen yourself," she sniffed.

"I mean it, Vashti. Are you allergic to bees?"

"I don't know. I've never been stung before. My throat feels weird, though." Vashti scratched her neck and left claw marks behind.

Everly fought to stay calm. If Vashti was allergic, the situation was dire. Back at the Root, Maria Jose might have something, but they were an hour's walk from the Bloodwood tree. Without proper medicine, Vashti might die before they made it back.

"We need help!" Everly shouted.

Vashti flinched. "So dramatic."

Pushing his way through the bush, Jax reappeared. He looked at Vashti, who was breaking out in shiny red hives. Her body trembled as a fever took hold. "That ain't good," he stated.

"Can you carry her?" It sounded like begging, but Everly didn't care.

"No, I have to carry Jolene."

"You can come back for Jolene," Everly insisted.

Jax scowled. "I'm not leaving my sister alone in the jungle. Your bandmate, your problem." Thick ferns closed behind him as he hiked away.

Vashti's eyelids were nearly swollen shut. "You go on ahead," she shuddered. "I'll rest here for a minute."

"I'll go get help," Everly said, struggling with the knowledge that Vashti might die before her return.

"Excellent plan," Vashti wheezed.

Branches whacked Everly from all directions as she sprinted through the jungle. Back at the bridge, she found Katak and Inés still on the bank. "Vashti needs help!" she shouted. "She's in the jungle. Twenty, thirty feet behind our hive. I'm going to find medicine!"

"Wait, what?!" Inés yelled back.

"She's allergic to bees. Katak, I know you're messed up, but can you carry her?"

"I'll try," he said, heaving himself from the muddy shore.

Everly crossed the bridge and turned onto the red dirt trail. In the distance, the top of the Bloodwood tree poked out above the canopy. If she ran flat out the whole way, would she make it back in time? Everly was grateful Micah had forced them to run to and from the beach every day as she took off at a sprint.

The trail was soft under her feet. The sun was unrelenting, as were the mosquitos that chased her. The stings on her body burned and throbbed, but she refused to let them slow her down. After a while, she turned a corner and spotted Min Jun picking leaves from a bush.

"Min Jun!" Everly shouted, breathless. "We need help!"

As they retraced her steps, Everly filled him in. She struggled to keep up with the Lemur's long, graceful strides. They didn't have to travel far before intercepting a group on the trail. Katak and Inés were among them. Vashti was semi-conscious in Katak's arms.

"Put her down," Min Jun instructed.

Above her collarbone, the flesh on Vashti's neck sucked in with each inhale. Her two stings were covered in a green paste.

"What is that?" Min Jun asked.

"Ephedra leaves," Inés explained. "I chewed them first. I didn't know what else to do."

"You did the right thing, but she needs something stronger." Min Jun dug in his satchel and pulled out a syringe with clear fluid. He jabbed the needle into the fabric covering Vashti's thigh.

She twitched and muttered something incoherent.

"We have to get her to the Root. Quickly," Min Jun said with a furrowed brow. "Where's Micah?"

"Dude took off an hour ago," Katak explained.

The Lemur bit his lip, his features tightening with an anger that had no present target. Min Jun scooped Vashti from the ground and cradled her in his arms. Too out of it to protest, Vashti rested her cheek against his chest.

The sound of footsteps scuffed the earth behind them. "Min Jun!" Micah called as he approached. He and Nikol raced up to them, looking utterly confused and mortified. "What happened?" he asked.

The concern in his voice sounded sincere, but Everly knew better. To Micah, she and her friends were completely disposable. Everly grinded her molars, fearful of what she might say if she opened her mouth.

Min Jun frowned. "Nikol, run ahead and find Maria Jose. Tell her we need more ephedrine. Hurry!"

Nikol took off down the road.

Min Jun turned his attention to the world's worst mentor. "They're newcomers, Micah!" he snapped with such force the whole group flinched. "You went directly against orders."

"I wasn't that far, Min Jun. I was only gone a couple minutes."

Everly scowled. The first part might be true, but the second part certainly wasn't. He and Nikol had been off sucking face for a long while before the arrow hit the hive. The spy had launched their first attack, and for all she knew, Micah was the one holding the bow.

"No excuses!" Min Jun boomed. "Of all the stupid, irresponsible, reprehensible moves!"

The Lemur chastised Micah all the way back to the Bloodwood tree. Everly thoroughly enjoyed it, and was sad when the tongue lashing was over. Micah deserved far worse than a public shaming. She wanted him flogged.

When Min Jun finally ran out of steam, Micah dropped his chin. "I hear what you're saying," he said, abashedly. "I'm sorry, Min Jun."

"Don't be sorry, just be better," the Lemur fumed. "You heard what Tazeen said at the Council meeting. The newcomers are to have eyes on them. Always. While you were looking away, a single arrow nearly took them all out."

"Who do you think fired it?" Everly asked the backs of their heads.

Min Jun and Micah stopped talking, remembering their audience.

"I'll find out," Micah said. Although how he planned to do that was a mystery, considering he wasn't even there to witness the crime.

"Leave the investigation to the Lemurs," Min Jun stated. He turned to look at Micah with a judgemental gaze. "I expect you to use your time building bridges rather than digging holes. Otherwise, if you ever need to be carried, the Naked Mole Rats might bury you instead. I've seen it happen before."

CHAPTER 14

The sky clouded over and warm rain filtered through the canopy. As they entered the clearing, the Bloodwood tree acted as a giant umbrella. Micah crossed the aerial roots with Vashti slung over his shoulder like a ragdoll. At the base of the tree, he stepped onto a square patch of moss that hid a trap door. The ground fell away and the two of them disappeared into the underworld.

When it was her turn, Everly stepped onto the lift and fell like a raindrop into the black column of the hollow trunk. Her knees gave out at the bottom, and she crumpled onto the floor. She could have happily stayed there, in a heap of her own bones, but several hands dragged her over to a pile of cushions. Maria Jose appeared and began applying a strong-smelling balm to Everly's stings.

"Is Vashti going to be okay?" Everly asked, unable to spot her bandmate in the crowded trunk.

"She'll live," Maria Jose confirmed. "Thanks to you."

Everly scanned the room but the haze of bee venom made it hard to focus. The Rooters were lounging on colourful cushions, chatting and laughing and playing cards. Off to the side, Micah and Nikol were talking to two other boys—a skinny kid with long hair and a boy with a purple birthmark covering half his face.

"Who are they?" she asked, motioning toward them with her chin.

Maria Jose looked up. "Ping's got the ponytail and Arseniy is rocking the badass port-wine stain. They're Fire Ants, too."

"How long have Micah and Nikol been a thing?"

"About a year. And they make sure the whole island knows it."

"I guess some people enjoy an audience," Everly clucked. The bee venom was loosening her tongue, an effect that she'd have to be cautious of as the night wore on. "Is this a party or something?"

"Or something," the Lemur said with a smirk.

The Umbo entered the trunk through one of the tunnels, drifting like a black cloud across the uneven floor. "I have to go," Maria Jose said. She met the rest of the Lemurs in the middle of the trunk. The Rooters all climbed to their feet as Tazeen stepped onto a wooden crate. Everly stayed in place, partially out of defiance, partially because her body wouldn't move.

The Umbo gestured for everyone to take their seats, and she waited until the crowd was settled comfortably before addressing them. "We're gathered tonight to celebrate the full moon, and our newcomers, who have shown great bravery and fortitude for the past four weeks. It's time for some formal introductions. I give you the Ghost Shrimp!"

Everly spotted Jax, Jolene, and their two bandmates, named Tusha and Jihad, near the back. As they stood up, Jax helped his sister to balance on one leg. The crowd cheered.

"The Nine-Banded Armadillos; the Funnel Web Spiders!" Two more groups were hailed like returning war heroes. When Taz announced the Burrowing Owls, five dejected newcomers climbed to their feet and waited out the applause with vacant expressions. Nikol's recruits had been harvesting honey at the hive next to Everly and her bandmates when the arrow struck; they were probably too pumped full of bee venom to care about the praise.

"And last but not least, I introduce to you, the Naked Mole Rats!"

Everly, Inés, and Katak struggled to their feet. The crowd erupted with laughter, clapping with appreciation. Their band name was a hit, apparently. Vashti would be pissed, if they ever saw her again. Everly rocked on her feet as the trunk pulsated around her.

"Let the feasting begin!" Tazeen proclaimed.

From the tunnels, Rooters appeared carrying platters of food; each tray was piled high with steaming bowls of rice, eggplant, fruit, and fish. Everly was starving, but what she really wanted was to go home and eat a whole box of cereal beside Shelby on the couch. What was Shelby doing right now? Was she lonely? Was she thinking about Everly, too? Was she even alive, or had she finally succumbed to the sickness and the Dust's cruelty? The thoughts made Everly want to cry. Instead, she focused on shovelling food into her mouth. It was the first hot meal she'd had in forever, and she planned to eat herself into a coma.

As night fell, the blue mushrooms came to life, glowing like constellations across the inner walls of the trunk and peeking between the floorboards. In the middle of the trunk, a drum circle formed. The air vibrated with rhythmic thumping. Ebimi stepped into the circle, casually swinging ropes at her side. Her long locs were pulled back into a braid as thick as a hawser. The shadows danced across her dark skin. The Rooters clapped and shouted her name as the Lemur began to sway her hips, swinging the ropes in circles.

She moved around in exaggerated steps as the drums accelerated. Out of nowhere, the ends of the ropes burst into flames. With undeniable confidence, Ebimi drew symbols in the darkness with the fireballs. With a jubilant scream, the Rooters on doumbeks, bongos, and tambourines kicked into full gear, pounding out a chaotic beat that Everly felt in the nerves of her teeth. Ebimi spun and twirled the burning ropes, throwing them in the air, catching them behind her back.

The music crescendoed and she landed on her knees as a trapdoor fell away. She dropped her ropes into the empty space and flames shot high into the inky blackness of the trunk. The heat was enough to singe Everly's eyelashes, and she wasn't even that close to it.

"Welcome to the bonfire!" Ebimi declared. The crowd roared.

As the next performers took their positions, Everly rubbed her collarbone nervously. An androgynous pair of Earthworms stepped into the circle. Their long hair fanned out as they twirled, spinning hoops around their necks and ankles. With each pass, they added more hoops to the mix. One formed a sphere, which they lifted jubilantly. The other transformed the hoops into wings that flapped to the beat of the drums.

By the time they finished, Everly's cheeks were aglow, and against her better judgement, she found herself swept up in the weird pageantry.

The performances lasted long into the night. Ping did sleight-of-hand tricks, releasing colourful birds into the humid air. They flew in a spiral around the bonfire's column of heat before disappearing through cracks in the walls. Andrew entered the trunk carrying a yellow python with creepy black marbles for eyes. The snake wove itself around his thick arms and legs, finally resting its sizable skull on top of Andrew's mop. Chen, a broad-chested mentor with a bowl cut, swallowed swords the length of his torso. As a grand finale, he filled his mouth with oil and spewed it through the flames, sending brilliant blasts of fire over the crowd.

Soon all of the Rooters were dancing around the bonfire in a kaleidoscope of hair, feathers, and limbs. Drunk off the party, or maybe it was the bee venom, Inés joined in, throwing her hips from side-to-side and twisting her wrists above her head. Not wanting to miss out, Katak lumbered around the circle with heavy feet and flailing arms.

In the middle of the crowd, Everly noticed Nikol dancing with Arseniy. Her movements were fluid and sensuous. The girl glanced over and caught Everly staring, abruptly abandoning her dance partner to move gracefully through the crowd, flashing her pretty smile and touching everyone she passed. Nikol sat down across from Everly on a frayed pillow and drained a cup of tea.

"You should be dancing!" Nikol insisted, wiping sweat from her brow. Her irises were different colours, one green and one blue, which made it hard to focus on both. Everly looked at her own hands instead.

"I don't dance," she admitted.

"I could teach you."

"Like you're teaching him?" Everly nodded toward the dejected-looking boy.

"Who, Arseniy? He'll be fine. Sorry about today. That went bad in a hurry."

"It wasn't your fault," Everly said, which was technically true.

Nikol cast her a suggestive smile. "It kind of was. But we were being selfish. It won't happen again."

"It probably will," Everly grumbled.

"No," Nikol insisted. "We're mentors. We're going to be more focused from now on."

"Focused on what?"

"The cause."

"The cause," Everly repeated, sitting up a little straighter. "What can you tell me about it? I know Rooters sometimes get summoned for special missions, like when Micah came to recruit me. Have you ever left the island for a mission?"

Nikol smiled. "If I had, I wouldn't be able to talk about it. Secrecy is security."

"So I've heard," Everly sighed. "But is there anyone here who actually knows what's going on with the rebellion out in the real world? Where I come from, the Bloodwood Society is a myth. No one has seen them in action for years."

"Bloodwood used to be a lot stronger, but there was a major breach ten years ago, and thousands of rebels were killed. We've been rebuilding ever since," Nikol explained.

"And the people in charge—"

"The Spearheads."

"Right, the Spearheads. How do you know they have a plan that will even work?"

Nikol selected a fried sardine and popped the whole thing in her mouth, speaking while she chewed. "I've seen what Bloodwood can do. They got me out of a bad situation, and I gave them my life in exchange. Joining the cause means believing in something greater than ourselves. I think Micah and I forgot that for a minute. Have you seen one of these before?" Nikol rolled up her pant leg. She plucked a mushroom from between two boards and used the pale blue light to reveal the rebellion's insignia—a silhouetted tree, what Everly now recognized as the Bloodwood, inside of a crescent moon.

"Who gave you that?" Everly asked.

"The Umbo."

"Risky move, branding all the rebels."

Nikol blinked. "It's only risky if you get caught."

"What are we talking about?" Micah asked, crashing between them on the cushions. He pulled Nikol into his lap and kissed her neck like that wasn't a totally gross thing to do in front of someone who wasn't about to participate.

"Commitment," Nikol replied, nuzzling him back.

Micah rubbed his thumb over the invisible tattoo on his girl-friend's thigh. "Don't worry, Everly. Only the initiated take the mark. The Naked Mole Rats won't make it that far. "

Everly felt the edges of her front teeth with her tongue. "If we fail, it'll be because we had a shitty teacher."

Micah shrugged. "The weak do not survive."

"Survival of the fittest, right?" Everly raised her eyebrows. "If you'd ever actually read a book, you'd know Darwin says it takes all types."

"You think you're smart, eh?" he tisked. "Just like your dad. Look where that got him."

Everly felt a familiar sensation in her core, like a match being struck near a propane leak. She took a swig of green tea from a metal cup, hoping to douse the flame.

"Micah, go easy," Nikol interjected. She reached for him, but he moved her hand away.

"You know what really pisses me off? I did what Tazeen asked, I got this kid away from the Dust, and I'm still trapped on this god-forsaken island. And to make matters worse, I'm stuck mentoring a bunch of rejects. Katak's an idiot, Vashti's a certified sociopath, Inés has literally no skills whatsoever, and Everly's only here because of the Bloodline Law."

"What do you mean?" Nikol asked.

Everly sat up so fast the tea spilled in her lap. "Yes, Micah, we'd all like to know."

Unfortunately, the Umbo chose that exact moment to appear beside the mat. "Never you mind," Tazeen interrupted. She turned to the Fire Ants. "Micah. Nikol. A word, if you will."

Micah glared at Everly. Apparently, it was somehow her fault he was about to be lambasted by the Umbo. Everything Nikol had said about him was garbage—he would never put anything, especially the newcomers in his charge, before himself.

The world's worst mentor and Nikol followed the Umbo away from the bonfire and into a tunnel. Everly could only hope Tazeen kept a torture chamber back there; it would be nice to see Micah actually punished for a change.

With a chest full of dynamite, Everly leaned back on a cushion. The grackle soared across the trunk. It twittered before diving into the tunnel, following its beloved Tazeen. The bird gave Everly an idea.

She made her way to the back of the trunk where she ducked into the tunnel marked with Roman numeral IV. A glowing mushroom plucked from the ground lit the way. Even without the grackle's help, Everly managed to locate the right opening in the wall. She folded herself into the crevasse. When she reached the ladder, Everly felt behind the bottom rung and exhaled with relief—the journal was still there.

Blue light flooded the pages as she opened the book. She couldn't be gone long, and unfortunately, she didn't have time to read the whole thing. But she wanted dirt on her mentor, and the best place to start was his scar. Something bad had clearly gone down and not long ago. Everly flipped to the last entry, dated two years earlier. It was a transcript.

Deep underground, with a luminous mushroom in hand, Everly learned the story, as told by Micah Kikwete himself.

CHAPTER 15

Interviewer: This is Bloodwood investigator XIB, interview number 2 with Micah Kikwete. May 11, 2073. Alright, Micah. Tell me what happened once you made it to the tracks.

Micah: It was so hot. I wasn't expecting that. The air smelled like grease and metal. And it was pitch black. Nobody warned me it would be that dark.

Interviewer: You were running down the tracks.

Micah: I was following the tracks, and the walls of the tunnel started to shake. I checked my watch. The train was a full minute early.

Interviewer: And this didn't concern you?

Micah: It did. I mean, we planned everything. To the second. I tried to contact Ezra, but my earpiece was full of static. So I kept running. The backpack they gave me was too heavy.

Interviewer: Micah, focus. The train.

Micah: The train shook the tunnel so hard that dirt was falling from the rafters. I was scared the whole thing would collapse. But I did what I was told. I counted the cross beams—three hundred and two. I stopped at the concrete ladder. Then Erza's voice was in my ear, saying something that sounded like "port...port" and I shouted for him to repeat, but all I could hear was clicks and pops.

The train rounded the corner. The lights were so bright they blinded me for a second. The engine, the wheels, the gears, it was so loud. I started climbing. I got to the top of the ladder, I swung the bag around, I took out the package, and I waited for the train to pass me. There was supposed to be an open window and a long hook. Simple. But, I mean, looking back, getting a package on a hook fed through the window of a moving train was never going to be simple, even if everything went according to plan. Which, clearly, it didn't.

Interviewer: What happened next?

Micah: The train went by me and the force of it nearly tore me off the wall. I counted the passenger cars as they passed. Further back on the train, a hand reached out. I saw it, holding the red bandanna. The go-ahead sign. But then the hand went slack and released it. The bandana kind of thrashed between the train and the walls. When I reached out and snagged it, the fabric was hot. And wet.

Interviewer: What was it?

Micah: Blood.

Interviewer: Do you need to take a minute to compose yourself?

Micah: No. I'm okay. I'm good.

Interviewer: Alright. What happened next.

Micah: The train was in front of me. The lights inside kept going on and off. I saw a man with a machete. There was a spray of blood across the glass. Our people on the train were already dead.

Interviewer: How did you know that?

Micah: I mean, I didn't *know it*, know it. I just knew I needed to get out of there. There was this loud squeal and the train started slowing down. I put the package in the backpack and I decided to keep climbing.

Interviewer: Were those your orders?

Micah: No. The orders were to retrace my steps back to the checkpoint, but that wasn't an option. If I did the wrong thing, I'm sorry, but my equipment was malfunctioning, I couldn't reach my mission leader, and I knew the drop was a bust. I had nowhere else to go, so I climbed. At the top of the ladder, there was a manhole cover, and I shoved it aside and pulled myself through. I popped out in the middle of a deserted city, but I had no idea where I was. That's when Ezra started screaming in my ear.

Interviewer: What did he say? Exact phrasing, please.

Micah: He said, "Micah, abort! Abort mission! We're compromised, get out of there!" I asked him which way I should go, but before he could answer, a hand shot up from the hole and grabbed the bag. I fell backwards and caught myself. I was lying across the manhole with my arms and legs spread out. A machete cut into my shoulder and the pain was like, white hot. I tried to roll away, but this huge guy climbed out of the hole.

Interviewer: Describe his appearance.

Micah: Six-foot-five. Gnarled face. Gold teeth.

Interviewer: Do you need to take a break?

Micah: No. I'm good.

Interviewer: Did you recognize the man?

Micah: Yes. He was a captain in the Lord's Freedom Army.

Interviewer: Did you know him?

Micah: Yes.

Interviewer: What did he say to you?

Micah: He called me Skull Crusher.

Interviewer: Skull Crusher?

Micah: It was my name...from my time in the army.

Interviewer: As a soldier.

Micah: A child soldier. I was kidnapped when I was twelve. I was their slave for more than two years. Bloodwood got me out.

Interviewer: I understand.

Micah: Do you?

Interviewer: Micah, that part...that part is not my job. Did you say anything to the man?

Micah: I said, "That's not my name!" Then he broke my nose with the back of the machete. He kicked me in the head. I saw sparks. After that, everything got real blurry.

Interviewer: Did he say anything to you before he took the package?

Micah: Yeah. He said, "Tell the Spearheads I say thanks."

Interviewer: I see.

Micah: You can ask Ezra. He heard the whole thing through my earpiece.

Interviewer: I've already spoken with Ezra. What happened next?

Micah: The guy dropped back into the manhole cover and rode the train back to hell.

Interviewer: Did you try to go after him?

Micah: No. Ezra told me to "stay put," like I had any other options.

My arm was hanging off my body, my nose was broken, my brain was rocked, and I'd lost a ton of blood. I started crying. I cried like a baby.

Interviewer (reading from radio transcript):

Ezra, "Stay put, we are coming to get you."

Micah, "What happened?"

Ezra, "We were compromised."

Micah, "Yeah, no shit. Ezra, what the hell was in that bag?"

Ezra, "Nothing that's any good to us now."

Micah: That's it. I waited for the team to extract me. Look, no matter what anyone says, I did exactly what I was told. No deviations. No mistakes.

Interviewer: That's for our investigation to determine. Why do you think you were chosen for this mission?

Micah: Oh, I know why. At first, I thought it was because I was special. But now I know better. The Spearheads sent me because I know the country and I know the LFA. I could have been kidnapped. Again. If that had happened, I would have killed myself. You don't know what these men are capable of. You have no fucking idea.

Interviewer: Micah, do you understand the consequences of losing that package?

Micah: A thousand deaths. Or so I'm told.

Interviewer: That's the estimate.

Micah: I know. I'll...I'll make up for it. I swear I will. Where are you sending me next?

Interviewer: Back to the island.

Micah: No.

Interviewer: To continue your training.

Micah: No! Give me another chance. Send me back to Ezra. I can help. Please, I'll go crazy on the island. Don't send me back there to rot!

Interviewer: It's done, Micah. This is Bloodwood investigator XIB interviewing Micah Kikwete. May 11, 2073. Interview 2 is complete.

CHAPTER 16

E verly spent the next week obsessing over all the questions she wanted to ask her mentor, who was nowhere to be found. According to Taz, he was in purgatory, but she offered no further explanation. Min Jun took charge of the band, which would have been nice, had he not dropped the Naked Mole Rats in a plantain grove and instructed them to pick the trees clean. Every aspect of the task—the heat, the mosquitos, the tree-dwelling snakes—made their lives terrible.

Milking her anaphylaxis for all it was worth, Vashti rejoined the group the morning after the harvest was complete. She sauntered into the trunk looking fresh as a daisy and joined them for a bowl of rice and coconut milk. "Don't all of you rush to greet me at once," she said.

"So, you didn't die," Katak noted with his mouth full.

"I'm immortal."

Everly was nose-deep in her bowl when she noticed Micah across the trunk. His fingers were wrapped in bandages, so however he'd spent his days away had taken a small toll. He finished his meal and made his way over to where his charges were eating in silence.

"Vacation's over. I hope you're ready for some real work," he stated.

"Micah, so lovely of you to drop by," Vashti schmoozed.

"You're looking better than when I last saw you," Micah replied.

"So nice of you to notice."

"I'll meet you all topside in five," their mentor said before walking away.

"Wow. He disappears for a week and now he's a totally different person," Katak said sarcastically.

Inés snorted into her bowl. Everly was too tired and annoyed to feel amused. Clearly, Micah could put them in whatever dangerous situation he wanted, and Tazeen would let him get away with it. Purgatory was a joke.

With heavy limbs and zero enthusiasm, Everly followed the others up the lift. They tailed Micah across the aerial roots and into the jungle. They hadn't gotten far when the underbrush split open and revealed the entrance to a staircase carved into the side of the cliff. Once they reached the riverbank, Everly saw a row of cedar kayaks sitting expectantly along the shore. Her mood improved. A day out on the river would be a welcome change.

Micah dragged a boat into knee-deep water and called out a lesson, demonstrating a technique that involved bracing a paddle into the riverbed and shimmying his legs inside the hull of the kayak.

"Don't turn your boat sideways or the current will dump you. If you flip, leave your boat. Swim to the shore, grab onto something—a branch, a rock, whatever you can find—and wait for help," he instructed. "The lake is a straight shot from here if you stay on the main river and avoid the tributaries. Stay close so you don't get lost." Micah paddled out to the middle of the river. The current grabbed the kayak and carried him swiftly downstream.

"I'm not the best swimmer," Inés admitted, fingernails in her mouth.

"You'll be okay. Look." Everly held up a frayed life vest that looked like a relic from the War and immediately doubted her own words.

Katak tugged on a vest that was clearly made for someone half his size. "You see? This is going to be great!" He shoved a kayak away from the bank and hopped into his boat without so much as a wobble.

"Have you done this before?" Everly called out to him.

"Are you joking? My people invented these things. My dad used to take me out on the inlet every summer."

Everly felt an invisible punch to her solar plexus. Katak's parents went through the ice and never resurfaced. How mad would

Katak be when he found out she knew? How long could she keep her knowledge hidden?

There were many things she hadn't told her bandmates. Everly had wanted to discuss Micah's failed mission with them, but she couldn't admit that one file existed without having to answer questions about the others. Keeping one secret meant keeping many.

Everly capsized her boat immediately, but was able to climb in with Inés's help on her second attempt. She leaned from side-to-side to test her balance.

Inés handed her a paddle. "At least we're going downstream," she offered.

"Sure, on the way there," Everly replied.

Inés paled. "What?"

At first, the sensations inside the boat were unsettling. The current slapped against the sides, and a few times, Everly came close to flipping. She sorted out how to use the paddle for balance and found a rhythm as the blade cut through the water. Everly rounded the first bend and caught sight of Micah. He was facing upstream in his kayak, using the rush of the current over a boulder to surf a continuous wave. Eventually, the current kicked him further downstream.

As they drifted along, Micah shouted out landmarks—a makeshift suspension bridge, a footpath leading away from a pebble beach to a place called the Cocoa Copse, a tributary that led to a waterfall which he called "the best make-out spot on the island." Everly kept mental notes, but that last location probably wasn't worth remembering.

Soon, the earth rose on either side of the river and funnelled them into a canyon, narrowing until they were forced to paddle in single file. The canyon walls were smooth and marbled with swirling blues and greens that shimmered and played with the light. The water slowed and became a milky turquoise colour. Far above them, the sky was an undulating strip of blue. Vines, thick and heavy with leaves and flowers, crawled the canyon walls. Everly had never seen a more beautiful place. Her heart ached, anticipating the instant they'd leave the canyon behind and it would change from a moment to a memory.

Movement along the vines snapped Everly out of her revelry. Black and white monkeys leapt between the hanging plants like trapeze artists. Chatter bounded through the canyon. With a long white beard and a crooked smile, one of them flipped from the vines and grabbed a handful of Vashti's hair as she floated by. Vashti shrieked. The capuchin hissed through yellow fangs. It released its grip and scurried back up the wall, disappearing over the top of the canyon.

"What the hell!" Vashti exclaimed, rubbing her scalp.

"Don't trust those guys," Micah said. "They'll steal your stuff."

Everly watched the animals with fascination. The most exotic creature she'd ever encountered before her recruitment was a moose, standing with its knobby knees in the middle of the road. Now, she'd seen a bonafide barrel of monkeys.

After a short distance, the canyon widened and the river spilled into a crystalline lake. Everly and the others paddled across its velvety surface, sending v-shaped ripples to the shore. She leaned over, staring into the depths of the clear, blue waters. With her nose almost touching, Everly tipped.

For a second, she was trapped underwater with her legs stuck in the hull. Water flooded her sinuses. Everly pushed hard against the wooden gunwales and wiggled her legs free. She burst from the water, gasping and sputtering. Her life vest barely offered the extra buoyancy needed to stay afloat.

Micah paddled over to her. "You good?" he asked.

"Never better," she coughed.

He waved the others over and began his instructions. "Welcome to Emerald Lake. We're here to catch Piraiba. They're a type of catfish. And just a warning, they can grow to be as big as sharks."

Everly squealed and swam as fast as she could for the shoreline, leaving her upside-down kayak behind.

The Naked Mole Rats spent the rest of the afternoon fishing with clear lines, stone hooks, and slimy grubs. The fish, which turned out to be no more than a foot in length, were caught with ease. Their challenge was fighting the wriggling bodies without falling from their kayaks.

The sun set behind the group as they dragged their boats to the eastern shore. Micah built a campfire, cleaned a pair of fish, laid the meat out on a flat piece of wood, and placed it across the fire. The lake blushed pink and orange as they feasted. Everly thought of Jordan, who often took a beating for illegal fishing. He would've loved this, the fresh-water lake, the cookout, all of it. She imagined Jordan seated beside her, teasing her about something ridiculous. Her heart twinged.

When the campfire had dwindled to red coals, Micah cleared his throat. He looked notably uncomfortable, which meant Everly needed to savour every word that was about to come out of his mouth.

"There's something I want to say," he started. "Look, I know I haven't been a good mentor so far. I've been angry at Taz for a lot of reasons, and I've been taking that anger out on you."

"Correct," said Katak, picking his teeth with a fishbone.

Micah sighed. "What I'm trying to say is, I'm sorry. Even though I didn't want to be a mentor in the first place, I'm going to make sure I do a good job of it from now on. It's not your fault I'm stuck here, and I won't make my problems your problems anymore. I promise."

Vashti smacked her lips. "Apologies are nice and all, but you know what would really make us feel better?"

Micah cocked his head.

"Dessert."

"No such luck."

"Fine, how about you answer one question about yourself?" Everly suggested. She tried to sound casual, even though she'd been waiting for ages for the opportunity to arise.

"Weird request, but fine. I'll play along."

Everly perked up. Micah's pink scar was visible through his shirt, but she already knew that morbid tale. "Tell us your recruitment story," she blurted out before anyone else had a chance.

"Everly! Do you think we could have discussed it first?" Inés scolded.

"Too late," Micah cut in. "I mean, I could have told you the meaning of life, or the secret location of a freezer full of ice cream, but sure, my recruitment will do."

"Way to go, Everly," Katak muttered, clearly disappointed.

Micah settled into the sand. "The Dust would never admit what I'm about to say, but they don't have complete control of the Afro-Continent. Places still exist that have been virtually untouched by the War. So, the Dust hires mercenaries from the poorest regions to round up the remaining villagers and relocate them to urban centres.

"We thought we were safe, so far out in the savanna. But we heard rumours that the mercenaries were getting closer, and my mother became afraid. She needed to stay behind to tend to the farm, but she sent me to stay with her cousins further north. After a lot of tears, she wrapped some food and sent me away. I walked for hours and hours. When I finally got there, I passed out on the floor with my shoes still on.

"The next morning, a *mzungu* stopped by the house. There aren't many white people where I'm from. He pulled me aside and told me the mercenaries had attacked our village in the night. He said my mother had been killed."

"Micah…" Everly hushed.

He held his hand up and pursed his lips, as if the sympathy in her voice might break him. "I couldn't accept it, not from a stranger, not without seeing the truth for myself. So I ran. I ran for half a day. I could barely feel my feet. When I got closer, I followed the smoke to the village. The stranger had been telling the truth. The huts had been burned to the ground. The beams that once held up our small home were still smouldering, and beneath them, I found what was left of my mother's corpse. Hours later, when I'd stopped sobbing, I buried her and marked her grave with a pile of rocks.

"Then, I set out to find the men responsible. I was in shock, and I don't remember it clearly. All I know is that I reached a mercenary campsite. One of the soldiers was sitting in front of a campfire with his back to me. I picked up a rock with jagged edges, I sprang from the brambles, and I hit him over the head. His skull cracked like an egg. He fell from the stump and didn't get up.

"The other men caught me and beat me within an inch of my life. They locked me up with some other kids from my village. After weeks of being tortured and starved, the mercenaries put us to work. I was twelve years old when I became a child soldier.

"It was two years before I saw the man from the road again. I came across him in a small town we were sent to ransack, and I had every intention of pumping him full of bullets as he approached me. But he shouted, "I can take you to Ezra!" so I stopped. My brother had left home years before, and I'd tucked his name so deep in my memory that I'd all but forgotten it. The man grabbed my weapon and jabbed a needle into my neck before I even knew what hit me. One minute I'm wielding a machine gun, calling myself Skull Crusher, the next I'm waking up in a box."

"That part I can relate to," Vashti said.

"It's the one thing we all have in common," Micah said with a nod.

Katak shook his head. "That shit is rough, man."

"Tell me about it." Unconsciously, he touched his scar, tracing it from his pec over the arch of his shoulder. "I've made a lot of mistakes in my life, and letting my mother send me away was one of them. I should have stayed to protect her. Since her death, I've been looking for ways to make up for that mistake. But I've failed, over and over. Unfortunately, I'm stuck on this island, and all I can do is wait around and let the past eat me up inside.

"I never wanted to be a mentor; Tazeen knows that. She knows I'm desperate to get back to fighting for the rebellion. But, since you all arrived, I've acted like a fool. I've let you down. Vashti almost died, and that would have been even more blood on my hands."

Micah climbed to his feet and walked over to his kayak. He opened a cubby in the bow of the boat and returned with his arms full. He handed out six woven hammocks. "Tazeen gave me a week to think about my actions, and to find a way to make amends. It's not much, but at least you don't have to sleep on the ground tonight."

Everly unfolded the beautiful gift. The yellow yarn was soft and flexible. It would wrap around her like a cocoon as she slept, and the weaving was tight enough to keep the insects away. The hammock did a lot more than get them off the ground—it was their ticket out of the burrow. It felt like Christmas morning.

"These must have taken you ages," she said.

Micah shrugged, hiding his bandaged fingers behind his back. "The trees behind us will do. Get some sleep, Naked Mole Rats. The paddle here was easy. The way back will be much harder."

CHAPTER 17

The following morning, just after sunrise, the Naked Mole Rats folded their hammocks and packed them into the kayaks before joining their mentor at the water's edge.

"We have two options and both of them suck," he explained. "The first is to paddle upstream, which will be basically impossible for most of you. The second option is to portage uphill, catch a tributary, and paddle downstream to the other side of the Bloodwood tree."

"Portage?" Inés repeated.

"It means carry the boat," Katak said.

Inés's face dropped.

"We can carry the boats one at a time if we have to," Everly added, to reassure herself as much as Inés.

Micah flipped a kayak upside-down and hoisted it above his head. "Let's go," he commanded, his voice muted by the wooden body of the boat.

Everly helped Inés lift her kayak into place. "It's too heavy," Inés whimpered. "I can't do this."

"We can stop every few minutes," Everly said.

"That's right," Katak conferred. "I can always double back and carry your boat, if you need me to."

"Okay," Inés agreed and took her first wobbly steps toward the jungle.

"I assume that offer extends to all three of us," Vashti said, fluttering her eyelashes.

Katak gave her a wry look before disappearing under his boat.

Everly struggled to hoist her own boat into place. She lowered the gunwales onto her shoulders. Her breath filled the empty hull.

Katak's cracked heels set the pace. Somewhere behind her, Vashti cursed and groaned beneath her kayak.

After a while, the trail steepened, and Everly lost track of Katak's feet. Her pulse pounded in her ears. She tried to hum a tune to distract herself from the gouges being dug into her flesh. Branches scratched along the underbelly of the kayak. A loud thump accompanied by chatter told Everly that a monkey had landed. "Hey! Get off, you little twerp!" she hollered. The monkey ignored her, rode for a bit, and eventually shimmied up a vine.

A crunch behind her told Everly that Vashti had ditched her boat.

"We have to keep going," Everly panted.

"I'm not…going…anywhere," Vashti huffed. "I might die. Right here."

Everly couldn't turn around. Looking down, she could see a packed clay wall to her left, and to her right, a steep slope that ended at the river. "I'm not stopping for you," she stated.

"But I can't do it!" Vashti whined.

"Vashti, move it!"

"Don't tell me what to do, loser."

Everly didn't see it, but she felt Vashti shove the stern of her boat, causing the bow to slam into the clay wall. The last of her patience dried up. She lifted the kayak above her and swung around to spit venom, but her stern caught Vashti in the side of the head. Vashti stumbled sideways and stepped off the slope.

Everly's kayak bounced and settled in the dirt in the time it took Vashti to slide down the incline and disappear into the rapids below.

"Micah!" Everly screamed. The ridge was empty. There wasn't any time to make a better plan. Swallowing her fear, Everly leapt from the path and half-ran, half-tumbled down the vertical drop. She shouted for help, hoping that the others weren't too far away to hear her cries. The terrain turned to mud, and her feet went out from under her. Fighting momentum and gravity, Everly clawed at a thin tree as it passed, but everything she touched bent and snapped. For a second, there was nothing beneath her. Then she hit the water.

The current was faster than it looked. It dragged her, kicking and flailing, to the riverbottom. She tore her way to the surface, but Everly gasped too early and water flushed her nose and throat until she retched. On the next breath, she filled her lungs with air before crashing against a sunken boulder and slipping around it.

"Micah!" she yelled again as the river flipped her up. Desolate, she coughed into the swirling rapids and tried to flutter her feet, but they collided with boulders along the bottom. She tried tucking into a ball, but it went against all her instincts not to swim. Sucked under again, the surface of the water folded like a warped mirror, obscuring the blue sky. Everly found air and took in a short gasp that did nothing to ease the ache in her lungs. The panic swelled and she fought it, trying with everything she had to move perpendicular to the current. The shore was close; she just couldn't reach it.

The bottom of the river dropped off. Everly had enough depth to kick, but she knew it wouldn't last long. Using her hands, she cut a pathway through the water. But when she looked up, she saw that the muddy incline had been replaced by a sheer marble wall that shot skyward. Like a mouse in the bottom of a bucket, Everly searched frenziedly with her hands. Her fingernails bent backwards against the cracks that might have saved her had they not been slick with algae.

Far above her, a dark figure ran along a ledge, but she couldn't process it before gulping a mouthful of water and being yanked below once again.

This was drowning. Everly didn't want to admit it, didn't want to stop fighting, didn't want to surrender. But she was so tired. She tried to swim, but her arms felt like rubber. Again, the river pulled her under. Her lungs burned. Every cell in her body begged for oxygen. Her skull cracked off of a boulder and sparks burst in front of her.

Everly felt herself going over the waterfall without actually seeing it. After a second of weightlessness, she crashed into the shallows below. Colliding with the riverbottom, her knees slammed into her chest. Fresh panic ignited. All she could see was bubbles, the fleeting flash of blue sky, and the large greyness of a massive rock the instant before she barreled into it. Her face dragged along the bottom; a soggy branch caught her cheek and sliced it open. Back at the surface, Everly gulped a mouthful of air before being pulled back down, yet again.

At the bottom of another waterfall, her right forearm snapped against the rocks. The ferocious pain told her the bone was no longer where it was meant to be, but she had bigger things to worry about as she slid limply over a smaller set of falls and back into the current.

Ahead, Everly spotted a willow tree, roots sprawled skyward and limbs wrenched downstream. She kicked hard, heaving and sputtering, and finally reached the fallen tree. Gasping and weak, Everly gripped the branches with her able hand. Her body became a blockade that the river tumbled over as if she were nothing more than a rock pressed into the silt.

The current was a thousand hands with long, sharp fingernails that scraped her legs and torso. Her right side bumped against the wall of the ravine. She tried to push away, but a separate force kept sucking her in. The tree bowed, splintering at its weakest joints, then the life-saving branch finally broke away. Everly clawed at the wall, but she couldn't find anything to grip. She felt the suction again before disappearing into an opening in the marble.

It was black. Hopeless. The tunnel pressed all around her. She screamed with the last of her air and choked on the bubbles that rushed up her nose. Seconds ticked by like a metronome. With empty lungs, Everly stopped lashing. Her burning muscles relaxed as she succumbed to exhaustion. She thought of Shelby. She thought of her parents. Something caught her wrist just as Everly opened her mouth and filled her chest with water.

CHAPTER 18

Never forget…
Why'd you do it?
Don't fall…

A force like a sledgehammer slammed against Everly's sternum, bringing her out of the fractured dream. She lurched toward the clearest sky she'd ever seen. Water gushed from her nose and mouth. A pair of hands rolled her onto her side. Her body convulsed, wringing her dry like a kitchen rag. Everly wanted to go back to the soft, dark place where every part of her wasn't in agony.

"You were d…dead," Vashti hiccupped beside her. "I did that thing. It brought you back."

Everly shifted onto her back. Her left arm didn't look right—the bone above her wrist protruded at an unnatural angle, and her fist was purple and swollen. With her working hand, Everly massaged her ribs, feeling the aftermath of the live-saving compressions. "Thank you," she croaked. "How did you—"

"I grabbed the ledge and you crashed into me. I caught you by accident." Vashti said, still shaking from the adrenaline. "You're welcome."

Everly chuckled painfully. She reached into the front pocket of her pants. It was empty. She checked the other pocket, even though she already knew what had happened. "It's gone."

"What is?"

"My badge. It must have fallen out in the river. It…it belonged to my dad."

"Oh," Vashti said, looking at the scratches on her hands. "That sucks."

Everly choked back her tears. It was the only memento she had from her former life. What if she never saw her family again? What if she had to move forward without a single physical object that connected her to them? The thought was stupid. The badge didn't bring her any closer to Shelby or their dad. It was a hunk of metal and glass, and now it belonged to the river.

From flat on her back, Everly looked around and quickly understood their predicament. The girls were perched on a marble ledge that jutted out above the whirlpool. How Vashti had climbed out was a mystery, but the act had saved them both. Everly counted twelve openings in the marble walls, each gushing with water. Far from reach, vines dangled over a perfectly circular opening. From their position in the chasm, it felt like sitting at the bottom of a well.

"We're trapped," she said.

"Yup."

"Quick question," she said, hugging herself with her good arm.

"What?"

"Did you give me mouth-to-mouth?"

"I had to. You were dead."

Maybe it was fallout from almost drowning, maybe it was shock, or maybe Everly was finally experiencing a nervous breakdown after too many traumas, but that was easily the funniest thing she'd ever heard. Once Everly started laughing, she couldn't stop.

Eventually, she was able to pause long enough to ask a very important question: "So, we kissed?"

"What?" Vashti finally shook free of her zombie-like stupor. The two girls turned to look at each other. Then they burst into a bizarre fit of giggles.

"That was my first kiss," Everly howled.

"You could've done worse!"

The hilarity bounded up the marble walls. They laughed until their cheeks hurt and their tongues went dry.

"If you tell anyone, like, *anyone*, I'll kick your face," Vashti wheezed.

"You'll *kiss* my face?" Everly squeaked.

"Kick! Kick!" Vashti fell backwards onto the slab and wrapped her arms around herself. They continued to cackle until a shadow blocked the light above them.

"I'm glad to see you're both in such high spirits," the cloaked figure interjected. "Considering the trip down the river should have killed you."

"Taz!" Everly rose into a seated position and paled from the pain.

"Stop moving around," the Umbo snapped. She knelt in front of Everly to examine her arm. "It's broken in two places. Shock is the only reason you aren't feeling it fully. Hold out your arm."

Everly obliged. Without a countdown or any warning, Tazeen pounced, bracing one hand on Everly's shoulder and yanking on her wrist with surprising force. The bones made a sound like cracking celery. Everly's vision turned red. She had to blink herself back into consciousness. Cradling her wrist in her good hand, Everly whimpered while the Umbo fashioned a sling from a piece of her garb.

"Taz, how did you get here?" Vashti asked, ready to move on to more important things.

"The same way that you did. That's the problem," said the Umbo. "I need you to tell me what happened, and I need you to be very specific."

Everly was still reeling, so Vashti took the lead. "We were portaging with Micah, but I needed a break. Everly stayed back with me. My foot slipped off the path, and I fell into the river. Everly… jumped in after me." She said the final line like it was something she only now understood to be true.

Taz waved her hand, dismissively. "When you were on the river, how many waterfalls did you go over?"

Everly squinted, trying to remember. Even her eyelids were sore. "Two waterfalls, maybe?"

"Three," Vashti corrected.

"Did you notice any landmarks?" the Umbo pressed.

"I grabbed onto a tree at some point," Everly recalled.

"We both got sucked in here. If it weren't for that vine growing over the ledge we'd be goners," Vashti explained, pointing to the life-saving plant near an opening.

Taz pursed her lips. She clearly wanted something from them, but what? "You need to listen very carefully," the Umbo said. "We are dealing with an unprecedented dilemma. Through carelessness and reckless behaviour, you've stumbled across a place that you were never supposed to find."

"Reckless?" Vashti balked. "It was an accident."

Everly looked around the chasm. The water spun like the arrows on a compass held too close to a magnet. Beyond flashes of sky and blurry images of the underwater world, she couldn't tell up from down for the majority of the way. But none of it would have happened if she'd gone for help instead of jumping in after Vashti.

"It may have been reckless on my part," Everly admitted.

Taz raised her hand. "Be quiet. I'm making a very important decision."

"What decision is that?" Vashti sassed.

"I'm deciding whether or not I'm going to kill you."

Vashti's shocked expression confirmed Everly wasn't crazy. Taz was contemplating homicide right in front of them. Vashti would fight back, but Everly was too beat up to defend herself. Even if the girls somehow managed to throw Taz into the whirlpool, what then? They'd starve to death in the chasm. They waited in silence, looking for clues in the Umbo's stoic face as to what was going on inside the mind of their could-be executioner.

Taz sighed heavily and interlaced her fingers. "Before I take you back—if I take you back—I need to know, beyond a shadow of a doubt, that you will tell no one of this location."

"It's not like we floated here peacefully," Everly coughed.

"We were drowning," Vashti said with a sneer.

"Be that as it may, we find ourselves here in this particular location. This whirlpool. The most important place. The only place that matters. You've disturbed a sacred spot. And there will undoubtedly be consequences."

Everly's brain felt swollen. "I don't understand," she said, resting her skull in her good hand. "What makes this place so important?"

"If I'm going to kill you, I might as well explain the existential crisis you have created."

Everly gasped. "You're not actually going to—"

"Shut up and listen," Tazeen said, cutting her off. "The water in this cavern has a number of unique qualities. It makes things grow in impossible situations, no matter how inhospitable the environment. Add it to sand and plants will root there. It can replenish lakes and rivers that have been stripped of all nutrients. When distilled and injected, it has healing properties that we are only beginning to comprehend. We call it the Cure, and it's a true marvel of mother nature."

"The Cure," Everly repeated. The word cleared the fog in her mind. Sharpened her senses. A cure was exactly what she needed.

"I swallowed the whole river. I don't feel all that cured," Vashti pushed back.

"Yes, well, you're not supposed to pump it into your lungs, now are you?" Tazeen said with a tisk. "But I ask, since your arrival on the island, have you noticed that you've not gotten sick and that injuries heal at an unusually rapid pace?"

"Bee stings," Everly realized aloud. "Vashti should have died, but Min Jun injected her."

"And Jolene's leg healed in a matter of weeks," Vashti added.

"Trace amounts of the Cure exist all over the island, so Maria Jose's herbs are especially potent."

Everly's heart sped up. "So, you can cure...anything?"

"We can, in theory. But it's not that simple. There are rules. The Cure is an incredible resource, but our supply is limited. We have to be careful about when and how we use it, especially because the Dust wants it so badly."

A tingling sensation swept through Everly's body. The answer she'd been searching for was right in front of her. It could solve the problem that had consumed Everly's life for years. She could save Shelby.

"How did you find it?" Vashti asked.

Tazeen folded her legs beneath her and settled in for a story. "Half a century ago, humanity was at the height of our technological capabilities and on the verge of ecological collapse," the Umbo said. "A team of scientists was searching for a way to fight back against the droughts and wildfires. When they discovered this island, untouched by both, they knew it was something special. They quickly uncovered its healing powers and were able to trace a pathway back to the source. This whirlpool. They knew they'd found something extraordinary, but they also knew human society was on the brink of collapse. So, they took an oath to protect the island. They named themselves the Bloodwood Society.

"When the Dust started overthrowing governments and controlling fresh water supplies, the scientists were among the first to ring the alarm. But no one listened. The War began, and the Bloodwood Society was forced underground and eventually became militant. Fifty years later, our priorities remain the same—fight the Dust, restore nature's balance, and protect the island and the Cure. No matter the cost."

A sickly feeling settled over Everly like a wet blanket. She tucked up her knees to keep warm. "That's the reason the Root exists," she said with a shiver. "To train the next generation to protect something, without ever telling them it's here."

"Exactly," Taz confirmed.

"So, when Micah was on his first mission, he was moving the Cure?" Everly asked. As the words left her mouth, she realized the misstep—she wasn't supposed to know about that.

Taz looked hard at Everly. "A small amount of knowledge is a dangerous thing," she stated, sourly. "Yes, Micah was tasked with transporting a small amount of the Cure between two checkpoints. But he failed. And many people died."

Vashti whistled. "No wonder he's so pissy."

"We have all made mistakes. Micah needs to pay for his."

Everly was surprised by the urge she felt to defend him, but there were more pressing issues at hand. "How do you decide where the Cure needs to go?" she asked.

"The Spearheads determine where the Cure will have the biggest impact. It could be anywhere around the world. I don't make the calls," the Umbo said. She looked at Everly and paused, letting the silence speak. Everly felt the hope evaporate through her pores.

The Umbo continued. "I've sworn on my life to enact the will of the Spearheads and to protect this island. Which is why you girls pose such a serious problem. We're only safe because the Dust does not know how to find the Cure. Their ignorance is our protection."

"I don't get it," Vashti spoke up. "The Dust has satellites and drones and infrared scanners. With all that tech, how come they haven't found the island already?"

"We have tech, too." Tazeen replied. "Like I said, our founders were scientists. The island is protected by a geo-magnetic force field that disables any electronics on the outside within five hundred miles. But we live with the knowledge that the Dust will eventually find a way around our defences."

The shock was either wearing off, or getting worse; Everly couldn't tell, but the pain in her arm was becoming unbearable. "I'm thirsty," she said, aware that it wasn't an appropriate comment for the moment. Her brain felt weird, like it had a mind of its own.

Taz pointed to the whirlpool.

Everly gristled. "It won't try to kill me again?"

"Only if you make it angry."

Everly scooted to the ledge, but with only one functioning arm, there was no way to scoop the water. She glanced back at the others, feeling broken and helpless.

"You're so pathetic," Vashti sighed. She knelt beside Everly on the edge and used her own cupped hands to bring the water to Everly's mouth.

"Thanks," Everly said when she'd had her fill.

"Don't mention it. Ever."

Tazeen looked into the sky; it was awash with pink and purple. "I've decided," she said, rising to her feet. "I will not dispose of two innocent girls for crimes that they may or may not commit. But, trust me, if you've ever trusted anyone in your life—betray me, and there is not a place on this round earth that I will not find you."

The Umbo produced two flower blossoms from inside her tunic.

Yellow at the bottom, the petals melted into pink and blood red. She crumbled the flowers in her fist.

"Chew this until the numbness sets it, then spit. Do not swallow any of it. It's highly toxic."

"Is this Other Death?" Everly asked, eyeing the petals wearily.

"No, Other Death wipes your memories, but the dosing is complicated. You can lose months or years, which clearly wouldn't do in our current circumstance. This is Devil's Trumpet. It has a different effect."

Vashti crossed her arms. "I'm not taking that. Not in an ass-jillion years."

"So you're choosing to stay here and starve?" Taz waited for the girls to hold out their upturned hands; she sprinkled the crushed flowers into their palms.

Everly glanced sideways at Vashti. "Are we doing this?"

"Yet again, we don't have a choice," Vashti frowned.

"On three?" Everly offered. "One…"

Vashti ignored her, popping the Devil's Trumpet into her mouth and chewing with a scrunched up face. Everly sighed, exasperated, and did the same.

The flower quickly dissolved. When Everly could no longer feel her lips, she spat messily into the water. Her tongue was missing, but at least the pain in her arm was melting away.

She looked over at Vashti, who was transfixed on her own fingers. "I'm on fiya" she gurgled. "Wook! Fwames…" She wiggled her fingers in front of her. Where Vashti saw fire, Everly saw colourful ribbons. The way back to the Root was going to be a long trip.

From her pocket, the Umbo removed a handkerchief. She unwrapped it, revealing a tiny glass prism. She caught Everly staring and answered an unspoken question: "This is Lunar glass, a gift given to the Umbos because of its special properties. Now, whatever you do, don't panic." Tazeen grabbed each girl by the wrist, and without further warning, dragged them into the whirlpool.

Everly opened her eyes underwater. The force whipped her in circles, while all around her, bubbles morphed into colourful birds from the pages of a textbook. Everly reached out to touch a goldfinch, but its flesh peeled away until all that was left was bones. The other birds dissolved, and their skeletons opened their beaks. The screams that came out belonged to her sister. Everly bellowed Shelby's name into the water.

Before she could break the surface, her body was hit with a blow that made her spinal cord vibrate like a guitar string. A geyser blasted her to the top of the chasm and beyond. Once the column of water reached its peak, Everly tumbled through the air and was caught, roughly, by the branches of the canopy.

Vashti hadn't been so lucky, although the spongy jungle floor had cushioned her landing. She lay there facedown, singing a song to the moss.

"This is our stop," Tazeen called to Everly from an upper branch. The Umbo's face had been replaced by a gnarled tree knot. When Tazeen reached her, Everly cowered, but reluctantly accepted the outstretched hand. Together, they climbed to safety.

Once on the ground, the Umbo tore two strips of fabric from her sleeves and used one to cover Everly's eyes.

"Bwindfolds?" she asked with a frozen jaw.

"An extra precaution," the Umbo said.

Behind the fabric covering, Everly's thoughts combined with strange hallucinations. Frothy waves crashed in fierce swells against the bluffs. Her dad in his study, his stubbled cheek pressed against the floor, two agents kneeling on his back. Shelby, young and healthy, running through the long grasses, her vibrant mane trailing behind her. The sensation of falling. Falling. Falling.

Vashti's fingers interlaced with Everly's, and her bandmate's hand became the only benchmark for what was real and what was imagined. Everly squeezed it hard. Hands clasped together, the girls stumbled through the underbrush, blindly following the sound of Tazeen's voice as they moved into the jungle in the unknowable direction of the Root.

CHAPTER 19

With bruises covering so much of her body, Everly found it impossible to get comfortable. The uneven bark of the Bloodwood tree dug into her back as she peered over the newcomers and struggled to focus on the fight. Nikol and Ebimi were locked in a sparring match. The goal was simple enough: see who could knock the other off an aerial root first using a bo staff. The sound of clashing sticks sent nearby birds flying for the safety of the canopy.

"How are you feeling?" Katak asked from beside her. Even though he was pretending to watch the fight, Everly could tell he was keeping her in his periphery.

"I'm fine," she replied. In fact, she looked far worse than she felt. Black stitches floated at the edge of her vision where Maria Jose had threaded part of her cheek back together. A goose egg protruded from her brow. Beneath yellowing bandages, she was missing three fingernails, and her shins looked like she'd lost a kicking contest with a horse. Wrapped in a plaster cast, her left forearm still throbbed a bit, but it was mild compared to the memory of having the bone set.

Her wounds would heal, but the rage simmering inside her wasn't going anywhere. She was livid. She was also very stupid. And shortsighted. She could have bartered with Tazeen. Begged. Lied. But Everly had wanted a way out of the chasm so badly, she hadn't fully considered the consequences of leaving it behind. Thanks to the Devil's Trumpet, which had fried her synapses, Everly had no idea how to find her way back to the Cure. She'd held the one thing that could save her sister in the palm of her hands, and she'd let it slip through her fingers.

"It was brave of you to jump in after Vashti," Inés offered from Everly's other side.

"I was the one who pushed her," Everly stated, her slouch deepening.

Inés spat out a sliver of fingernail. "I bet she deserved it."

"Guaranteed," Katak chuckled.

Sitting closer to the action, Vashti tossed a scowl over her shoulder. Her two black eyes made the expression even more aggressive. Everly returned the look. She wasn't in the mood.

"Truth hurts," Katak said under his breath.

The truth. What a concept. As far as her bandmates knew, Tazeen had miraculously appeared to pull the girls from the river, and they'd spent the night in a cave, which is why nobody from the search party found them. Katak and Inés had spent hours combing the shoreline for any trace of their bandmates, and Micah had even risked shooting the rapids in his kayak. Everly felt bad lying to them, but if she wanted to stay alive, she didn't have a choice.

Katak nudged her gently. "Seriously, Everly, what happened out there?"

Vashti whipped her head around again. "Excuse me, but some of us are trying to learn."

"Hard to learn to fight without actually fighting," Katak huffed.

From the aerial root, Ebimi shouted, "Truce!" loud enough that everyone in the clearing jumped.

Nikol either ignored the command or wasn't in control of her reflexes, because as Ebimi lowered her weapon, the Fire Ant thrusted hers forward. The Lemur responded with lightning speed, using her opponent's own momentum to throw her off balance and whacking her bo staff off the bridge of Nikol's nose. Her nostrils exploded with a mist of blood as she slipped off the root.

"I said truce," Ebimi barked, sweat dripping from her chin.

Crouched on the uneven terrain, Nikol lifted the hem of her shirt to her nose. "My bad," she mumbled.

The mentors were gathered near the front of the crowd, and Micah stood up, looking concerned. He walked over to Nikol. When he reached for her face, she swatted his hand away in a clear rebuff before storming off. He was clearly surprised by the response, but

Micah turned back to the rest of the mentors with a cool shrug, as if her rejection were more ridiculous than humiliating. But Everly could feel the sting from all the way back at the trunk.

"Trouble in paradise," Katak noted. "I hear Nikol dumped his ass."

"Who told you that?" Everly asked.

"Just the word on the street."

"He seems to be taking it well," Inés observed.

"Sure, but I bet Arseniy is about to make his move," Katak said. "I wonder who will throw the first punch?"

"Do you ever shut up?" Vashti snapped. She'd been in a piss-poor mood since they'd come down from Tazeen's floral fever pitch. Likely, the two-day-long hangover wasn't helping.

They were about to start spitting insults when Ebimi called their names. "Katak and Vashti, how nice of you to volunteer. Why don't you join me?"

Katak looked sheepish as he tossed his cap into Inés's lap. As they made their way through the crowd, Katak's oversized feet made it impossible to move gracefully. Vashti, on the other hand, moved like a lynx across the overlapping roots to where the Lemur was waiting.

Ebimi sized up the Naked Mole Rats and handed each a bo staff. The stick looked thin and breakable in Katak's hands, but as Vashti twirled hers, it came to life with homicidal potential.

He chewed his lip. "Not your first rodeo?"

"Giddy up." Vashti grinned.

Ebimi thumped the butt of her bo staff against the root to get their attention. "Remember," she said, "a rebel must avoid capture at all cost. If you have to fight, you fight to kill. Make it quick and clean. Begin!"

Everly covered her mouth with her hand and prepared for a blood bath as her bandmates squared off. Vashti was the first to strike. She lunged forward and rapped Katak on the knuckles so hard the skin split.

He yelped and dropped his bo staff. "Hey! That's cheating!"

Ebimi clicked her tongue. "She disarmed you, fair and square.

Go again."

Before the words had left the Lemur's mouth, Vashti was already mid-stride. She used her bo staff like a pole vault, planting it into a soft spot in the root and flinging herself onto Katak's back. She caught him by the neck with the crook of her elbow and trapped him in a headlock. Katak tried to buck her off, but Vashti locked her legs around him and squeezed.

"Say mercy," she gritted.

"Let me go," he rasped.

"Or what?"

"I'll tell them."

Vashti threw her weight to the side, trying to knock him from the root.

"The red dot…when you got here…what it means…" he squeaked with the veins in his forehead bulging.

Vashti froze. She looked out across the crowd like she'd already been exposed. Her expression was a mix of shock and anger, but Everly was sure she saw fear in there, too. Whatever Katak knew, Vashti did not want it spoken aloud. She released her grip and dropped. Katak fell to his knees, coughing and wheezing.

She picked up her bo staff and looked ready to kill. Lucky for Katak, Ebimi got in her way. "Very well done, Vashti. Next time, don't drop your weapon."

"I won't," she said, breathing hard.

The Lemur dismissed them with a wave and surveyed the new-comers for her next matchup. "Inés and Jolene," she selected. "You girls are about the same size."

The statement wasn't true; the same weight, maybe, but Inés was four inches shorter than the Ghost Shrimp. As the two went about selecting their weapons, Everly caught Jax staring at her from across the crowd. His dark expression was a warning, but what did he expect her to do? She couldn't very well force Inés to throw the match, and anyway, the only chance Inés had was if Jolene's leg, which was no longer wrapped in a cast, decided to give out. Everly kept her eyes lowered, doing her best to ignore his sinister gaze.

The match between the girls was over practically before it got started. Their bo staffs clashed, with Inés on the defensive, but Jolene took a false step and slipped off the root. The newcomers booed.

"Who wants to fight me, then?" Jax snapped. No one replied. Ebimi elected an Armadillo to be his opponent.

While Ebimi armed the newcomers, Vashti made her way to the base of the Bloodwood tree. She plopped down beside Everly and drained a canteen. Everly had been waiting for this moment—she and Vashti hadn't had a chance to talk, and with everyone focused on combat training, this might be their only opportunity.

"Where'd you learn to fight like that?" Everly asked, casually.

"Dharavi." She said the word as if it should mean something, but Everly had never heard it before.

"Is that a town?"

"A slum. There was nothing to do there but play soccer and fight. I did both."

It explained why the girl could sprint and defend herself, but Everly knew from history books—both legal and otherwise—that a slum meant something worse than rotting clapboard and boarded up windows. That didn't add up with the other details Vashti had shared about her life back home.

"I thought you lived in a hotel with your uncle," Everly challenged.

"We moved there after my dad died. He was a builder. Some scaffolding collapsed." Vashti wiped her lips with the back of her hand. Her face stayed neutral.

"I'm sorry," Everly said, because there was nothing else to say.

Vashti shrugged. "If you tell the others I grew up in a slum, I'll end you."

"Secrets and death threats," Everly said with a tisk. "That's your whole personality."

Vashti looked around to make sure no one was eavesdropping. She lowered her voice. "Speaking of secrets, I hear Satan is quite musical."

The corner of Everly's mouth twitched. "I hear he plays the

trumpet."

"How's your arm?"

Everly met her bandmate's inquisitive stare. "Cured," she replied.

"They're going to kill us, you know that right?" Vashti whispered.

"Not if we keep our mouths shut."

Vashti sucked her teeth. "So says Tazeen."

Everly hated sharing anything with Vashti, let alone a secret that their joint survival depended upon. It wasn't smart to trust a wolf to guard the sheep. She felt a sudden desperation to change the subject. It was risky to be talking about it at all.

"What was Katak going on about?"

"Do you really need to know everything about everybody?"

"Nice deflection," Everly said with a frown.

Vashti simpered. She reached up and rubbed the space between her eyebrows. It was a self-conscious motion, one that triggered Everly's memory—Vashti in the storeroom, with a dab of red paint on her forehead. Everly had seen Vashti make the gesture before, like she was checking to make sure she hadn't forgotten to wash the mark away. Whatever it symbolized, Vashti was willing to risk her own pride to keep Katak from revealing it.

"You're really not going to tell me?" Everly pushed.

"I could, but I'd have to cut out your tongue."

Hidden somewhere on her person, Vashti had the tool required to make good on the promise, so Everly decided to drop it. Vashti could keep a secret, but only when it suited her. How many others were kept locked away? And how many of them, like the red paint, had left behind invisible scars?

🔨

In the dead of night, with the sky full of stars, Everly startled in her hammock. She put her good hand on her chest and felt the quickened rhythm of her pulse. Inhale. Exhale. She allowed the gentle sway of the hammock between palm trees to calm her. The moonlight filtered through the fronds, casting geometric shadows across the jungle floor. The air was warm and damp, sweet with the scent of citronella. Since the incident on the river, all of the newcomers had been invited to sleep in the grove with the rest of the Rooters. A precaution disguised as a privilege.

With the nightmare of Shelby's arrest threatening to return the second she fell back to sleep, Everly sat up and looked around the grove. Multi-coloured hammocks hung like pregnant cocoons. They twitched and bobbed as the Rooters navigated sleep. Some held two occupants, their bodies intertwined in a night-long embrace. Back home, being caught out at night with anyone was a crime; here, there was no punishment for being young and in love. Everly thought of Jordan. Where had he ended up? What was he doing right now? Did he miss her, too?

Hoping to escape the loneliness, Everly climbed from her hammock. She weaved between the sleeping Rooters, careful not to wake them. In the middle of the grove, a lone campfire burned. There she found Min Jun sitting by himself on a stump. He was examining an old book; the firelight showed the creases in its worn pages.

"Hey," she said to his back, not wanting to scare him. The Lemur didn't flinch, which suggested Everly needed to practise her stealth.

"It's late," he said with a smile. "You should be resting."

"Can't sleep," Everly shrugged, taking a seat on the stump next to him. The dead wood gave beneath her, softened by years of rot. "What are you reading?"

"For decades, Rooters have been trying to record every species of plant and animal on the island. Whenever I find something I don't recognize, I check the logbook."

"Did you make a new discovery?"

"Perhaps," he said, closing the book. "Your surname is Dahl, right?"

"Yep. Like dollhouse, only spelled differently."

"Such an interesting name," he mused.

"Oh yeah, how so?"

"In my mother tongue, it's close to our word for moon."

"Really?" Everly sat up a bit straighter. "I like the sound of that."

"Ever Moon," he smiled. "It sounds poetic. May I?" Min Jun held up a stick of graphite and motioned to her cast.

"What, you want to sign it?" She wasn't sure why, but the idea made her blush. It felt intimate, somehow, even though there would be layers of fabric and glue between them.

Min Jun swivelled on his stump and rested the book on his knees. "I can decorate it, but only if you want."

Everly held out her arm. He positioned it atop the book and got to work, starting with a small sketch of the Bloodwood tree. For a while, they were silent, but it was the good kind that felt relaxing instead of awkward. Maybe it was the late hour or the dying camp-fire.

"What did you find that wasn't in the logbook?" Everly eventually asked to keep herself from falling asleep.

"A red feather," he replied. "It's not native to the island, as far as I can tell. But there are a few different ways it could have ended up here. Birds tend to go wherever their wings take them."

"You'd think so," Everly yawned, "but most birds have set territories, and the ones who migrate tend to stick to specific routes."

Min Jun paused his artwork to consider her.

"My dad is an ornithologist," she explained. "Or, he was. Now he's a prisoner."

"The Dust does not approve of free minds," Min Jun said.

"He's sure paid the price for it."

"Him and millions of others." Min Jun rotated her cast to examine his work by the firelight. "There. My masterpiece."

Everly looked at the sketch. Surrounding the tree were a series of dots intercut by short, wavy dashes. "Thanks," she said. "It's... abstract."

He smiled. "Some of the best art is, Ever Moon."

"I wouldn't know," she said as stood up. "Thanks for the chat. I should get some sleep."

"You should. But before you go, there is something else I'd like to show you." Min Jun lowered his voice and looked around the grove.

"But I probably shouldn't…"

"I can keep a secret," Everly replied.

Min Jun's face became serious. "For your sake, I hope that's true."

He reached into his satchel and revealed an arrow. Everly recognized it right away. It was the same arrow, wooden with three bright red feather fletchings, that had pierced the hive and nearly sent Vashti to an early grave.

"Do you know where I got this?"

She nodded.

"Do you know who shot it?"

Everly shook her head, no. She didn't know their identity, but she suspected the spy was responsible. Was the Lemur thinking the same thing? The fire had dwindled to embers. She could barely make out Min Jun's features in the dim, orange light. "Why are you asking me this?"

Min Jun used a rag to rub the graphite from his fingertips. "Your fifth trial is tomorrow," he said. "And now, you and Vashti both have targets on your backs. The shots will be coming from all directions. I thought it only fair to warn you."

CHAPTER 20

The next morning at sunrise, the newcomers gathered in the trunk with the Lemurs and mentors all in attendance. In the middle of the group, Everly was huddled between Katak and Inés. Vashti stayed off to the side. Close, but not too close. Everly's muscles were tightly coiled. Meeting in the trunk meant only one thing—they were headed back into the tunnels, where the shadows could be harmless or filled with monsters, depending on what the day held in store.

From high up in the hollow trunk, the grackle dive-bombed with a whistle and came to rest on the Umbo's sharp shoulder. "Welcome!" Tazeen called above the nervous crowd. "Today marks your fifth trial. We call it the Lost Souls. Each band will be given provisions and a map. You will use these to reach your assigned destinations, collect proof of arrival, and return safely to the Root. I needn't remind you that if you get lost, or hurt, or if anything else happens to prevent your full band from returning to this exact spot before sunset, you will all be banished. Watch your steps and keep your wits about you. The challenge begins now!"

With that, the mentors split up and jogged over to their respective bands. Micah tossed Everly a backpack. "Good luck, Naked Mole Rats. Don't do anything I wouldn't do," he joked with a toothy grin.

"Here we go again," Everly muttered to herself. She unzipped the pack and searched it. Four canteens, bags of fruit and nuts, and a map, as promised. She unfolded the map on the floor. The parchment boasted a series of lines and arrows away from a circle, representing the trunk. Near the top of the map was an X with the word 'Hangar' scribbled above it.

With maps in hand, the newcomers took off in all directions. Jax and his crew ran for the lifts, which gave Everly some hope that, at the very least, they wouldn't have any run-ins with the Ghost Shrimp underground.

"Where are we headed?" Inés asked.

"Tunnel eight," Everly said, pointing to the placard. Vashti yawned. Her black eyes had faded, but the dark circles remained. She looked ready to curl up in the dirt and fall asleep. Everly hoped they wouldn't have to carry her back. Again.

"Let's get this abuse over with," Katak huffed.

Everly kept glancing over her shoulder, feeling skittish and uneasy as they moved through the mouth of the tunnel. The air here was particularly thick with sulphur, and soon they knew why—the aquifer's shimmering back appeared beneath a makeshift crossing. Inés stopped to fill their canteens, which was smart, since they had no idea how long the route might be. The map didn't have a scale, so an inch could represent one mile or ten.

Deeper underground, the mud gave way to flat slabs. Surrounded on all sides by smooth stone felt like walking through a subway. Everly shivered, recalling Micah's transcript. Her anxious thoughts betrayed her, sending a vision of an unexpected train hurtling around the corner. Her veins filled with wasted adrenaline.

Calm down. Focus. Stay alert.

After half an hour, the ceiling lifted and cracked open, letting in the daylight. The jungle climbed through the slits, with roots and vines claiming the space as their own. Groundwater from a recent rain dripped down the stone walls and disappeared into seams in the floor. Songbirds chirped from clay nests. Everly paused underneath a fissure, absorbing the warmth of the sun. But a displaced sound prickled the hairs on her neck.

A chill swept through her. Katak and Inés were discussing the map, and Everly put up a hand to silence them. "Be quiet," she hissed.

The Naked Mole Rats froze.

"What's wrong?" Inés whispered.

Everly waited, straining hard to hear through the sounds of the subterranean world. The sick feeling eased up. "It's nothing," she decided. "But I don't want to be in the tunnels any longer than we have to."

"Hey, what's that?" Vashti asked, pointing to the markings on Everly's cast.

Everly turned her cast over in the sunlight. She rotated so the real Bloodwood tree was at her back, and the dots and dashes took on new meaning—the dots were the tunnels and the lines were the aquifer, which at the moment was hidden underfoot.

"I spoke with Min Jun last night," Everly said. "I thought he was just being nice, but I think he drew us a map."

"But we already have one." Inés said, holding it up.

"Let me see that." Vashti snatched the map from Inés's hands. She stepped into the sunlight and compared it to the one on Everly's cast. "They start off the same, but you see here, up ahead…this one says go right and Min Jun's says go left."

"How do we know they even lead to the same place?" Inés challenged.

"We don't. But Min Jun must have given me the map for a reason," said Everly.

Katak yanked the map from Vashti and performed his own analysis. "Tazeen's route looks shorter, so that one's got my vote."

Everly frowned. "It may be shorter, but I'd bet Tazeen's route is booby-trapped."

"I mean, it's a trial, so probably," Vashti grumbled.

"But why would Min Jun want to help us? I don't understand," said Inés.

"I have no idea," Everly admitted. "But maybe he's the mentor we should have had all along."

Katak chewed his bottom lip, thinking. "If we're wrong and he sends us on a wild goose chase, we'll fail the trial."

"And be banished," Inés chirped.

"And brain-wiped," Everly concluded. She'd already had a taste of Tazeen's mind-altering meds; they were to be avoided. She looked at the maps, considering their diverging paths. Min Jun said there were targets on their backs. And he'd saved Vashti once before. If Tazeen had changed her mind and decided she wanted the girls eliminated without raising any red flags with the rest of the Root, an accident during a trial was a decent cover.

"It's your map, Everly. You make the call," said Katak.

"Alright," she said with a confidence she didn't actually feel. "We'll go with Min Jun. Sorry in advance if I'm wrong."

"That would suck," Katak sulked.

Inés touched her crucifix.

"We've wasted enough time," Vashti urged. "Let's go."

Leaving the daylight behind, they followed the tunnel and turned left down Min Jun's pathway. The air was quiet, except for the occasional flutter of insect wings. The floor sloped, carrying them deeper into the earth. As the walls closed in, Everly did her best to ignore the growing sense of claustrophobia that threatened to overcome her.

They weaved through the underground for what felt like an hour and reached a spot where a huge boulder nearly blocked the tunnel. They had to squeeze between the boulder and the wall to clear it. On its far side, a troop of mushrooms was growing at its base. Everly plucked a fat one from the soil, revealing its bright, bulbous underbody. The mushroom gave off just enough light to read the map.

Everly squinted and pointed to a small opening just up ahead, one that they could have easily overlooked. Fear bloomed within her—if they missed a turn and wound up lost, both of their maps would be useless. On the list of fates worse than banishment, dying of starvation in the tunnels would be near the top.

In the small tunnel, the ceiling dipped so low, Katak had to walk with his head ducked beneath his shoulders. "Are you sure we're going the right way?" he asked, irritation creeping into his voice.

"The map says one more turn," Everly replied. "We must be getting close."

"I hope you're right," Katak groaned.

A short distance later, they cut to the right, and the tunnel opened into a vast cavern. It was coolly lit with thousands of blue mushrooms, but they weren't the only source of light; cracks in the ceiling allowed the sun's rays to reach the cavern floor, which was covered in overlapping flat slabs. On their surfaces, water gathered in hundreds of silvery pools.

"This must be the Hangar. Min Jun led us right to it!" Everly gushed.

"Look!" Inés shouted. In the middle of the space was a bamboo rod with a burlap flag. On the rough weaving, painted in black, was the outline of what Everly had to assume was a naked mole rat.

Katak clapped his hands. "It must be our sigil. It's beautiful!"

"It's ugly as sin," Vashti clucked. "But that flag is our proof that we made it here."

The foursome spread out to explore the expansive cavern. Hanging down from the ceiling were dramatic columns of dripstone, formed by millennia of water droplets depositing minerals and building new rock on their way to the ground. At the bottom of the stone icicles, the droplets fell, rippling the silver pools in perfect concentric circles. Where the water met dry land, pillar-like sculptures grew up from the cavern floor. In a few places, the oldest formations met in the middle and fused into hour-glass shapes that looked like they held up the weight of the entire cavern.

"This place is amazing," Inés mused.

"This place is boring," Vashti yawned.

Katak rolled his eyes. "Seriously, what does it take to impress you?"

"More than a few rocks."

Everly was only half paying attention to the conversation as she roamed the Hangar, taking in the layered compositions of the dripstones. Smooth and cool to the touch, the mineral formations were mostly white, with swirls of rusty orange, cobalt blue, and charcoal grey.

"How long did it take us to get here?" Vashti asked.

"Three hours, maybe," Everly replied.

"Perfect." Vashti removed a canteen from the bag. "We've got time to kill before sundown."

"What are you suggesting we do?" Inés asked.

"I'm not suggesting *we* do anything," Vashti corrected. "I, how-ever, intend to make the most of my afternoon. I'll meet you all back at the trunk."

"Sure, Vashti," Everly chuckled. There was no way the girl was serious. Splitting up during a trial would be insane. But Vashti's grin made Everly nervous.

"I know what you're up to," Katak cawed. "I saw you sneak out of the grove last night. You're meeting up with someone."

"Oh yeah, who?" Vashti countered.

Katak raised his eyebrows. "*What* is a better question."

"Vashti, you can't leave us just to *enrollarte* with someone," Inés interjected. "Is that worth risking banishment?"

"If *enrollarte* means get off several times, then, yes, it most defi-nitely is," Vashti said with a suggestive shimmy.

"Don't," Katak warned. "I'll barf."

Everly chewed the inside of her cheek, trying to stay calm. Vashti's proposal was deranged and dangerous. Min Jun's warning was ringing in her ears, a warning she hadn't yet been able to share with Vashti. "We'll all go back right now, together," Everly suggested. "You can spend the rest of the afternoon doing whatever you want."

"No way! You know they'll put us right to work the second we get back. Look, just hang out here for a few hours, okay? Take a nap, tell ghost stories, Katak and Inés can make a weird mutant baby, whatever works."

"Vashti!" Everly barked. From across the cave, she tried to com-municate the unspoken truth between them, without tipping off the others. "Don't be stupid. It's not safe out there. Not for us."

Vashti ignored her and crossed to the tunnel. "I'll see you at sun-set. And don't forget our hideous flag." Before anyone could argue further, Vashti left.

Everly groaned with frustration.

"We should have forced her to stay," Katak tisked.

Inés sighed. "I don't see how."

"Who do you think she's hooking up with, anyway?" he asked.

"Nobody," Everly stated. "She's allergic to bees and physical touch."

Inés sucked her teeth. "That girl is up to something. I just know it."

"She's always up to something. And now we're stuck here all day, so we might as well make the best of it." Katak moved over to a trio of short pillars and sat on one of the rounded tops. "Can we eat something, please? I'm calling dibs on Vashti's rations. Non-negotiable."

Everly and Inés joined him on the make-shift chairs, munching on dried coconut and cashews. Once the food had taken the edge off, Katak spoke up with his mouth full. "Hypothetical question," he chewed. "If you weren't on the island, what would you be doing right now back home?"

Everly took a few seconds to think about it. "Assuming I wasn't arrested with my sister?"

"Sure," said Katak.

"I'd probably be in the basement of the archive, trying to figure out how to get my family out of jail. Which is such a joke. I used to believe that if I could prove my dad wasn't a traitor, the Dust would set him free. But Shelby never once stepped out of line, and they took her, too."

"Do you think she's okay?" Inés asked, gently.

"She's sick," Everly admitted. "Really sick. So, I'm not sure."

"Screw the Dust," Katak growled.

Everly lifted her canteen. "Cheers to that."

"SCREW THE DUST!" Katak bellowed. His words echoed around the Hangar. The girls laughed.

"What about you both?" Everly asked. "Your families must be worried." Katak looked away, and she immediately wished she could stuff the thoughtless words back into her mouth.

"Not mine," he sniffed.

"Don't you have any family?" Inés nudged.

"Nope. My folks died a few years ago. We never found their bodies. The ice is brutal like that."

"*Ay Dios mio*," Inés whispered. "Katak, I'm so sorry."

"Thanks. It was rough. I lived with my grandma for a while, but when she got sick, I was tossed into Union care. I ran away a lot. Sometimes I camped, which is illegal, so I got arrested a lot, too. Sometimes I crashed on couches. But this year, I finally landed in a decent home. Before getting recruited, I'd been staying with Mrs. Kumar for six months or so, and there were two other fosters living at her house. The youngest was Napatsi. This other was this asshole named Dave."

Everly already knew the rest. She kicked off a shoe and dipped her toes into the pool beside her, using it to draw circles on the slab while Katak laid everything out in his own words. It was much worse than reading the recruiter's factual summary.

By the end, Inés had tears in her eyes. "Poor Napatsi. That poor little kid," she sniffled.

"Don't worry. Dave isn't going to hurt her anymore. I made sure of that."

Inés wiped her nose with the back of her hand. "You protected a child, Katak. You're a hero."

Katak looked away. "I'm not a hero. But I know there are things you can get away with in this world, and there are things that will take you out of it."

Everly set her jaw. "Can't argue with that."

"Can I tell you both something terrible?" Inés asked. "Something I've never told a living soul?"

"Of course," Everly said.

Katak nodded.

Inés sighed, shakily. "I set the fire on purpose. I was…desperate." She buried her face in her hands and broke down into sobs.

"It's okay, Inés," Katak said, trying to offer some comfort.

"It gets w…worse," Inés stammered. "When Sister Antoinette passed out, I had a chance to save her, but I just stood there. She was a bad person. She'd done bad things to me. I could not find grace or forgiveness. Then the priest showed up and carried me away. I don't know what happened to her, but I hope she's dead. That's terrible, yes?"

"No," Katak insisted. "Monsters should burn."

Everly felt hot and agitated, like her clothes were too tight. "You were defending yourself, too, Inés," she pointed out. "If Katak's a hero, so are you."

"No doubt," he said, sweetly, taking Inés's hand in his own.

Everly couldn't help but smile. How long would it take them to figure out something already so abundantly clear?

Inés wiped her tears with her free hand. "Your turn, Everly," she said, weakly. "We both shared something."

"You pretty much know it all already," Everly replied.

"We don't know what really happened on the river," said Inés.

The comment caught Everly off guard. She knew her fake version of the story was too sparse to satisfy them, but she had nothing more to offer. "I'm sorry. I can't tell you."

"Why not?" Katak pushed.

"I swore on my life," Everly stated. "And if I tell you anything, Tazeen will kill me."

Katak scratched his head. "Vashti's in on it, too?"

She nodded.

"Do you trust her to keep her mouth shut?"

"I don't have a choice."

Inés looked at Everly. "It's okay. We understand. We won't ask again."

"Thanks," Everly said with a weighty exhale. She stood up and stretched her back. "Now, we've got this place all to ourselves. You both hide. I'll seek."

"Are you serious?" Inés giggled.

"Yep. Here are the rules. You have to stay in the Hangar, and you have to stay on the ground. No climbing. You both have thirty seconds to hide."

Katak looked back and forth between them. "Is this really happening?"

"Thirty, twenty-nine, twenty-eight..." Everly began her countdown.

The other two scrambled in opposite directions. When she ran out of numbers, Everly spun in circles and began her search. She jogged over to where two pillars had fused together halfway up. She crouched to look between them, but the space was empty.

From the far side of the cavern, Katak chortled. "You're not even close!" he called to her.

Everly jumped from slab to slab, avoiding the silver pools, and peering between boulders and dripstones as she moved. The cavern was big, but there were only so many places they could be.

"Are you two making out?" Everly shouted.

Inés's giggle sent her running in a different direction. She tried to be stealthy, in case her bandmates were moving around while she searched, which wasn't against the rules, but would have been if she'd thought it through. Several minutes passed, and Everly started to worry that she might be stuck seeking for the rest of the afternoon. At this point, she figured the others probably weren't having much fun, either, and she was about to call 'olly olly oxen free' to bring them back out into the open. But before she could, Inés's scream ricocheted across the cavern.

Everly sprinted toward the sound. She yelled Inés's name, but there was no response beyond an echo. Finally, Everly spotted her, curled into a ball between two boulders.

Everly crouched in front of her bandmate. "Inés," she whispered. "Are you okay?"

Katak appeared at Everly's side. He spun around in circles trying to spot the unknown danger. "What happened?" he snapped.

Inés looked up with a ghost-white visage. Her cheekbone was cut open; blood streamed down her face. All at once, she seemed to return to reality, colour flooding her cheeks, sweat breaking from her pores.

"I'm not sure," she croaked. "Someone grabbed me. They pinned me." She wiped blood from her chin. "They cut me," she whispered in disbelief.

Katak took off running, chasing the unseen attacker.

"Katak, get back here!" Everly shouted. Her skin crawled like they were kneeling on an anthill. Katak returned, heaving with exertion and fury.

Inés shivered. She struggled to stand. They helped her climb out from between the boulders. Her shorts were wet, and she tried to pull her t-shirt down to hide it.

"We don't care about that," Everly insisted. Her heart stuttered in her chest. Her ears registered every plink of water dripping from the ceiling, every flap of a wing, every unidentifiable shuffle. The attacker could still be in the Hangar, could still be watching them.

Katak took off his shirt and pressed it against Inés's cheek as her whole body began to shake. He put his arm around her waist to steady her.

"I honestly d...don't know what happened," Inés stuttered. "They...they came up behind me. They twisted my arm behind my back and pushed me between the boulders. They had a knife. I...I didn't see who it was. I'm sorry...I'm so sorry..."

"It's okay, Inés. Everything is going to be okay. You're going into shock. Take some deep breaths." Everly removed the t-shirt to check the bleeding. That's when she saw it. The shape of a small but purposeful letter. Katak saw it too, and they locked eyes with sudden fearful recognition.

Everly glanced at Min Jun's map on her cast, now distrusting it. To the east, it indicated a tunnel that led out into the jungle, connecting with a footpath that would take them to the beach, the grove, and eventually the Root. But the jungle left them fully exposed.

"We'll backtrack through the tunnels," Everly decided, whispering so unwelcome ears wouldn't overhear their plan. "Let's go."

Making as little noise as possible, the trio scuttled through the Hangar. But once they were back in the tunnel, Everly regretted her choice. The shadows had an edge to them, like the walls were made of broken glass. Ages passed before she saw the boulder up ahead. It made Everly feel better, for a second, to know where she was.

"Did they say anything?" Everly whispered to Inés as they squeezed around the blockade.

They cleared the boulder, and Inés glanced nervously over her shoulder. She froze. Everly followed her gaze and couldn't stop the sharp scream that escaped from her throat. Katak forced his way in front of them to see.

A message dripped down the backside of the boulder, the handwritten letters scrawled in glowing blue ink:

DUST IS COMING. GET OUT NOW.

"That," Inés whispered, touching the letter D carved into her cheek. "They said that."

CHAPTER 21

The hours they were forced to stay hidden just outside the trunk were some of the longest of Everly's life. At some point, Inés's wound stopped bleeding, which hopefully was not a sign that it was too far gone for stitches. A permanent reminder was the last thing she needed.

When the world's least desirable bandmate finally appeared mere minutes before sunset, it took everything Everly had not to smack her. Katak explained the situation to Vashti using aggressive hand gestures and multiple expletives.

Instead of her usual antics, Vashti surprised with a different approach. "Look, I'm sorry about what happened," she said, holding her hands up in surrender. "But I'm not the one who carved Inés's face."

"Aren't you?" Everly glowered. "You've got a blade and no alibi. It could have been you."

For a second, Vashti looked genuinely hurt, but she quickly replaced the expression with smugness, saying, "I do have an alibi."

"Oh yeah, who?" Katak smouldered.

"As if I'd tell."

"Don't push me, Vashti." The crease that cut his brow in half was deep enough to hold a dime.

"That's enough," said Everly, stepping between them to prevent a brawl. "We need to finish this trial and tell Taz what happened."

Off to the side, Inés stood with her arms wrapped protectively around her torso. She hadn't spoken since the boulder. Katak moved closer to her and spoke with a tenderness his imposing form shouldn't logically possess. "Are you ready?" he asked her.

Inés nodded, keeping her eyes on the floor.

The Rooters cheered when the Naked Mole Rats entered the trunk. Everly wished she could mute the noise. She spotted some of the other newcomer bands, but five people were missing. The sun had nearly set, and Funnel Web Spiders hadn't made it back. Assuming something hadn't killed them during the trial, they'd be facing banishment upon their return. The number of recruits had dwindled to twenty-one. The island was ruthless.

Near the back of the trunk, Tazeen was chatting with Andrew and Maria Jose. Everly pushed her way through the Rooters and approached them.

The Umbo clapped her hands in a slow applause. "Welcome back," she purred.

"Inés was attacked in the Hangar," Everly stated.

"Attacked by whom?" Tazeen demanded.

"We don't know. But the cut is deep."

"Clear the trunk!" the Umbo shouted. The Rooters halted whatever they were doing and followed her command, quickly exiting in all directions. Tazeen waited, fingertips in the shape of a pyramid. When the trunk was empty, she summoned the Naked Mole Rats to her with the flick of a wrist.

"Tell me what happened."

Katak stepped forward. "We were in the Hangar—"

"Not you," Tazeen said, cutting him off. "Inés."

The girl looked up like a startled doe. Her voice cracked when she opened her mouth to speak. Her small frame collapsed inward, and she covered her mouth with mud-stained fists.

"You are safe, Inés. You are surrounded by friends," Tazeen cooed, placing her hands on Inés's shoulders and attempting to meet her eyes. If the Umbo recognized the shape of the cut, Tazeen didn't respond to it.

Inés gulped and dropped her hands, eyes wide and brimming. As she recounted the events, it was as if the act of retelling forced her to relive the moment again, to physically feel the pain and terror. When she reached the part about the message on the boulder, Inés could barely get the words out.

"Thank you," the Umbo said when Inés's story was done. "I am glad you are alright."

Everly almost sputtered aloud at that description. Nothing about Inés's posture, movements, or stammer suggested she was alright. Alive and unscathed were not the same thing.

"I have some questions," said Tazeen. "And please know that I am not doubting you or your recollection. I believe you. I am simply looking for additional details that might be helpful. You said you did not see your attacker, but was there anything memorable about the way they spoke? Their accent, perhaps?"

"They were whispering, so it was hard to tell. I didn't notice an accent, I don't think. But he had a deeper voice."

"Did you get a sense of his size? Was he tall? Did you see his hands?"

Inés shook her head, no. "I didn't. He left bruises on my arms. Also my back, I think."

"Show me."

Inés glanced at her bandmates with an expression of shame that nearly broke Everly in half.

"I won't look," Katak offered, turning around.

Inés pulled up her shirt so Taz could examine the marks. There was a dark purple bruise the size of an apple between her shoulder blades. Rage heated Everly's body; the attacker had used his knee to keep Inés on the ground.

"How many people knew we were going to the Hangar?" Everly asked, abruptly.

"Too many," the Umbo replied. "The Lemurs, the mentors, and whoever they told."

"Min Jun gave me another map," Everly said. She stepped forward to show the Umbo her cast. "We followed this route."

"Which saved you from multiple obstacles," Tazeen explained. "His map was a gift, not a setup."

Everly exhaled, feeling some relief. She didn't want to believe that Min Jun could be responsible, but she wasn't ready to cross anyone off the suspect list.

The Umbo watched Inés closely, like she could read something in her tremors. "Inés, when the attacker spoke to you, what were their exact words?"

Inés touched her crucifix and closed her eyes. "'The Dust is coming. The Blood Moon will be bloody. Everyone is going to die. You and your friends must leave the island. One of you knows the way.'"

Everly bit her tongue. The message was ominous, but was it true?

Tazeen's eyes narrowed. "Do you know what that last part is supposed to mean?"

Inés shook her head. "We can't m…move between moons, I thought?"

"That's correct." Tazeen's gaze flicked between Vashti and Everly. The girls certainly knew more about the island than their bandmates did, but a way to leave wasn't one of the secrets they kept. As far as Everly knew, the only way off the island was through Tazeen. The attacker's warning, the words clearly delivered by the Dust's spy, didn't make any sense.

"What does that mean, anyway, 'move between moons'?" Katak asked.

Tazeen pursed her lips. "It's a complicated matter, one that I'm not going to explain right now. I will only say that there are certain methods we use to travel to and from the island. If the moon is not in the right phase, the door is closed. The Rooters know this."

"So, you know who comes to the island, and who leaves, and when," Everly elaborated.

"Indeed."

The information confirmed an important fact—the spy-turned-attacker had been with them since day one.

The Umbo pinched the bridge of her nose. "Inés de la Rosa, I am proud of how you have handled yourself. You have been brave. I just have one final question for you. There were four newcomers in the Hangar—"

"Three. I wasn't there," Vashti admitted. Everly looked at her, surprised by the honesty.

"And why is that?" Tazeen frowned.

Vashti shrugged, sheepishly.

Tazeen's face darkened. "Vashti Jahanara, how do I know it was not you—"

"I was with Chen. He'll vouch for me," Vashti muttered.

The Umbo stared at her, looking confused and clearly unimpressed. "I will have words with the Armadillos' mentor."

"Dude's what, thirty years old?" Katak said with disgust.

"What do you care?" Vashti hissed.

"Enough!" Once again, Tazeen looked to Inés for answers. "Three in the Hangar, in that case. Do you have any idea why you were targeted?"

"I don't know. I don't think he could have pinned Katak, and Everly would have at least tried to fight back…"

Everly wanted to argue the point, but she knew now wasn't the time. Weeks before, she'd been cornered and overpowered by Jax in the tunnels, and Everly had felt helpless and frozen. Inés wasn't giving herself enough credit. Bravery wasn't always measured by the number of punches thrown.

"A crime of opportunity," Tazeen said. "I want you to know that the attack was in no way your fault. You have done nothing wrong. I want you to see Maria Jose about that cut."

Inés nodded, shakily.

"Katak, Everly, did either of you see or hear anything else?"

They looked at each other, then both shook their heads, no.

"Alright. For now, Inés fell in the tunnels and cut herself on a rock. I need you to keep your wits about you. And stick together, understood?" The Umbo paused and honed in on Vashti.

"Understood," Vashti said.

"But what are you going to do about the attacker?" Katak pressed. "One of your Rooters has come after us twice."

"The Lemurs will investigate on our own terms."

"Like how you investigated what happened at the hives?" Katak said with a cluck.

"Katak's right," Everly said, feeling her temperature rise. "There's a spy on the island. A spy working for the Dust. And they hurt our friend. What are you going to do about it?" Everly didn't care about her tone or the consequences of speaking the truth. Katak and Inés deserved to know the attack was a symptom of a much bigger problem.

"Careful, Everly Dahl," the Umbo warned. "There are forces at play here far above your paygrade. I am asking you to trust me. We will do our best to protect you. But you must also look out for each other. I cannot be everywhere at once."

Everly looked at the floor so the Umbo wouldn't see the anger and resentment in her eyes. Trust was earned, and so far, the Bloodwood Society was zero for two when it came to their safety.

"I trust you all to inform me if there are any further developments," Tazeen concluded. "Until then, keep your eyes peeled and your teeth sharp. And get some rest."

With that, the Umbo of an infiltrated island stepped into a tunnel, leaving the Naked Mole Rats behind to fend for themselves.

CHAPTER 22

They spent the next week going through the motions. The Naked Mole Rats ran every morning with Micah. They practised hand-to-hand combat with Nikol (who still wanted nothing to do with their mentor). In the galley, they peeled a mountain of taro root for Andrew, which made Everly's hands so itchy she begged Maria Jose to cut off the cast. The stitches on Inés's cheek healed quickly, leaving behind a faint pink scar that would fade from her flesh but not her memory.

Much to the annoyance of some older Rooters, Micah instructed the Naked Mole Rats to relocate their hammocks to the middle of the grove—prime real estate, close enough to the campfire to keep the bugs away. They kept Inés in the centre, with her bandmates and Micah forming a perimeter around her. Eventually, after a few rough nights, Inés was able to sleep.

On the eve of the New Moon, the grove was lit with sweet-smelling torches. A pair of Rooters strummed guitars and sang a lullaby in a language Everly couldn't name. Nearby, a small group was settled on stumps, weaving colourful threads through each other's hair. The others were already asleep in their hammocks.

Without the brightness of the moon, the sky performed its solar dance with dazzling clarity. Everly could tell which stars were near and which ones were eons away as she gazed through the fronds. A single star fell and burned with a brilliant white arc. Bands of light gathered into the Milky Way, which Everly knew contained the earth and the sun. But the galaxy felt distant and separate from her position in space.

Everly stirred to the sound of whispers. How long had she been out? The sky was still black, but the grove was filled with a glow that didn't belong to the torches. She sat up in her hammock and looked around. Hanging from the palm trees were dozens of glowing paper lanterns, each one shaped like an animal and illuminated from the inside by a small candle. Somewhere in the distance, a drumbeat sounded. The glowing creatures formed a pathway into the jungle. The Rooters were following the lanterns.

"What's going on?" Everly asked, reaching for the mossy floor. The other Naked Mole Rats were already on their feet.

"I don't know," Vashti replied.

Inés wrung her hands. "I don't like this."

"We could just stay here," Everly suggested.

"Naw, strength in numbers." Katak threw Vashti a wry glare.

"I get it already. You guys are helpless without me."

Staying close together, the Naked Mole Rats joined the migration. Everly felt Inés's hand slip into her own as they stepped onto the trail. Everly squeezed it, glad for the reminder that she wasn't alone. They followed the path around a bend, where more lanterns came into view. Everly took in their intricate shapes as they passed—a flying squirrel with arms stretched wide, a coiled python with a forked tongue, a jaguar with its fangs on display.

"What do you think we're doing out here?" Inés whispered as they left behind a toucan lantern.

"No idea," Everly said. The mystery of it felt exhilarating, but after the Hangar, she'd had enough excitement to last her a lifetime. What was Tazeen up to?

After the glow of a monkey lantern faded behind them, the trail went cold. Katak knocked into the girls from behind and steadied himself with his hands on Everly's shoulders. Beside them, an enormous leaf pulsed an iridescent green. Everly pushed it aside and revealed a lantern shaped like a sloth bear, illuminating a freshly-stomped footpath that cut deeper into the jungle.

Everly wrestled with a growing sense of discomfort. She had no idea where she was, no sense of where the Bloodwood tree or the grove were in relation to her. The slightest breeze could snuff out the candles and leave them completely lost. She focused on Inés's warm hand, small within her own. She felt sweaty and tense as a coati guided them into a small clearing where five cloaked figures were waiting. The one in the middle held a lantern shaped like a grackle.

Two hundred Rooters crowded together. The mood was jittery. The bright sound of a high-pitched bell silenced the chatter. Everly was still gripping Inés's hand, and Katak stood so close behind them she could feel the heat radiating from his body. Flanking Inés, and staying true to her word—so far—Vashti stood with her fists clenched, keeping one eye on the exit.

The figure with the grackle began to speak with the familiar voice of the Umbo: "To pay homage to the New Moon, tonight we will begin a special challenge…"

Tazeen held the bird lantern over her head and released it into the air. As it drifted upward, the real grackle swooped in from the trees and pierced through it. The lantern crashed to the ground, igniting a circle of flames so bright, Everly had to turn away. Within the fiery ring, a human-like figure appeared. A creepier scarecrow had never existed. Had it been there the whole time?

"Moon Tracker," someone hushed, as if the stickman were a sacred shrine.

"Moon Tracker," another whispered.

"Yes, Moon Tracker, indeed," Tazeen confirmed.

Rooters vibrated in place, hissing with excitement.

Taz raised her hands to steady the crowd. "Most of us know the rules already, but allow me to inform the newcomers," the Umbo said. "The game is played under the light of the moon, or in this case, the lack thereof. Anyone within the trunk and the grove is in the safe zone and will be considered out of play. But once you enter the tunnels or jungle, the game is on. Each night, for as long as it takes, you must go out in search of this, the Sapien."

Taz reached through the smoke and removed a loop of twine from around the stickman's neck. Hanging from the bottom was a single bead, painted crimson red. "Every night, from now to the end of the game, you will collect a different token. Successfully carry it back with you to the safe zone and you will have survived to play another round."

"Sounds too easy," Katak whispered, dipping his head between Inés and Everly's.

"But that is not all," Tazeen continued. "Each of you will play two roles—the hunter and the prey. Or, as we call them, the tracker and the mark." Taz walked in front of the flames and revealed a pouch from within her cloak. "I hold in my hands the names of every Rooter and newcomer. You will each draw a name, and that person will become your prey. Your mark. Sharing this name with someone else will result in your elimination from the game. It is for you to know, and you alone. While searching for the Sapien, you must also hunt your mark, and avoid getting marked, yourself. Marking someone means capturing or subduing them and stating the Moon Tracker's mantra…"

"I am what I am!" the Rooters shouted in unison.

Everly jumped. Goosebumps swept across her arms and legs.

"That's right," Taz cooed, firelight catching the concealed contours of her face. "Upon uttering these hallowed words, 'I am what I am,' you will have successfully eliminated your mark and will take over their mark as your own. As your collection of names grows, so too increases your odds of winning.

"Starting at dusk tomorrow, each of you will be eliminated, one by one. Until that fateful night when the last two players will hunt each other. When the final mark has been captured, the game will be over. However, should the final mark be in possession of more tokens than their tracker—proof they were more successful at locating the Sapien throughout the challenge—they shall be granted the title of Moon Tracker."

Everly looked over and caught Vashti's eye. Her expression was stern, but there was an unmistakable glint of mischief there.

The explanation wore on: "For the newcomers in the crowd, a complete collection of tokens—each a different colour—will be proof positive that you have passed your sixth trial, meaning even after you have been eliminated, you still have to make it to the Sapien and back. Every night."

The Rooters murmured and chuckled at the newcomers' expense. At least if a Rooter got eliminated, the game was over for them. No matter what, the newest bands were in it for the long haul. To the bitter end.

"And one last thing," said Tazeen. "The winner will earn more than bragging rights. This year, our victorious Moon Tracker will be given the most valuable prize there is—an additional wish."

The response to the news swelled like a thunderstorm. The mood in the clearing became charged. Manic. The Rooters shuffled their feet and yipped and howled at the invisible moon, preparing for a bloody hunt.

"Good luck!" the Umbo shouted above the fray. "And may the best tracker win! The root of the root…"

"The salt of the earth," the Rooters chanted.

Tazeen moved to the footpath. The Rooters followed, chattering skittishly, eager to reach into the pouch and pull a name.

"What the hell is all this?" Katak asked the girls as they shuffled to take their place in line.

"Don't you get it?" Inés hissed. "The game is the fishing rod; we're the bait."

Everly sucked in her lips. Inés was right.

Katak glanced suspiciously around the clearing as if every person posed a unique threat. "So, what do we do?"

"We outplay them," Everly stated. "We have no other choice."

The selection ceremony was sombre. Each Rooter drew a name and moved solemnly along without comment. Everly's heart fluttered as her turn approached. The stakes felt way too high. Who among them had the best shot at claiming the title? Who would be the easiest mark? She realized, with a shudder, that many would be glad to pull Everly's name; the thought made her feel vulnerable.

When it was her turn with the Umbo, Everly hesitated. She stood with her hand hovering above the pouch.

"Choose carefully, Everly Dahl."

Everly shivered. "This doesn't feel right."

Taz pulled back her cloak enough that the fire danced across on her skin. "Don't worry. What hides in the darkness shall be seen in the light."

Everly desperately wanted to believe that the Umbo had a plan. But the game was putting everyone, not just the newcomers, in danger. Everly inhaled slowly and held the air in her lungs. She reached into the bag and selected a scrap of parchment, worried that if she fumbled it, she'd alter her destiny completely.

When she read the name, Everly felt like she was falling. The sensation stayed with her as she made her way back to the grove. To keep her mind from spiraling, Everly did her best to sort through the facts. The spy had already struck twice, and both times, the Naked Mole Rats had been the target. So why, with a Dust spy on the loose, would Tazeen host a hunt-or-be-hunted challenge and invite the whole island to join? If Inés was right and their band was the bait, it meant Tazeen considered them to be expendable. Maria Jose had issued the warning weeks before—if necessary, she'd said, the Rooters would sacrifice the few for the sake of the many.

Everly was only three trials away from getting her wish and seeing her dad and sister again. And another wish was now on the table. But the Bloodwood Society had yet to prove they were capable of following through on their promises. Her dad used to say, if wishes were dolphins then sailors would ride. A wish was only valuable if it came true.

She kept the parchment clenched in her fist as she climbed into her hammock. Under the starlight, Everly peeled it from the palm of her hand. Her sweat had rubbed most of the ink away, but the name was still legible. It wasn't an impossible mark, but the name came with baggage Everly did not want to carry. She had less than twenty-four hours to figure out how to take the name and turn it into an advantage. Come sunset tomorrow night, she'd be hunting Jolene.

Jax's twin sister.

CHAPTER 23

At dinner the next night, the mood throbbed like a low-grade fever. In the busy trunk, the various bands kept to themselves, conversing at a murmur so others wouldn't overhear. A few anxious Rooters drifted aimlessly. As the speckled sunlight crept across the walls, Everly battled internally with a sense of dread. She and her bandmates were seated on square cushions, staring at dishes with playful names—Tracker Crackers, Hide and Go Pecans, Catch Me if You Canapés. Everly couldn't stomach any of it. Moon Tracker didn't feel like a game or even a trial. It felt like a trap.

But for whom?

Beside her, Inés thumped an empty wooden bowl on the floor. "I won't do it," she declared. "I won't go out there and get another letter carved into my face."

"You don't have a choice," Vashti said, blandly. "It's a trial."

"I don't care!" Inés snapped with more force than Everly had ever heard her use.

Everly didn't want to agitate her further, but she couldn't think of anything to quell her friend's legitimate concerns. "What can we do?" she asked, earnestly. "Our hands are being forced."

"We could let ourselves get marked tonight," Katak suggested.

"That doesn't make it any less dangerous," Everly pointed out. "We still have to go out every night to collect tokens."

"And Chen told me the further we make it in Moon Tracker, the better our chances are of getting initiated," Vashti chimed in.

Katak snorted. "Chen doesn't even talk to you."

Vashti flicked her eyebrows up. "He does more than talk."

The likely-fictional romance with the Armadillo's mentor was not currently a topic Everly cared to discuss, so she shifted the conversation back to the trial that would begin any minute. "We need to focus," she chided. "We have no idea how many nights we'll have to search for the Sapien. Moon Tracker could take us all the way to the Blood Moon, for all we know."

Inés wrapped her arms around herself. "The spy said the Blood Moon will be bloody. They never said it would be peaceful between now and then. Why is Tazeen doing this to us? She knows what could happen."

"The spy's already hit us twice," Katak emphasized.

"That's true," Everly agreed, although she still hadn't parsed out why the spy had targeted the Naked Mole Rats, specifically. "The spy found us at the hives because all of the newcomers were there. And they somehow knew we'd be in the Hangar. But Moon Tracker is different. They won't know where we are. We just have to make sure we get to the Sapien first."

Since getting her cast removed, Everly had developed a habit of rolling her wrist around in its socket whenever she was thinking hard about something. The two bones in her forearm shifted in place as she tried to formulate some sort of plan to keep them all safe. Thanks to the Cure, the breaks had healed in less than a week. Inés's cheek had taken days. The others hadn't questioned the unusual rates, but now that Everly knew the truth, there were signs of it everywhere.

Vashti leaned back on her elbows and casually looked around the mat. "So," she clucked, "who do you all have?"

"We're not allowed to say," Everly reminded her. The trial hadn't even started yet, and already Vashti was trying to break the rules.

"Come on!" she whined. "If we want one of us to win this thing, we have to work together."

"You probably have one of our names and are planning your kill as we speak," Katak said through a mouthful of rice.

Vashti put her chin in the air, harrumphing at the injustice. Who was she trying to fool? In a kill-or-be-killed challenge, the girl was a lit fuse—it was only a matter of time before she took everyone out.

The shadows on the walls stretched long as the last fleeting moments of daylight vanished from the trunk. Everly wanted to capture the rays, to carry them with her through the long, frightful night. Her muscles tightened as she spotted Tazeen crossing the trunk and coming to a standstill in the centre.

"My friends, the night is upon us! Before we begin our moonless hunt, a gift for all of you. A poem." She cleared her throat. "*There's a tree in Italy wherein the quinces grew. The fruit fell to the soil as the summer winds blew. But when I went to pick them, no quinces could be found. No quinces in the branches. No quinces on the ground.*"

Katak leaned over, whispering, "What the hell's a quince?"

Everly shrugged. Back home in Cape Fundy, only apple trees were hardy enough to survive the winter. She'd never tasted a quince.

Tazeen continued. "When the final mark is captured, the last hunter will reveal themselves by saying the hallowed words of the victor. I invite Micah, our reigning champion, to formally begin the challenge…"

Across the trunk, Micah stood. "I am what I am!" he hollered. "I am the Moon Tracker!"

The column of the tree shook with the tight-throated voices of the Rooters who joined him in his call. They bayed on the word 'moon' and cracked the word 'tracker' like a hide whip. The hairs on Everly's neck stood on end as the group transformed into a pack of wild dogs, growling, snarling, and gnashing their teeth with anticipation.

"I will see you at first light!" Taz declared.

Moon Tracker had begun. The Rooters abandoned their mats and raced for the exits, some using the lift, some climbing the walls, others sprinting into the tunnels.

Inés gripped Everly's arm so tightly her fingertips dug in. Everly locked eyes with her. The girl's face was creased with fear.

Katak jumped to his feet. "What do we do?"

Everly swiveled from side to side. Using a lift was the fastest way out of the Root, but it would leave them exposed at the base of the Bloodwood tree, where their trackers, whoever they were, could already be waiting. They needed to get out of the trunk, to use the chaos as cover and slip away unnoticed. But no matter which direction they went, danger could be lurking.

"What was Tazeen saying about quinces?" Everly asked, heart pounding against her ribs.

"I wasn't listening," Katak admitted. "I was too busy trying not to piss myself."

"You're so helpful," Vashti frowned. "Taz said something about quinces. In a tree."

"And they fell when the wind blew," Everly added.

"*No quinces in the branches, no quinces on the ground,*" Inés repeated. Of course, she'd been listening when it counted.

"What the hell's a quince?" Katak asked again.

"Fruit," Inés explained. "Tazeen said Italy. Why would she say Italy?"

"I have no idea," Everly said, already feeling defeated.

"Not quinces, means…just one quince…" Inés muttered.

"Let's go!" Vashti said, bouncing on her toes. The trunk was almost empty. "We're sitting ducks if we stay. Our trackers are probably watching us right now."

Inspiration flashed in Inés's dark irises. "Follow me, I have an idea." She led them to the mouth of tunnel V and boldly left the safety of the Root behind as she stepped into the shadows.

"Are you sure about this?" Katak whispered. "We don't know our way around without a map."

Inés kept walking, her upper body rigid, her gaze fixed straight ahead. "There were no quinces in the tree or on the ground, because there was only one quince in either place."

"So?!" Katak wheezed.

"So, Taz said Italy, right? *Cinque* is Italian for five. This is tunnel five."

"What the hell are you talking about?" Vashti spat.

"It's another anagram, like Skeleton Drama. Quince and *cinque*. Same letters."

The pieces of the puzzle clicked together in Everly's mind. Inés had somehow solved a multi-layered riddle in mere minutes. "How did you know that?"

"The nuns at my school only spoke Italian," she said with a self-conscious giggle.

"You're a child prodigy," Katak gushed.

"Stop," Vashti hissed. She put out her hands to prevent her bandmates from moving any further. "Listen."

Standing there in the tunnel, it felt like they'd been swallowed—the hiss of steam was the breath of the underworld, the gurgle of the unseen aquifer, its digestive juices. Everly strained to pick up on other sounds, noises that didn't belong, pockets of silence, muffled footfall. A rock skipped behind them. A tracker, a spy, or something else entirely was hot on their heels.

"Run!" Everly barked.

The Naked Mole Rats sprinted through the tunnel. They turned a corner and Katak dragged Everly and Inés into a crevasse with Vashti close behind them.

"Great, now we're trapped," Vashti hissed.

"Over there." Katak pointed to where the shadows were interrupted by a soft, orange glow.

Moving as quietly as possible, they followed the light. Around a bend in the rock, an owl-shaped lantern came into view. Its beak pointed toward another tunnel.

"You were right, Inés," Katak whispered.

"You're the one who saw the light through the opening," she replied.

Vashti sucked her teeth. "Would you two get a room?"

The others shushed her.

The owl led them to a row of candles. Their low flames guided the Naked Mole Rats through even more twists and turns in the underworld. As they progressed, the smell of sulphur was replaced by the scent of brine and seaweed. Up ahead, the ground flooded.

"Woah," Everly gasped as the ocean soaked through her shoes.

"Are we going to have to swim our way out?" Inés said, teeth chattering nervously.

"I hope not," Everly whispered. "But it'll be harder for anyone to track us through water."

The further they trekked, the deeper the water became. As it reached Everly's armpits, she was about to start swimming, but the low ceiling was replaced by a clear night sky. Starlight reflected off of the ocean's surface, making it shimmer like black diamonds. Gentle waves lapped against the cliffs and funnelled into the mouth of the tunnel. Luckily, the water was calm, otherwise crashing waves would have blocked their passage.

In the distance, where the cliffs ended and the beach began, Everly saw a pair of bonfires. A figure stood between them. It was the Sapien.

"We found it!" Everly shouted. The exclamation jumped from her mouth.

Vashti splashed her. "Shut up, idiot. Do you want to be marked?"

Everly wiped the saltwater from her eyes and glared at Vashti.

"You're telling me there's a shortcut to the beach?" Katak sighed. "I can't believe we've been running our asses off through the bush every morning."

With the stickman in sight, the Naked Mole Rats waded through the waves and climbed onto dry sand. They hid behind a dune. Solving the riddle meant they'd beaten the rest of the Rooters to the Sapien. As far as Everly could tell, the beach was deserted.

"Now what?" Katak asked.

"We each need a token," Everly stated. "Now might be our only chance."

Through the inky darkness, a blurry figure appeared at the fringe of the jungle. He moved carefully across the sand toward the bonfires. Everly recognized his muscular build and rounded shoulders. Without a word to her bandmates, she took off running. The Moon Tracker gods had given her a chance, and she wasn't about to waste it.

As she closed the distance between them, Everly saw Jax stop in front of the Sapien. He removed a wooden bead from the stickman's neck. With a quick glance around, Jax turned and ran in the opposite direction of the cliffs.

Everly started to follow him, but quickly backtracked to collect her own token. The black ocean rolled in the faceless idol's eye sockets. She hesitated before touching it, feeling like the wrong move could release an ancient curse. Her bandmates appeared in the firelight as she snatched a bead and put the string around her neck.

Scanning the darkness for Jax's shadow, she caught sight of him just as he reached the far end of the beach and cut into the jungle. Everly had a plan, but it was now or never. There was no time to explain. "I'll meet you back at the grove," she shouted to her band-mates as she took off running.

The ground transitioned from sand to packed mud as she reached the footpath. The trail bent sharply, and Everly spotted Jax and Jolene just up the trail. She was about to side-step into the jungle when two other Ghost Shrimp appeared, grabbing each of her arms.

"Look who we've got here, Jihad," Tusha sneered.

"A lost little moley-mole," her bandmate taunted.

Jax sauntered over to them. "Why am I not surprised?" he clucked when he realized who they'd nabbed from the shadows. "You've been making problems for us since day one."

Everly twitched. She didn't need to look around to know she was on her own. Regret flooded her body; she should have stayed with her band.

"What should we do with her?" Tusha growled.

"You should let me go," Everly said, speaking directly to Jax between rattling breaths. "So we can trade marks."

Jax tilted his head. "Why would we do that?"

"Trade me and you'll find out."

He stepped in front of Everly, boxing her in. Jax's hooded eyes were shiny and menacing. "Or we could strip you naked and find your parchment wherever you have it hidden."

His bandmates laughed. Everly's lip curled with disgust.

"Tell me your mark and it won't go that far," he goaded.

"If I tell you, we're risking banishment. But if you trade with me, sight unseen—"

"A loophole," Jax said with a nod, seeming to grasp the concept. "But how do I know you don't have some impossible mark?"

"You don't," Everly stated. "But if I screw you over, you and your bandmates can kick my ass. I won't fight back."

"As if you could," Tusha snarled.

Everly ignored her and kept her focus on Jax. "I'm offering you a truce."

"A truce?" he scoffed. "I don't care about truces. All I care about is getting my band to the other side of the Blood Moon."

"We all want the same thing," Everly said. How could she make him understand what she was offering without words? She leaned as far to the side as his bandmates' grips would allow, pointing her chin to where Jolene was waiting.

"We're wasting time," his sister grumbled, hands on her hips.

Jax glanced at his sister, then back to Everly. He motioned for his bandmates to release her. Everly reached into her back pocket and delivered her parchment with an outstretched hand.

Jax unrolled it and squinted to make out the name. "Holy shit," he chuckled.

He untied his parchment from the knot in his headband and tossed it to her. The stars offered enough light to make the name of Everly's new mark legible: Min Jun.

"You asked for it," Jax smirked.

"I did," she sighed.

Jax pulled the token over his head and handed it to Jolene. She looked confused as she put the string around her own neck. "Tusha, Ji and I will go back for more tokens," her brother explained. "You and Everly get back to the grove. It isn't far. Just stay off the trails."

"That's a plan," Jolene said, noncommittally.

"We owe her," Jax reinforced. "Keep her safe."

The siblings parted ways. The girl seemed to know where she was going, so Everly opted to follow. Jolene pointed out a tiny creek and they balanced with one foot on each side all the way to a running path. She and Jolene hid in the underbrush as a pair of Rooters trotted by.

"Can I ask you something?" Jolene whispered once the coast was clear.

"Sure."

"Is Inés okay?"

Everly's breath caught behind her voice box. "What do you mean?"

Jolene tapped her own cheekbone. "That cut was too clean to be from a fall."

The darkness around them changed; what had seemed a protective cloak just seconds before was now thick with dangerous potential. Everly balled her hands into fists. How could she be so stupid? She'd been so swept up in the game, she'd forgotten to treat everyone as a suspect. Now she was alone with a Ghost Shrimp, and Jolene knew more than she should. Everly searched the path, willing her bandmates to appear.

"Who did it?" Jolene pushed.

"I don't know."

"None of you saw anything?"

"No." Everly watched the girl in her periphery. What was she digging for?

"It wasn't the Ghost Shrimp. You should know that. We were in the middle of the jungle at a rock formation called the Stone Witch. And I don't want to tell you your business or anything, but you should keep an eye on Vashti."

"Why?"

"Because she's lying to you. I've heard her bragging about hooking up with Chen."

"Stranger things have happened."

"Sure, but Chen has a boyfriend. I've seen them sneak off together at night. His name is Ping."

"The Fire Ant?"

"Yeah."

The doubt had always been there, but now it was undeniable. The secrets between Everly and Vashti should have been a bond. But Vashti had other secrets, too. She collected them like playing cards, to build a house around herself, no matter how flimsy. Everly hadn't believed the story about Chen from the start, but she'd never bothered to check Vashti's alibi.

Jolene and Everly picked their way through the jungle. When the grove came into view, Everly sighed with relief, saying, "We live to track another day."

"It's the least I can do, seeing as you gave Jax my name," Jolene said.

"How did you know?"

"Please. Dude never smiles. I'm the only person he cares about that much."

The girls grinned at each other. Through the branches, Everly spotted her bandmates standing near the campfire. They'd made it back in one piece, no thanks to her. Hopefully, they wouldn't be too mad. Everly turned to thank Jolene, but the girl was gone, so she climbed from the underbrush and approached her friends.

"You get your mark?" Katak asked as she joined them by the fire.

Everly nodded. She wanted to tell them about the trade, but wasn't sure she could, based on Tazeen's vague rules.

Inés folded her arms. "You left us," she huffed. "I hope it was worth it."

"I'm sorry, Inés. It won't happen again."

"Spoken like a bonafide ditcher," Vashti tisked.

Each of them sported a red bead around their necks, evidence they'd survived the first night of Moon Tracker. Everly wished she could explain her actions, but her body was heavy with exhaustion, and all she wanted to do was pass out. "Let's get some rest," she suggested.

The Naked Mole Rats climbed into their hammocks. Through the gaps in the yarn, Everly saw Inés and Katak interlace their fingers across the divide. Despite everything that she'd been through, despite multiple betrayals, Inés still found a way to keep her heart open. Appropriately, Vashti slept with her back to the group, close enough to benefit from the protection, but far enough away to be an island unto herself. Everly pictured Vashti surrounded by her house of cards—not safe, just separate.

Everly went over Jolene's revelation in her mind. Where was Vashti, really, when Inés fell victim to the spy? Had she somehow put the rest of the band at risk? Despite the blood that had been spilled alongside the silver pools of the Hangar, Vashti still hadn't come forward with the truth. Come the morning, Everly decided, she would bring down the house.

CHAPTER 24

Everly spent the next seventy-two hours trying to approach Vashti, but they were never alone together for long enough. Even if they had been, casually mentioning the fact that Chen was only interested in guys and Vashti had been lying to her bandmates for weeks probably wouldn't go over well. As far as Everly could deduce, Vashti was lying for one of two reasons: one, she was somehow responsible for what had happened in the Hangar, or two, she had a specific reason for not wanting anyone to know the details of her mid-trial rendezvous. Either way, she was hiding something.

There was a possibility that Everly kept coming back to, even though she didn't want to admit it—Vashti could be the spy. If that were the case, how far would the Bloodwood Society go to punish her? What would be considered justice after such a betrayal?

Everly was lost in her thoughts when Inés addressed her bandmates at dinner. "I have a confession to make," she stated. "Something happened last night."

Everly leaned in with a furrowed brow. "Are you alright?"

"I'm fine. I had to pee, so I stepped out of the grove."

Katak nearly choked on his rice. "Inés! What is it about not going places by yourself that you don't understand?"

"Excuse me for wanting a little privacy. Anyway, the second I stepped outside of the grove, I was marked."

Everly smacked her own forehead so hard it stung. "So, you're out?"

"I'm afraid so," Inés sighed.

"Who got you?" Vashti asked, casually. As if she wasn't dying to know.

Inés pretended to zip her lip and lock the corner of her mouth.

"Unbelievable," Katak huffed.

"Isn't that a tad hypocritical?" Vashti asked him. She blew across the top of a steaming mug of tea. "I have it on good authority that you were also recently marked."

Everly stared at him in disbelief. "Is this true?"

Katak took a keen interest in his fraying cap.

"Katak!" Everly barked.

"Alright, fine," he groaned. "I went out just before sunrise, because I heard that's when my mark goes for the Sapien. Turns out, I was given bad information."

Vashti rolled her eyes. "I can't believe Everly is the only Naked Mole Rat left in Moon Tracker. How embarrassing for us."

Everly blinked at her.

"What?"

"You're out, too?"

"I don't want to talk about it."

Everly smacked her lips. "So much for playing as a team."

"We were all just taking a page out of your book," Inés shot. She was clearly still sore about Everly's antics on the first night, which was fair. But instead of learning from Everly's mistake, her bandmates had all wandered off into the bush by themselves only to be taken out.

Everly touched the trio of beads resting at the notch in her clavicle. Each night, the Sapien was moved to a new location, but there hadn't been any more clues to help them along. The Naked Mole Rats sneakily followed the Burrowing Owls to a waterfall on the second night, and Jolene had tipped them off about the location of the Sapien at the base of the Stone Witch the night before. Looking around the trunk, the challenge was clearly taking its toll. The Rooters sported puffy faces and listless limbs from lack of sleep. Half of them looked ready to pass out in their bowls.

At dusk, Tazeen's appearance in the mouth of tunnel II instantly charged the dozy atmosphere. As the Umbo made her way to the centre of the trunk, the Rooters straightened their backs and quieted. "My fellow Rooters," she said. "I wish to announce that only five remain in the hunt for Moon Tracker."

The information zapped the Root like a defibrillator. The crowd whooped at the news, quickly turning to their neighbours to discuss who the finalists might be.

A wave of exhilaration crashed over Everly, leaving her shaky and breathless. She did her best to hide it. The fewer people who knew she was still in the game, the better.

"And now, a poem," Taz called above the commotion. " '*Twas once a knight wrapped up in tin, but best was what he held within. Complex was he, both sweet and dark. Maidens consumed him as a lark. At night he slept far from the hearth. Touched by the heat, he lost his worth.*"

Everly tried to repeat the lines to herself. But the words were already getting mixed up in her mind.

"The root of the root!" the Umbo shouted.

"The salt of the earth," they all roared in return. The Rooters raced for the lifts and tunnels.

Everly scanned the room, confused by the bedlam. "I thought almost everyone was eliminated. Where are they all going?"

On his way by, Micah overheard her and paused. "We're not going to make it easy on the final five. It's going to be total mayhem!"

Katak offered Everly a hand and dragged her to her feet. "You could win this thing!" he buzzed in her ear.

Everly cracked her knuckles and tried to slow her pulse with concentrated breaths. "What's one more night of jungle terror?" she joked through her jitters.

"That's the spirit!" Katak said, clapping her on the back.

"Hurry up! We need to solve the clue," Vashti urged.

The three looked over at Inés.

"How should I know?" she shrugged.

"Don't hold out on me now," Everly teased. It came out more desperate than she wanted.

"I'm not holding out. I need more time."

"Please, whenever you're ready," Vashti sassed.

Inés and Vashti stared daggers at each other, but more pressure wasn't going to get them any closer to an answer.

"Guys, focus," Everly begged. "We have to figure out where to go next. There was a knight in shining armour…"

"With goodness inside him. He was dark and sweet. The maidens were into him," Katak said, clearly having paid closer attention this round.

"And he couldn't sleep too close to the fire," Everly finished.

Katak snapped his fingers with a loud click. "I've got it!"

"Highly doubtful," Vashti muttered.

"The knight is made of chocolate," he exclaimed. "Wrapped in tin, right? As in tin foil. And he can't go close to the fire because he'll melt."

Everly dug her fingernails into her scalp. "So where is the—"

"The Sapien is in the Cocoa Copse," Inés yipped, shooting up. "Remember? Micah pointed it out when we were on the river."

"I know where it is," Katak said, gravely. "But I only know one way to get there."

Everly took a second to interpret his words. She rubbed her eyes and saw sparks—like she'd just smashed her skull on a submerged boulder. When she'd last set foot in the river, it had almost killed her. Her windpipe shrank to the size of a straw.

"Everly, are you okay?" Inés asked.

Katak frowned. "You look like you're about to chunder."

Everly dropped her ears between her knees. "I can't," she gasped. "I can't go back out on the river."

"You don't have to if you don't want to," Inés consoled her.

Katak went slack-jawed. "Yes she does! She's our only hope. Vashti, back me up."

There was no smartass response. Everly didn't need to look around to know for sure, but she did anyway. Vashti had bailed.

"Seriously?!" Katak barked. "She said she was out of the game."

"And you believed her?" Inés said with an eye roll. "We don't need Vashti. Everly, what do you want to do?"

At that moment, surviving what felt like a heart attack was her top priority. Everly broke out in a cold sweat. Her tongue went dry.

"Everly, are you dying?" Katak asked.

"I'm fine," she lied.

"We'll use the lift," Inés said, taking control. "We have to cross the aerial roots quickly, in case anyone is watching. Are you ready?"

"Just get me out of here," Everly wheezed.

They rode separate lifts to the surface and met on the aerial roots. Everly gasped as a pair crossed in front of her wearing crow masks. The Rooters were out in full force—and costume—for what might prove to be the final night of the challenge. As if Moon Tracker wasn't freaky enough, now there were monsters in the mix. Everly's first horrifying moments on the island came to her in flashes.

"Disguises," Katak groaned. "Why didn't I think of that?"

A haunting howl rang out from the jungle. The sound sent goosebumps across Everly's flesh. She watched as two Rooters entered a footpath, only to be swept up by a net. They dangled in a cluster of arms and legs ten feet above the earth. Somewhere in the unseeable distance, a loud voice called out: "I am what I am!"

"Only four left!" Inés yelped. "You're almost there."

The trio picked their way through the jungle and carefully scaled the carved steps to the bottom of the ravine. Thunderclouds billowed above the Bloodwood's canopy. The clouds rumbled and flashed with lightning as a storm brewed within them.

"That's not good," Everly noted as they reached the water's edge.

"We can outrun the storm," Inés insisted.

Everly looked out across the river. It seemed so calm, so trustworthy from the bank, but she knew better. Bile rose in her throat.

Katak whistled. He pointed to the fleet of kayaks along the rocks. Gouged into the shoreline were the imprints of three missing boats. "Looks like someone beat us to it."

Everly shivered in her sweat-soaked clothes.

"Are you sure you want to do this?" Inés asked.

Despite her organs twisting inside her, Everly dragged a kayak into knee-deep water. Maybe it wouldn't be that bad. Maybe she wouldn't drown. She bent at the waist and vomited into the river. After a minute, she leaned back and wiped her mouth on her sleeve.

"You good?" Katak asked.

Everly coughed and nodded.

"Let's tie our boats together," Inés offered. "Moon Tracker stays in the middle."

Once they were out on the water, the panic loosened its grip. The paddle felt smooth and reassuring in Everly's hands. Whenever the anxiety swelled, Everly repeated, 'I am what I am' over and over, padding to the rhythm of the words. Risking the river and winning the game would put Everly that much closer to her wish, closer to being reunited with Shelby.

But it wasn't just about Everly or her sister; back on day one, Tazeen had promised the bands would be punished and rewarded as a team. Beside her, Katak and Inés were fighting just as hard for their wishes, for their own destinies. She wanted the win for all of them. As for Vashti, the girl needed a new band name. She wasn't a Naked Mole Rat; she'd been a lone wolf from the start.

"All good, Moon Tracker?" Katak asked, his boat bobbing on the other end of the rope.

"I'm good," Everly replied.

"Look!" Inés pointed to the treeline.

The missing kayaks were on the bank, one carelessly discarded on the rocks near the mouth of a small cave, the other two pulled further onto the soft shore. A fox-shaped lantern sat at the start of a footpath that would lead them directly to the Cocoa Copse. Where the three remaining hunters were probably waiting.

Everly paddled hard across the current and beached her kayak. She used the rope to drag Katak and Inés onto the shore.

"You can't take that route," Katak said, climbing from his boat.

"What choice do I have?"

The clouds rumbled ominously. "The storm is coming. Once it starts, the jungle will be pitch black. We won't be able to find our way back," Inés warned.

"We have to hurry," Everly agreed. "But how do I avoid getting ambushed in the Cocoa Copse?"

"I have an idea," said Inés. "Give me your shirt."

"What?"

"Maybe your tracker will think I'm you. I can lure them out."

"We're not using you as bait, Inés!" Katak blared.

"Shut up and give me your hat," she demanded.

"This is stupid," Katak stated, but he handed over his baseball cap and turned away while the girls swapped shirts. Inés tucked up her thick hair and spun around, looking nothing like Everly, but maybe the darkness would tell a different story.

With Katak acting as their bodyguard out in front, the trio moved stealthily up the footpath. It was overgrown with thick bushes, giant fronds, and creeping vines from the low canopy. They made it to the end, where a cluster of cocoa trees grew closely together. Everly scanned the spaces between their slender trunks. A tiny crescent moon between clouds offered just enough light to make out the Sapien's form, standing with the untamed jungle at its back.

"There it is," Everly whispered.

Without discussing the plan further, Inés stepped into the copse. Slouched over and moving with quick, uncertain steps, Inés kept her face to the ground as she scuttled across the jungle floor. Everly tried not to dwell on the impression, but if she actually walked like that, her entire being needed work.

"Wait here," Everly whispered to Katak. Doing her best to stay hidden, Everly crept along the tree line, keeping her body-double and the stickman in sight.

Nearing the far side of the Cocoa Copse, Inés-as-Everly paused and looked around. She stepped up to the Sapien and touched the collection of yellow beads. As Inés lifted a token, a shadow fell from the branches above and knocked her to the ground.

"I am what—What the? Inés?" Min Jun stood. "You're supposed to be Ping!"

Everly ran between the trees and jumped on Min Jun's back, giving Inés a chance to duck into the jungle. The Lemur tried to flip her, But Everly held firm with her knees long enough to shout, "I am what I am!"

Min Jun fell backward and Everly landed with a thud at the base of a cocoa tree. Chuckling, the Lemur rolled away, propping himself up on his elbows. "No, you're not," he said.

The air above Everly whooshed as a second figure fell from the treetops, landing hard on her back. After a brief squirmish, Ebimi was kneeling on Everly's torso. She whispered the five dreaded words, and just like that, Everly was eliminated from Moon Tracker.

"Did you have to be so rough?" she wheezed.

"Yep," Ebimi laughed.

Everly climbed to her feet and brushed dirt from her knees. "That did not go as planned," she grumbled.

"Yes it did," Ebimi grinned. The two Lemurs ran off into the jungle, bushwhacking in the direction of the distant Bloodwood tree.

"Talk about a classic backfire," Katak said with a frustrated sigh.

Inés stepped in from the fringe. "I'll say."

Everly looked around the Cocoa Copse with a gnawing feeling. "Wait, this doesn't make sense."

"Sure it does. You had Min Jun, Min Jun had Ping. Now Ebimi and Ping have each other," Inés tallied. "They're the final two."

"No, not that," Everly said. "They're not going to the river."

"So?" Katak asked.

"So, who brought the kayaks?"

Like ice splitting across a frozen lake, a scream cracked through the night air. Everly flinched and spun in a circle, trying to locate its source. The terrified wails rattled the small bones in Everly's ear canals. The caller was nearby, but impossible to pinpoint.

"Where's it coming from?" Katak yelled.

The voice cried out again: "Somebody help me!"

"Oh no…" Inés whispered.

The blood drained from Everly's face. "It's Vashti."

CHAPTER 25

When the screaming stopped, the atmosphere in the copse felt charged, as if they'd just witnessed a lightning strike and were waiting for another.

Inés stood with her hands in her mouth, trembling. "They've got Vashti," she whimpered. "The spy…they took her."

"We don't know that," Katak countered as he frantically searched the area.

Everly didn't want to jump to conclusions, but Inés's assumption was likely. Who else but the spy would come after Vashti? Behind the Sapien was a low outcrop of rocks. Everly dropped to all fours and searched, unsure of exactly what she was looking for. When her arm disappeared into a fissure, hot steam dampened her palm.

"There are tunnels beneath us," Everly shouted. "Vashti was right under our feet."

"There's a cave by the river," Inés stated, her voice monotone.

"We have to get to her!" Katak blared.

A whooshing sound filled the copse. Everly spun around just in time to see the stickman burst into flames. The Sapien looked menacing as it burned; its eye sockets glowed red. The grass around its feet curled away as the fire spread. But how could a pile of twigs ignite itself? Before Everly could figure it out, something stung her shoulder; she slapped at an insect that wasn't there. Another spot burned on her forearm, and she brushed a live spark from her skin.

Everly looked up into the night sky—embers were falling like apocalyptic snowflakes.

"Get to the river!" she yelled.

The trio took off, leaving the stickman to its fiery fate. Everly ran as hard as she could, feet pounding the packed earth, arms thrashing through branches and vines. Back on the pebble beach, thunder-clouds blocked out the moon and stars. The river should have been black; instead, it was orange. Everly plunged into the water until she was waist deep. She looked upstream and gasped.

The Bloodwood tree was ablaze. The entire column of the trunk was engulfed in flames. Ancient tree knots were transformed into blood-orange demons, the roar of dying wood escaping from their mouths. A black cloud spread out from the suffering giant, raining ash and fire onto the jungle below. Just then, a massive limb gave way, breaking from the tree with an ear-splitting crack and tumbling down the cliff. It crashed into the river. Even though she was a mile away, Everly felt the heat of the blast as the elements collided.

The Rooters were in trouble. The fire was spreading quickly, and there were only a few trails that led away from the Bloodwood tree. If they were blocked by debris, people could be trapped.

"We need to get the kayaks back to the Root," Everly shouted with a violent shudder. "They might need them to get people out."

"What about Vashti?" Katak asked, eyes wide and afraid.

"I'll go after her," Everly stated. She clawed her way back to the shore. "We'll tie up the boats and you two can tow them back."

Inés stood at the water's edge, crucifix clasped in her fist. "We can't leave you. This feels wrong. Everything's wrong!"

"Please, Inés," Everly begged. "Vashti needs help, and Rooters could be dying in that fire. We have to split up. There's no other way."

"She's right," Katak urged. "I can't tow six boats by myself. We have to work together."

Inés's face was crumpled with angst. She stared hard at the Bloodwood tree and made up her mind. "We'll tow the boats and come back for you right after. Mark your path through the tunnel. We'll find you. I promise."

"Okay," Everly said, hiding her shaking hands behind her back.

Inés pulled Everly into a tight hug. Everly returned the embrace, fighting the urge to cry.

The girls parted and moved quickly to string the kayaks together. Inés and Katak pushed them onto the river and climbed into the boats on either end.

"We'll be right behind you!" Inés called over her shoulder as they began their difficult journey upstream.

Everly took one last mournful look at the Bloodwood tree. It had become a giant torch, towering high above the canopy. Thunder cracked above the jungle. Everly looked up and felt the drizzle on her cheeks. She willed the sky to open, to douse the flames, to protect the bandmates she'd come to love. The orange glow turned Katak and Inés into silhouettes. Was this the last time she'd ever see them? It was too late to go after them now; she couldn't swim against the current.

A wail—guttural and desperate—spilled out from the mouth of the cave. Everly refocused. She wasn't going to lose any people tonight. Not if she could help it.

The downpour began as Everly crossed the threshold. Thunder clapped and lightning flashed; the storm clouds had the power to start a fire and put one out. She prayed the rain would help. Moving deeper into the narrow tunnel, she dragged her hands along the walls on either side of her, ignoring the familiar sensation of being squeezed. Up ahead, a cluster of mushrooms bloomed. She crouched and plucked one by the stem, using the stipe to draw an X on the wall. If Katak and Inés ever made it back, hopefully they'd notice the breadcrumb.

From the depths of the tunnel came another shriek. Fear corkscrewed down Everly's spine, but she set her jaw and followed the sound to a dead end. Everly stopped. She listened. A whisper of air drew her into a crevasse. Before ducking inside, she smeared another blue X on the wall.

"Come on, guys," she whispered. "Come and find me."

In response, Vashti's voice echoed off the walls. Her bandmate was moving—or being moved—deeper into the subterranean world. A new tunnel beckoned with a blue glow. As she turned the corner, Everly's heart filled with hope. Blue handprints covered the stone walls. There were thousands of them, all different sizes, some faded, some glowing brightly enough to guide her with certainty—the Rooters of the past were showing her the way.

Everly splayed her fingers above an aged print; their outlines matched almost perfectly. Were their lifelines connected, too? Using the last of the mushroom stipe, Everly painted her palm blue and added her own print to the wall. She placed the mushroom gills-up in the dirt as a marker, so her friends would know she was here.

Drifting through the tunnel felt like being in outer space—the handprints were five-point stars glowing against infinite darkness. Time crawled by as if the continuum had lost its shape. But then a cry—"Let me go!"—broke through the void. Everly stopped and listened, trying to judge Vashti's distance and direction. Her voice sounded close.

As Everly turned another corner, a rumbling sound filled the tunnel. The aquifer picked up its pace as the floor began to tremble. Other veins of the aquifer crashed through openings in the walls and flowed into the larger river, adding to its speed and force. The water was roaring, but there was another sound, too, something mechanical and out of place. Everly followed the droning noise to where the tunnel lifted.

In the middle of the cave was a machine the size of a small house. Enclosed within it was a turbine with blades as big as airplane pro-pellers. As the swollen aquifer flowed into the machine, the force of the current turned the blades and cranked a metal shaft that went through a hole in the ceiling. Framing the turbine was an opening that swirled with steam and spray. Everly squinted and suddenly understood where she was. The turbine was perched at the top of the waterfall that blasted from the roots of the Bloodwood tree.

She was staring at a hydro-electric generator. If Tazeen was tell-ing the truth about a force field protecting the island, this turbine was powering it. The heat and humidity were suffocating, and the vibrations from the spinning blades rattled Everly's teeth. And there was a scent that shouldn't be there. Smoke. Above her, unseen, a wild inferno was blazing. If the tree fell, would it bring the cave down with it?

Panic made it hard to think clearly. She could run. She could return to the pebble beach and wait for her bandmates. But then

Everly saw Vashti.

On a boulder in the middle of the aquifer, dangerously close to the turbine and its whirling blades, Vashti was laying on her side. Her frame looked so small, Everly hadn't even noticed her before. Vashti's hands were tied behind her back. She was blindfolded. One wrong move and Vashti could easily tumble into the water and be sucked into the blades of the turbine. Did she realize how close she was to death?

"Hello?" Vashti cried. "Is anyone there? Somebody help me!"

Everly wanted to call out to her, but she hesitated. Against the wall, she spotted a ladder. Was it long enough for a make-shift bridge? Vashti had a rope wrapped around her torso that arched upward. Everly followed the line and held a gasp in her chest. On a rock shelf above the aquifer, a figure in a black cloak gripped the far end of the rope; they were wearing a crow mask made of leather and metal studs. A second figure, also masked but wrapped in a red cloak, flipped a rock in their bare, human hand.

Vashti tried to stand, but her bloodied knees buckled. The Red Cloak whipped the stone. It bounced off the boulder and clipped Vashti's ear. She fell back onto her tailbone.

Rage erupted in Everly's core—the kind that turned to brimstone in her gullet.

"What do you want?!" Vashti bellowed.

A raspy voice called from the overhang. "Just tell the truth, Vashti."

"I don't know anything!"

"You need us," said the Black Cloak. "We know people. People who can steal your mother and sisters away in the night and hide them where they cannot be found."

Vashti bristled. "That's impossible."

"You got yourself into this mess. After all your uncle has done for you. He took you in. He paid for your schooling. He gave you a life of prosperity. You owe him, Vashti."

"I owe him nothing!" she screamed.

Everly's blood pooled in her feet. There was a reason Vashti's eyes turned black whenever someone touched her, but Everly had never let herself wonder why for long. The crows knew her backstory, and were about to use it to get whatever they were after. And Vashti would do anything—*anything*—to protect her own secrets.

Everly scanned the cave for a weapon, but there was nothing to wield beyond a few stray rocks. Even if Everly could reach Vashti and get her untied, as soon as the crows dropped from the ledge, they'd block the only exit.

The Black Cloak elaborated: "Your uncle is a powerful man with powerful connections within the Dust. He is determined to find you, no matter the cost. And so is your husband."

"That man is not my husband!" Vashti boomed.

The scarlet sari. The gold jewellery. The red mark on her forehead. Could it be that Vashti had escaped not only the Dust on the day of her recruitment, but a marriage? Everly's guts churned with revulsion. Vashti was only sixteen. A child bride.

"They will find you, Vashti," said the Black Cloak. "You can't stay hidden on the island forever. But if you agree to help us, we can protect you."

"No one can protect me," she cried.

"All you have to do is tell us how to move between moons, and this will all be over."

The statement revealed a much larger problem for the girls. Her captors thought Vashti knew how to leave the island without the help of the Umbo. They wanted information that Vashti didn't have, which put her in even greater danger, because the truth and a lie would sound the same.

Maybe she wasn't thinking straight, or maybe she just didn't care anymore, but Vashti's maniacal laughter filled the cave. "Move between moons?" she wheezed. "If you want to leave the island so badly, go ask the Umbo yourself."

"Tazeen never gives, she only takes. You've put your faith in the wrong people," snarled the Black Cloak.

"I put my faith in no one but myself."

A stone whizzed through the air and hit Vashti in the ribs. She fell to her knees, moaning in pain. Everly covered her mouth to keep from screaming. Vashti was inches from the water, oblivious to the added danger of the turbine blades.

"You'll have to stone me to death," Vashti chuckled. "Because I can't tell you something I don't know."

The monsters on the overhang began to whisper. Everly silently willed Vashti to stop provoking them. Her big mouth could very well get her killed.

"That day on the river, you didn't find a way off the island?" prodded the Black Cloak.

"Not even close," Vashti snarled.

"But Taz has been watching you ever since. So, you must have found something. Something important."

The Red Cloak knocked a pile of stones from the ledge. They clanged against the cave floor, sounding off like exploding buckshots. Vashti's head snapped wildly from side to side.

The Black Cloak swooped from the ledge, arms spread wide, fabric rustling. They landed beside the aquifer with the end of the rope still in hand.

"You found the Cure," the Black Cloak said. "Even better."

CHAPTER 26

"I don't…I don't know what you're talking about," Vashti said, stumbling over her words.

"I'm going to give you one more chance," growled her captor. "You're going to tell me everything, or you're going to die with your secrets."

"Either you'll kill me now, or Taz kills me later," Vashti replied. "It's all the same."

The Black Cloak gave the rope a hard yank. Vashti slipped on the algae-covered boulder and landed on her hip. It was everything Everly had to stay in the shadows, to not throw herself at the crow and use her fingernails to claw out their eyes. But one false move could send her bandmate into the spinning blades.

From deep in the tunnels, Katak's voice reached the cave, calling out to her: "Everly, where are you?!" Her bandmates had come back for her, just as they'd promised. But their presence meant the captors were out of time, making the situation even more dire.

"Someone's coming," called the crow from the overhang.

"It's now or never, Vashti," the Black Cloak warned.

Vashti dragged her brow along the rock, forcing the blindfold up. With equal parts bravery and defiance, Vashti snarled: "I guess you'll just have to kill me."

"Have it your way."

The Black Cloak pulled the rope with full force and sent Vashti tumbling into the aquifer. When she broke the surface, the current pinned her against the boulder with her hands still bound behind her back. The rushing water cascaded over her before it was sucked into the turbine.

"I'm here!" Everly shouted as loud as her lungs could manage.

"Katak, Inés, I'm here!"

The Black Cloak reeled around as the other crow dropped to the floor.

"Everly?!" Katak's voice called, closer than before.

"I'm here! I'm here!" Everly cried, revealing her position. "There's two of them, hurry!"

"We have to go," the Red Cloak insisted.

In a slow pivot, the Black Cloak turned to face the uninvited guest. The crow tilted its monstrous head to the side. "Her death is on you," they growled as they dropped the rope.

It slithered across the cave floor. Everly dived to catch it. The crow jumped on Everly's back, forcing her face into the ground. Her nose exploded with blood and her vision sparked. The weight of the crow lifted, and Everly looked back to see Min Jun fighting with both captors.

"Everly, pull Vashti out!" the Lemur screamed.

From her belly, she reached further up on the rope. The fibres shredded her palms. Inch by inch, Everly dragged Vashti from the boulder, her bandmate's mouth wide in a silent cry as the water arched over her.

"I've got you!" Everly shouted, teeth dark with blood.

The Black Cloak shoved Min Jun hard against the cave wall and spun around on one foot to deliver a perfectly placed heel kick to his sternum. Min Jun buckled over. The captor hoisted the ladder from the ground and broke it over the Lemur's back, sending pieces scattering across the floor and into the water.

The Red Cloak grabbed their accomplice by the arm, trying to drag them to the tunnels. But the Black Cloak shoved them away. Faster than Everly could process, the crow grabbed Min Jun by the tunic, rolled backward with their feet on his chest, and launched the Lemur into the aquifer.

Everly screamed—"No! No! No!"—as the captors ran from the cave. Min Jun fought against the current, face contorted with terror. He clawed at the boulder as he was pulled toward the turbine, but it was too slick to offer salvation. The Lemur yelled something inaudibly before being sucked underwater and passing through the blades like a bird through a fan. The river churned red.

"Min Jun!" Everly bellowed. As the sound finished echoing around the cave, the water cleared, leaving behind no trace of the Lemur.

Shaking and sobbing, Everly clutched the rope in both hands and pulled with all of her strength. The force of the current tried to tear her arms from their sockets. Her lungs were on fire. Her muscles burned.

She heard Katak shout her name again. Everly followed the sound and saw her bandmates and Ebimi running along the ledge.

"Help me!" Everly cried, her voice warped with agony.

Ebimi and Katak appeared by her side. They grabbed the rope and heaved Vashti within arm's reach. Katak dragged her from the aquifer like a half-drowned rat. She coughed up water as Inés worked on the knots at her wrists.

"Where's Min Jun?" Ebimi barked.

"He's gone," Everly whispered in a daze, letting the blood drip from her chin.

"Where?" the Lemur snapped.

Everly opened her mouth to respond, but nothing came out. Her vision blurred with tears. Min Jun was dead. His body was shredded. She'd seen his eyes. She'd watched him die.

Ebimi crouched in front of her, shaking her into focus. "Everly, where is Min Jun?"

She lifted a quaking hand and pointed at the turbine blades. "He's gone," Everly repeated.

Ebimi's expression went stone cold. As the understanding took hold, it mutated with agony. "No," she bellowed. "No!"

The earth trembled above them. A wide fissure split the ceiling. Chunks of the cave fell and crashed into the aquifer and onto the generator, jamming the turbine blades with a screech of rock against metal. The weight of the Bloodwood was about to crash down on them.

"Move!" Ebimi yelled.

Fear shocked Everly from her stupor. She climbed to her feet and ran. The group sprinted for the exit, but with an ear-splitting boom, a section of the ceiling fell and blocked their path. Everly spun in circles. There was no way out.

"There!" Katak shouted. The turbine was jammed by a large rock, and there was enough space to slip between the blades. Vashti was the first to hit the water and squeeze through the opening. Ebimi was next.

"Hurry!" Katak shouted before crashing into the water.

"But the…the waterfall, the fire…" Inés stammered from the ledge.

"If we don't go, we die," Everly urged.

She grabbed Inés's hand and dragged her into the aquifer. The force of the current carried them to the turbine, where Katak shoved them through the opening before managing, just barely, to fit his shoulders between the blades.

As the cave collapsed, crushing the generator and sending an eruption of water out over the expanse, Everly felt herself thrown over the waterfall. She became weightless, for an instant, before gravity wrapped its heavy hands around her. As she fell, pummelled by the weight of the vertical aquifer, she was glad that, unlike Min Jun, at least she'd die in one piece.

CHAPTER 27

Never forget how much I love you…

The ghostly words woke Everly with a start. A gasp rattled her lungs like she'd been holding it for days. Her hands were numb and tightly fastened behind her. Something hard and unforgiving dug into her spine—a stake sticking up in the earth. A haze of low-hanging smoke floated away on a soft breeze. Everly was in a crater. The hole in the earth was deep, the walls were charred, and the ground was covered in ash as fine as the powder on the surface of the moon.

Dazed and disoriented, Everly coughed weakly. She was thirsty. She leaned back, longing for rain. There was nothing above her. No branches. No trees. Only a grey sky at dusk or dawn, she couldn't tell.

"Where am I?" Everly croaked.

"At the end of the line," replied Tazeen.

Everly blinked several times before the face came into focus. The Umbo's skin was blackened with soot, lines washed clean by tears and sweat. Tazeen looked like she'd aged a decade and lost all hope in the process.

"Taz, what happened? Where are the others?"

"You are alive because of the nets strung across the falls, put there long ago as a precaution. Ebimi pulled you and your bandmates to safety, avoiding death by water and fire."

Everly sighed with relief; her friends were okay. But there was so much the Umbo didn't know. "Tazeen, the spies…"

"It is not your turn to speak," the Umbo snapped.

The smoke dissipated, revealing the rest of the Lemurs. They looked haggard, as though they'd gone days without food or rest.

They formed a semi-circle around the stake, staring at Everly through sunken eyes. Maria Jose was crying. Andrew and Ebimi looked ready to kill.

"Umbo, what's going on?" Everly whispered.

"We are standing in what is left of the Root. Above us is what is left of the Bloodwood tree. You're here to be held accountable for your crimes."

"Crimes?" Everly repeated.

"Everly Dahl, this is your Bloodwood Council tribunal. You are hereby charged with espionage. We know you have been working for the Dust. I only wish I had figured it out sooner, so I could have prevented the immeasurable damage you have done."

Everly understood the words coming from Tazeen's downturned mouth, but she couldn't make sense of them. "You think *I'm* the spy? That's...that's insane."

"Is it? I might have been inclined to agree, except you left a key piece of evidence behind last night. We found this at the fire's ignition point." Taz drew closer to Everly. Nathaniel Dahl's badge sat in the centre of her palm, fastened to a length of twine. Tazeen slipped the loop over Everly's head.

Everly looked down at the badge, utterly baffled. "It's mine. But I lost it when Vashti and I were swept down the river weeks ago. Where did you get it?"

"Jax came forward with the evidence."

The truth was immediately clear, as if Everly was staring cross-eyed at a stereogram and the shape finally jumped off the page. "Jax," she scoffed. "The night of the Council meeting, I caught him in the tunnels. He said he'd burn the island to the ground to get what he wants. And here we are. Jax must have seen me use the badge to start a fire at the hives. And there were two attackers at the generator. Jax and Jolene. It makes sense. They're siblings. The Dust could have approached them together."

Tazeen's weathered expression didn't change. "Ebimi, when you arrived at the generator, what did you see?"

"I saw Everly, holding Vashti on the end of a rope," the Lemur replied.

"No one else?"

"No one else. She'd already killed Min Jun at that point."

Everly's windpipe spasmed. It wasn't just espionage she was accused of; they thought she was a killer.

"Min Jun was my friend," Everly said. "And I would never work for the Dust. They ruined my life. They took everything from me. I want to destroy them." Everly was talking loud and fast, but it felt like no one in the crater could even hear her. She tried another line of reasoning: "Why would I go after my own bandmates? They're newcomers; they don't know anything."

"The attack on Inés was an act of terror, designed to destabilize the Root. With Vashti, it was because she had something that you needed. When the two of you were swept down the river, you were knocked unconscious. Vashti wasn't. She knew the exact location of the whirlpool. You tracked her to the generator, you tortured her, and when Min Jun showed up, you eliminated him to protect your cover."

"No," Everly insisted. "There were two crows in the cave—"

"Katak and Inés, come forward," the Umbo summoned. Everly's bandmates stepped into the crater, guided—or maybe guarded—by Micah. They shuffled across the ash to the middle of the semi-circle. Their eyes were swollen and bloodshot. Inés looked at her with an expression that tore at Everly's heart. She wanted to comfort her friend.

"Inés, tell us what you saw at the generator," said Tazeen.

Inés turned to address the Council. "We…we all got separated during the fire—"

The Umbo cut her off. "Only the relevant details."

Inés flinched and tried to gather her thoughts. "We saw Everly holding a rope, and Vashti was in the water, but—"

"But Everly was trying to help her," Katak stepped in. "Everly was with us in the copse when we heard Vashti start screaming. She was with us when the fire started. It couldn't have been her!"

"We believe she positioned the magnifying glass in such a way that the fire would start on its own," the Umbo explained. "And it's possible Everly wasn't working alone."

"You're not listening," Katak yelled. "She didn't do this!"

Tazeen held up her hand to silence him. "Katak, you want to believe that Everly was trying to help. But when Inés was attacked in the Hangar, you didn't see anyone else there, did you? Just Everly."

His shoulders slumped, slightly, and that barely perceptible response hurt Everly more than a savage beating would have. "She would never do something like this," he said, softly.

"Thank you for your testimony."

"You can't—" Inés started.

"Inés, did you see anyone else at the Hangar or the generator?"

"No," Inés cried. "I didn't see anybody, but, Taz—"

"That's enough."

"Please!" Inés begged.

"Leave us," Tazeen boomed. "Return to the grove. Tend to the wounded."

"Everly, I'm so sorry," Inés wailed as Micah led her away.

Katak struggled with Andrew, but the imposing Lemur twisted Katak's limb into submission. "Everly run!" Katak shouted before being swallowed by a tunnel. "Run! They're going to kill you. You have to get out of here!"

Everly started hyperventilating. The Lemurs had filled in the blanks with the wrong information, but how could she convince them otherwise? None of it made any sense. Everly had been plucked from obscurity, recruited at random the very same day that the Dust took her sister. How could she betray a rebellion that, before her recruitment, she couldn't even prove was real?

Everly raised her chin. "I didn't do this," she snarled. "I didn't hurt my friends. I didn't burn down the Bloodwood tree. You recruited me, and I fought hard to stay on the island for one reason."

"And what reason is that?"

"Because you said you could free my family!" Everly cried.

"And what did the Dust promise you, exactly?"

Everly scoffed, bitterly. "They promised a life without my father and my sister. A life with no prospects or hope. A life without freedom. Which is why I left it all behind the day I met Micah. I risked everything. I did everything you asked. Because I believe in the rebellion."

The Umbo darted forward and slapped Everly across the face. "You killed Min Jun! When Katak and Inés came back for you, Min Jun and Ebimi met them on the beach. Your bandmates said you and Vashti were still in the tunnels. Min Jun knew the whole structure was unstable. My friend risked his life to try and save you, and you murdered him!"

"No," Everly said, tasting blood. "The spy in the black cloak killed Min Jun. I…I would never do anything to hurt him. He was kind to me."

Everly couldn't fight it anymore; a torrent of tears flooded her face. Min Jun was good. He was kind. He'd saved Vashti. His map was meant to protect them during the Lost Souls trial; she knew that now. The person who should have been her mentor was dead, but even as grief filled her body like wet cement, she could not mourn him. Not with her own life hanging in the balance.

"Min Jun died trying to help us," Everly said, her heart hardening. "He's dead because you let two spies onto your island. And they're still out there."

"That's enough!" Taz screamed, her voice breaking. "Min Jun was my family. He didn't deserve to die while you scrambled to cover your tracks. We didn't deserve to lose our home because you were looking for a payout."

"What payout? Every witness is telling you your story doesn't add up. Ask Vashti who attacked her at the generator."

"Vashti is not a reliable source," Tazeen replied. "We have reason to believe she was engaged in spygames of her own."

Everly thrashed against the restraint. The stake shook in place. "You're so desperate to blame someone, you don't even care if you've got the right person," Everly blasted. "More Rooters are going to get hurt, Taz. The spies aren't done. They said the Blood Moon will be bloody—"

"The Bloodwood Council will now pass judgement," the Umbo decreed. "A Rooter is dead, and we must avenge him. An eye for an eye. A life for a life. But there is a chance for mercy here. In the case of Everly Dahl, for the crimes of espionage and murder, it is time to vote. Death or exile."

Everly looked around. The Lemurs, who'd been her teachers and guides, had become her enemies. They were blinded by grief and rage. By loss. There was nothing she could do, no way to defend herself. The truth had failed.

Tazeen clenched her jaw. "Andrew McPherson, what is your vote?"

"Death," Andrew said without hesitation. The air left Everly's lungs with a shudder.

"Marie Jose Colmenero?"

The healer was sobbing. "Exile," she choked. "Killing her won't bring Min Jun back."

The Umbo moved on. "Ebimi Adeyemi."

Her expression was cold and stoic. "Death," Ebimi said.

"Micah Kikwete."

Everly's mentor looked up, surprised.

"You're not a Council member, but she is your recruit. You should have a say in her fate."

Micah nodded, solemnly. "Exile," he replied. Everly was grateful for that, at least. As much as she could be.

"It is up to me to break the tie." The Umbo gazed up where the hollow trunk used to be. She righted herself to look her prisoner directly in the eye. "Everly Dahl, by order of the Bloodwood Council, you are hereby sentenced to death for espionage and the murder of Min Jun Park."

"No!" Everly struggled against the ropes, twisting her wrists as the restraints drew blood.

Tazeen pointed at her with an executioner's finger. "You will suffer the same fate as the Bloodwood tree. Death by fire. At sunrise."

"Taz, you can't do this! I'm innocent!" Everly cried. She looked at each juror, but they'd already decided her guilt and held firm in their resolve. She tried to lock eyes with Micah, but he stared at the earth.

It was no use. The Rooters followed the laws of the island. Their rules were sacrosanct. Everly's fate was sealed.

"The root of the root," the Umbo said, coldly.

"The salt of the earth," the others replied.

The wind picked up, swirling ash around her like a cyclone. Everly imagined herself transformed into particles, carried on an updraft into the endless sky. She wouldn't have to wait long, once the fire claimed her, to fade to dust. In that moment, she felt everything and nothing—terror and numbness, panic and paralysis, devastation and detachment.

But the truth of her reality was undeniable. The Bloodwood Society had deemed her a witch, and come sunrise, they would burn her at the stake.

CHAPTER 28

Ebimi and Andrew dragged Everly's limp body through a smoky tunnel. They'd covered at least a mile before they turned into a small cave that was cut in half by a wall of bars. A fissure in the ceiling let in a dull ribbon of light.

Vashti stood on the far side of the bars, gripping the partitions with scuffed knuckles. "Let me out of here!" she shrieked as the Lemurs appeared with their new prisoner in tow.

Andrew produced an ancient-looking key and used it to crack open the padlock. "Get back!" he boomed. Vashti raised her hands and took two careful steps away from the bars. Andrew opened the gate and grabbed her by the elbow, pulling her across the threshold.

"Don't touch me!" Vashti spat, clawing at his hands. He wrenched her wrists behind her, securing them with a short loop of rope before dragging Vashti from the cave.

"You have to tell them the truth," Everly coughed as she took Vashti's place in the cell. "They think I'm the spy…"

"What?!" Vashti cawed.

"Shut up!" Andrew bellowed.

"Get off of me! Everly, what's going on?"

Everly screamed her friend's name until Vashti's cries were absorbed by the tunnels. The air became eerily still. Was this where the banished newcomers had ended up? Since they couldn't move between moons, the eleven rejects probably spent some time behind the same bars. It was ironic, in a way, that Everly had ended up in the very place she feared the most. Despite everything she'd done in the name of freedom, she was still a prisoner.

Everly sunk to the floor and struggled with the ropes until they loosened. Her wrists were raw and blistered. Her lungs ached from inhaling smoke and water. Ash burned in her eyes. Everly's body was a mess, but her soul felt battered beyond repair. She'd seen rock bottom before, but now she knew sorrow and suffering had no limits.

Everything she'd hoped for, sacrificed for, was gone. Everly forced herself to take stock, to reconcile what was with what had come to be. The Bloodwood tree, the birthplace of the rebellion, was gone. It was the Rooters' shelter, but it had also become her home. The island and the rebellion had represented a future full of promise, but all of that went up in smoke.

Min Jun was gone. He'd been decent to her from the start, when Micah was still deciding the type of mentor he wanted to be. Min Jun was a leader. A philosopher. A gardener who tended not only to the needs of plants, but people, too. Min Jun didn't deserve to die. And knowing he'd lost his life trying to save her and Vashti made it so much worse. Was it her fault? If she's stayed with Katak and Inés, maybe things would have turned out differently.

The thought of her bandmates was heart-wrenching. At the tribunal, Tazeen had planted seeds of doubt that would take root as the story of Everly's treachery became part of rebel lore. She wished Katak and Inés had seen the crows; at least then they'd know for sure—no matter what anyone else believed—that their friend was innocent.

For most of her life, friendship had been an abstract concept. But Katak and Inés had helped her uncover parts of herself she actually liked—parts that were brave, trusting, parts that believed good things could happen. Before the island, she'd never let people in, never shown her soft side and stayed around long enough to understand what it meant to be loved anyway.

Even with Jordan. She'd always kept him at a safe distance. They were friends, sure, but she'd always wanted more. Maybe if she'd told him how she felt. Maybe if she'd grabbed his face and kissed him the way she'd dreamed of doing a thousand times. If she hadn't been so afraid. If she hadn't squandered so many precious moments. Maybe then she could have experienced what happens when friendship evolves into something miraculous. Something extraordinary.

But she was lucky enough to have known an exceptional bond. Through it all, Shelby was there. Their connection was unconditional, unfaltering. But now, Everly would never learn what happened to her sister. If it meant Shelby would be free and would go on to live a long, happy life, Everly would gladly accept her own death. If she still had a wish, it would be to hug her sister one last time. Everly had held out hope that she might see Shelby again. Now, Everly knew for certain that she would never get to speak the words of her heart—that there was only love between them.

The air in the cell was hot, but she couldn't stop shivering. She thought of her dad, locked up for years. Nathaniel was a good dad. He'd given her the gift of books, of knowledge and curiosity. He'd played games and peeled her apples in long, curly strands. After their mom died, he'd stroked Everly's hair for hours, until she fell asleep between sobs. She missed him so badly. Alone in the cave, she said goodbye in her heart, hoping somehow, somewhere, he would sense it.

A low moan swelled inside her, growing so painful she couldn't contain it anymore. She fell to her side and hugged her knees. Everly cried as misery and regret washed over her, as the grief she'd been repressing for a decade finally hit like a tidal wave. When her tears ran dry, Everly stared blankly at the bars that separated her from the rest of the world, that kept her from the truth and its unfulfilled promises. Her cheek was pressed against the dirt floor, and she felt the almost imperceptible rumble of the aquifer. It was always close.

Maybe it was her tears, her body's own expression of the water; maybe it was the low murmur of the underground river. Whatever it was, a memory flickered. Everly tried to focus on it, hearing the whisper of her dad's ghostly words. The distant recollection was clearest whenever she'd been in the water. At the Wishing Well and the whirlpool. And now, after the waterfall. Like the aquifer was trying to bring something to the surface.

She closed her eyes.

It was storming. Everly was sitting on the stairs, listening to her parents argue. Things had been bad for months, but something about this fight felt different. Dad's voice was louder. He sounded desperate. Mom was saying the world was ending. Dad was saying they just needed to keep their heads down.

Mom was crying when she came upstairs. She carried seven-year-old Everly back to bed. She smoothed her daughter's curls. Then Everly felt a sharp pain in her neck, followed by a sick, dizzy sensation. Mom told her to stay in bed. She kissed the bridge of her freckled nose.

"Never forget how much I love you," Mom whispered.

Everly tried to go back to sleep, but she heard the back door slam. Her legs felt heavy as she stumbled to the windowsill. Mom was parting the tall grasses, moving toward the bluffs. Dad was waiting for her there with his back to the house. Something was wrong. Mom wasn't wearing a coat or shoes. A hurricane was just about to make landfall; there was no reason for them to be out in the storm.

From the hall, Everly could see Shelby passed out with her head hanging off the side of the bed. Everly called to her, but her sister didn't move. She dragged herself downstairs and to the kitchen, using the railing and walls to keep her balance.

Once outside, the rain hit her bare arms like hailstones. Dad was facing the sea. Mom was screaming at him, tearing at his shirt. Everly pushed her way through the overgrowth, stumbling on the uneven earth. Halfway to them, she slipped and fell hard in the mud. She tried to get up, but her legs wouldn't work anymore. Panicking, Everly called for her parents: "Mom! Dad!"

Her father's head snapped around, his face wracked with despair.

"I have to go, Nate," Mom shouted.

He looked back at his wife. "Melody, please, don't do this!" he wailed.

"Please, Nate!" She stepped backwards. Her heels touched the edge of the bluffs.

"I can't do it!"

Her mom's long auburn hair thrashed in the wind. "I need you to tell me it will all be okay…"

Vashti's angry voice echoed from the tunnel, snapping Everly out of the past. Ebimi and Andrew dragged Vashti around the corner, and judging by her cursing, her tribunal had not gone well.

"You can't do this. If you send me back, he'll kill me!" Vashti shrieked as they locked her in the cell with Everly. Vashti threw herself against the bars. The Lemurs left without a word.

"What happened?" Everly asked, wiping her tears away with a filthy cuff.

Vashti slumped onto the floor beside her. "They're making me take Other Death in the morning and sending me home. I'd rather be dead."

"What did you tell them?"

"The truth. But it didn't matter. Taz got word from the Spearheads. Apparently, all of a sudden, the Dust knows the location of the Cure."

"Shit."

"Yep. Tazeen thinks I blabbed. That I somehow got a message off the island. Which is totally possible, because apparently I'm the proud owner of a courier pigeon!" Vashti screamed after the Lemurs.

"But at the generator, I know you didn't tell the crows about the Cure," Everly said.

"Are you sure? I was stuck on the rock for a while before you showed up. Maybe stuff happened that you don't know about."

"I heard the whole thing."

"Everything?" Vashti asked with a wince.

"Yeah," Everly replied, sheepishly.

"So, you know. About my life before I came here."

"Only what they said about your uncle."

Vashti picked at her fingernails. "Right. Him. He's not a good guy. He's not really my uncle. He's not even Indian. Just some white dude who married my mom's cousin. But we needed help, and he took us in. It was okay for a while. He made sure we were fed and got my sisters and I back in school. But nothing is ever free. He called it an arranged marriage, but that's not what it was. My uncle sold me to a Dust handler."

"What do you mean he sold you?"

"I mean some old man paid my uncle lots and lots of money to marry me. I said I'd run away, but my uncle threatened to marry off my sisters, too, if I disobeyed him. They're younger than me."

"That's disgusting," Everly cringed.

"Child marriages were illegal before. But the War sent us back two hundred years. I was recruited on my wedding day. The man who bought me came to see me before the ceremony. He was at least forty years old. He gave me a bag of diamonds as a wedding gift, as if that would somehow seduce me. When he tried to kiss me, I smashed his teeth with an incense holder."

"I would pay to see that," Everly said, approvingly.

"It was pretty great," Vashti sighed. "I grabbed the bag off the table and ran, but my uncle's thugs chased me through the hotel. I could barely move in that stupid sari, but I made it to my mom's room. She and my sisters forced me down the laundry chute. One of the maids hid me in a cart and smuggled me outside. She started saying crazy things about how she could make me disappear. I was so freaked out about everything that I agreed. She shot me up, I blacked out, and this," Vashti gestured around their cell, "is what I get for trusting people."

Everly gawked at her. "Vashti, that's…I'm so sorry that happened. All of it."

"And it's the truth."

"Wait, how did Katak figure out you were a child bride? When you were sparring, he said something about red paint."

"Dude is not as dumb as he looks," Vashti clucked. "Somehow, he knew what the bindi on my forehead meant. Can you imagine if I was actually married right now? To an old man?! How weird would that be?"

"Incredibly weird."

"Incredibly impossible to get a boyfriend."

Everly tisked. "You don't want a boyfriend, Vashti. You threaten any guy who comes near you."

"Fine, impossible to get a girlfriend, then."

The statement caught Everly off guard. "You like girls?"

"Whatever. It doesn't matter."

"It matters to me."

"Do you think it would have mattered to my uncle? Or my fiancé? It wouldn't have changed a thing," Vashti scowled.

"So, the day you left us in the Hangar, you weren't with Chen," Everly surmised.

"I was with him and Ping. And Ebimi."

"Oh!" Everly exclaimed. An uninitiated newcomer hooking up with a Lemur would have been a scandal, for sure. No wonder they'd both wanted to keep it a secret. She imagined the girls sneaking off into the moonlit jungle, united in their shared joy.

"It was fun while it lasted," Vashti huffed, kicking a pebble across the cave.

"I get it now," Everly said. "Why you left us last night. You went to tell Ebimi about the riddle. She was still in the hunt for Moon Tracker. You wanted to help her."

"All's fair in love and war," Vashti shrugged.

"Agreed, but during the vote, did she…?"

"My girlfriend voted for me to be exiled. So, I'd say we're pretty much broken up at this point."

"That sucks," Everly said, puffing out her cheeks. "Thanks for telling me. I know you and the truth have a complicated relationship."

Vashti sucked her teeth. "Why do you have to make everything so uncomfortable?"

Everly chuckled.

"Alright, I spilled my guts. It's your turn now."

"What do you want to know?"

"Something I can use to blackmail you."

"Fine," Everly sighed. "I remembered something about the night my mom died. She drugged me right before, but I was there. I saw it happen. Something about being in the aquifer brought the memories back." Everly told Vashti about the storm, about following her parents out to the bluffs.

"I had no idea what they were doing out there," she said. "My parents were screaming at each other. The wind was howling. The storm and the ocean were behind them. My mom looked so small. My dad told me to close my eyes.

"The storm went silent. My body went numb. Mom smiled at me. She made this sign with her hands." Everly bent her ring and middle fingers. "It's how we say, 'I love you.' I laid there in the mud, paralyzed, looking through the blades of grass as my parents wrapped their arms around each other. They kissed. And then my dad threw my mom over the bluffs."

Vashti gasped, raising a hand to her mouth. "He killed her?"

"She…she asked him to. She wanted to die, but he could have stopped her. I don't know why he didn't."

"Maybe…he loved her enough to let her go."

Everly sighed, shakily. "I don't know."

Vashti waited a few seconds before elbowing Everly in the ribs. "Thanks a lot for one-upping my story. 'I'm Everly Dahl, my trauma is better than your trauma, everybody look at me.'"

"You're deeply unlikable, you know that?" Everly quipped.

Vashti fidgeted in her pocket and pulled out Micah's knife, flipping it in her hand. "Unlikable, but useful." She got to work picking the padlock.

"Wait, you were alone in this cell for hours before the tribunal," Everly noted. "Why didn't you leave before?"

"I don't know."

"Vashti."

"What?"

"Were you waiting for me?"

"Shut your hole!" she cawed.

Everly climbed to her feet and watched her bandmate wiggle the blade within the lock. The prospect of escape made her pulse quicken, but the hope quickly faded. They could hide in the tunnels and survive for a little while, but how long would it take for the Rooters to track them down? Running would only delay the inevitable.

"Vashti," she said, softly, "there's nowhere for us to go."

"We'll figure something out."

Everly put a careful hand on Vashti's shoulder. "I'm not going to run anymore."

Vashti scowled. "You're still holding out hope that they'll come to their senses. But Tazeen held a kangaroo court and found us guilty. Face it, the Bloodwood Society is just as bad as the Dust."

"I don't want to believe that," Everly hushed.

"Tazeen is not the hero you want her to be." The shank popped. The lock dropped to the ground as the gate swung open with a clang. "Come with me," Vashti said.

"And do what?"

"I don't know, stupid, maybe find a way to clear our names?" Vashti pocketed the knife and stepped out of the cell. Her sandalled feet left imprints in the ash. She paused, deciding which direction to take. Everly made up her mind and moved to follow her, but something stopped Vashti in her tracks. She raised her hands and took slow, precise steps backward, like she'd crossed paths with a bear.

A human shadow stepped into the mouth of the cave, blocking the exit. "And just where do you think you're going?" he asked.

Everly knew the voice; it belonged to the Red Cloak. The boy held a stone in his hand, flipping it like an idea he was toying with. As he stepped into the cave, a sliver of light cut across his bare face, revealing a dangerous expression and an unmistakable purple birthmark.

It was Arseniy.

CHAPTER 29

E verly's eyes were locked on the stone in Arseniy's hand, following its path through the air and back to his palm. The stone was the same size as the bruises all over Vashti's body.

"It was you. You nearly killed me," hissed Vashti, drawing the same conclusion.

"I'm here to get you out," Arseniy stated.

Vashti gestured to the open gate. "We're good."

Everly stepped out of the cell and stood shoulder-to-shoulder with her bandmate. The Fire Ant wasn't that big. They could probably take him. Stones and all.

Arseniy frowned, reading the violence in their expressions. "Don't be stupid. The Lemurs turned on you. You girls don't stand a chance without my help."

"Tazeen won't punish us when she finds out you're the one who's been working for the Dust," Everly growled.

He grinned. "Have I?"

The girls exchanged confused glances. Before they could respond, a slender figure appeared in the entrance to the cave. The moonlight shimmered in her long white-blonde hair. Nikol glowed like an elf against the darkness.

"He's working for me, actually," she said, smiling like everything was right in the world.

Everly reached for the cell bars behind her. She wanted to pull them from the ground and start swinging. Crowbars. Seemed appropriate. Nikol and Arseniy weren't disguised as crows anymore, but the duo had already proven how far they were willing to go. Everly looked beyond them, wishing Andrew and Ebimi would reappear.

"Your guards won't be joining us," Nikol said, noting the

direction of her gaze. "It took a little extra oomph, but they both went down, eventually."

Vashti's breath caught, almost inaudibly. Was Ebimi dead? What about the rest of the Lemurs?

"We should go," Arseniy said, urgency creeping into his voice.

"We're not going anywhere with you," Everly hissed.

Nikol rolled her eyes. "Can we stop wasting time? Look, Bloodwood isn't what you think it is, okay? I was brainwashed, too. But you saw what happened today. Tazeen isn't the great and mighty Umbo she's pretending to be. She's a liar and a tyrant."

"Tazeen has always kept her word. You're the liar," Everly snarled.

"Tazeen literally just sentenced you to death, and you're still defending her," the spy jeered. "She doesn't care if you're innocent. So long as she can convince the Rooters that everything is under control, Taz gets to keep playing queen of the jungle."

Everly's head was spinning, trying to come up with a plan. The longer they stayed in the cave, the better the odds someone would come find them. If she could keep the spy talking, maybe help would arrive. "I don't understand," she said. "You're initiated. You had your wish granted. The Bloodwood Society came through for you. How could you turn your back on them?"

Nikol sighed. "A funny thing happens when you get the one thing you want most. You realize it isn't all that great. You still have problems. The world is still broken. The person you love most will get sick. The doctors will run out of options. She'll lay in a hospital bed, dying a slow, painful death. And you'll have to sit there and watch. Completely helpless."

The revelation hit Everly like a gutpunch. Was Nikol describing her own life, or Everly's?

"People die from sickness everyday," Vashti spat. "The Dust does nothing for them."

"That's where you're wrong. When my aunt got sick this year, Tazeen let me go visit her. The Dust arrested me at the hospital. They didn't lock me up, though. Instead, they offered me a miracle cure. So I said yes, okay, I'll do whatever it takes. And wouldn't you know it, the Dust tells me the Bloodwood Society has the Cure. That my own people, my fellow rebels, have been holding out on me."

Everly held her breath until it turned to spiders. Nikol had done monstrous things, but now, Everly understood why. They shared a common suffering, and Everly knew that brand of desperation all too well. But wanting to save a family member didn't justify inflicting violence and death on the Rooters. Or did it? Was it the smoke, the ash, or the recent traumas that were blurring the line between right and wrong? The murkiness was frightening.

"The Umbo doesn't control the Cure," Everly said, both to the spy and to herself. "Taz can't just give it away to whoever she wants. That's not how it works."

"Wow," Nikol scoffed. "What a good little soldier. And who are the Spearheads, exactly? Why should they decide who gets the Cure? Why should they get to play god?"

"It's for the greater good," Everly said, but the words sounded flat. It was a justification espoused by the Rooters, but what did it even mean? What was the criteria? Who were the judges?

Nikol humphed. "The greater good means whatever the Spearheads say it means. They've been fighting the Dust for decades, and how much good have they done? How many rebels have died or been imprisoned? How many innocent people have had their lives destroyed by association? Meanwhile, Bloodwood has been withholding the Cure from the rest of the world. From people like my aunt. People like Shelby."

Everly twitched.

"As if I wouldn't read your file," Nikol simpered. "Come on, Everly. You know where the Cure is. And I know how to get us off the island. Let's help each other get what we want."

"How would you do that?" Everly heard herself asking. She was almost as shocked as Vashti, who was staring at her, wide-eyed and confused.

Nikol produced an ovoid capsule the size of her thumb. Its cap pulsed with a red light. "Don't ask me how I smuggled this onto the island. It wasn't pretty. But now that the generator is no longer an issue, all I have to do is turn on the locator and the Dust will come for us."

"How do you know they aren't already tracking you?" Everly asked.

"The force field would have fried it," Arseniy piped in.

Everly felt like electric currents were flowing through her. Since the day she was recruited, she'd been on a set course, with little room for deviation. The decisions had mostly been made for her. But here was an actual choice. Here was a chance to get back to Shelby, to bring her the Cure, and to return to life as it was before.

"Once they know where we are, what makes you so sure the Dust won't nuke the whole island?" Everly asked.

"What are you doing?" Vashti muttered through her teeth.

"They won't," Nikol insisted, ignoring her. "The Cure is too valuable."

"Exactly," Vashti snapped. "It's liquid gold. Do you really think the Dust will just give it away? You can't trust them. The minute they have the Cure, they'll murder everyone on the island. Us included."

"I have my assurances," Nikol said. "A full pardon for me, and anyone who helps me. All sins forgiven." She smiled softly at Arseniy and the boy practically turned to mush.

"You know what I'm finding hard to forgive?" Vashti clucked. "The way you carved up Inés's face. The way you tossed Min Jun into the turbine. I may be cutthroat, but you…"

"I don't like hurting people. But I do what's necessary to get what I want," the spy replied. "You, Vashti, of all people, should understand that."

Vashti looked away.

"Did she tell you?" Nikol asked, considering Everly. "Back at the generator, Vashti offered me a trade: your badge for her freedom. Apparently, after pulling you out of the river, Vashti robbed your lifeless body. Classic, right? Without Vashti's help, I wouldn't have been able to frame you for what happened to the Bloodwood tree."

Everly didn't need to see the regret on Vashti's face to know the spy was telling the truth. Her badge wasn't lost to the river; Vashti had been holding onto it this whole time.

"I'm sorry," Vashti whispered.

Everly looked at the ground, a volcanic rage rising within her.

"I gave you the badge," Vashti said to the spy, "and instead of letting me go, you pelted me with rocks."

"Things are different now," Nikol replied.

"Different how?" Vashti seethed.

"Now you've seen Tazeen's true colours. And you have nothing left to lose."

"Thanks to you," Vashti said. "You, who left me to die." Without warning, Vashti lunged across the cave with Micah's blade in hand. Arseniy stepped in her way. She thrust the knife at his torso, but the Fire Ant pushed her hand aside and kneed her in the gut. Vashti dropped to the ground. The knife skidded across the floor and stopped at the spy's feet.

Moving casually, Nikol picked it up. She straddled Vashti, hand gripping the handle, teeth bared.

"Don't!" Everly shouted. "We need her."

Nikol paused. "For what?"

Everly hesitated. Was she really doing this? "Vashti knows the way to the Cure. I don't."

"Then why do we need you?" Arseniy snarled.

"Because," Everly said, "I know how to make her talk."

Nikol's mismatched eyes flickered with possibility. She flipped the knife in her hand. "Alright. Give me your badge."

"Why?"

"It's collateral."

Confused, Everly pulled the twine over her hair and tossed the badge to the spy. Nikol tucked it away in her shirt pocket. "Just so you know, if you try to double-cross me, I'll slit both your throats from ear to ear."

"Vivid," Vashti coughed from the floor.

Nikol snapped her fingers. Arseniy grabbed a fistful of Vashti's hair and dragged her to her feet. The Naked Mole Rat yelped and squirmed. She glowered at Everly, eyes dark and hostile.

Nikol pocketed the knife and tucked her hair behind her ear. "Let's make quick work of this, shall we?"

Blood pulsed in Everly's temples as the group moved through the abandoned tunnels. She wasn't sure what she was doing—not exactly—but at least she was free. Unlike Vashti, whose wrists were bound with rope, yet again. The once untamable girl walked a few paces ahead of them; Arseniy jerked on the leash to remind her who was in charge. Everly couldn't believe it had come to this. Come hell or high water, their fates were intertwined.

Near the entrance to the crater, Ebimi and Andrew were unconscious on the floor. Arseniy nudged Andrew with his toe on the way by. "Impressive," he praised.

"Thanks," Nikol smirked. "Maria Jose isn't the only herbalist on the island."

Everly's gaze flicked over to Ebimi's crumpled form. The Lemurs were still breathing, but just barely.

As the fugitives reached the centre of the pit, Everly looked up where the column of the Bloodwood tree used to stand. "No lifts," she noted.

"Lifts are gone and most of the tunnels collapsed when the tree fell," Arseniy explained. "One and eight are still clear."

Everly's eyes fell on the opening once marked with a VIII placard. Min Jun's charcoal map had led the Naked Mole Rats safely through it. They'd only followed it as far as the Hangar, but beyond it, the map's squiggly lines had indicated a passageway leading out into the open jungle. It was a long walk, but it might get them above ground. It would also give her time to think.

"This way," Everly said.

"Where are we going?" Arseniy asked.

Everly put a finger to her lips and looked nervously around the crater. Someone might be listening. She pointed to the smokey opening.

In the mouth of tunnel VIII, the scratch of a match was followed by the whoosh of a torch coming to life. The sight of flames made Everly shudder. The heat from the wildfire was still radiating from the walls. Arseniy handed the torch to Nikol. "It'll be hard to see without the mushrooms," he said with a shrug. "Most of them burned up."

"Good thinking," she gushed. Nikol pointed the lit end at Everly. "Tread carefully."

With the spy and her minion close behind, Everly began the long trek. The tunnel was eerily quiet; the jungle fire had driven away what little life could thrive underground. There were no fluttering wings from cave swallows, no squeaks from bats or clicks from insects. The only sound was their muted footfall on ash and the occasional splash through black puddles left behind by the thunderstorm.

They passed the spot where cracks in the ceiling let in the daylight. The hanging vines, once green and fragrant, were crumpled and charred. The smoke choked out everything in its path. A dull sky was visible through the fissures. Soon, the moon would be out, somewhere behind the brown haze.

As they moved on, the silence grew insufferable, and Everly decided to voice a question. "So, Arseniy," she said, trying to sound calm. "How'd you get caught up in all this?"

"I didn't get caught up in anything," he countered. "Nikol helped me see the truth."

Vashti sucked her teeth.

"So, you two are together now?" Everly asked.

"We've always been together," Nikol replied, dreamily.

Arseniy took the spy's hand. "Forever. 'Til the end."

Everly hesitated to state the obvious, but she needed to understand the situation in order to navigate it. "But, Nikol was with Micah for a while."

"I was using him," Nikol stated, "for information."

"Exactly," said Arseniy. "It was all an act."

"Micah was very useful," Nikol mused. "He told me what happened on the river. When Tazeen brought you back the next day all bugged out on her medicine, I knew you must have seen something. At first, I thought it was a way to move between moons. I figured if we scared you bad enough, one of you might try to leave the island on your own."

"But why go after Inés? She didn't know anything." Everly tried not to dwell on the image of Arseniy kneeling on Inés's back, dragging a blade along her upturned cheek.

"You were my target," he replied. "But you all started playing that stupid game, and I couldn't grab you out in the open. I had to settle for Inés."

"How'd you know we'd be in the Hangar?"

Nikol chuckled. "Micah might have let that slip, too. The mentors knew where the flags were hidden. Pillow talk, am I right?"

"Ha!" Vashti's bark of vindication echoed off the walls. Maybe if she hadn't lied about her alibi, it would have been easier to believe her. But Vashti had repeatedly proven herself a liar and a thief.

"That's funny, is it?" Nikol jeered. "After the Hangar, the rest of your bandmates never left each other's side. Lucky for us, on the last night of Moon Tracker, Vashti Jahanara decided to follow her heart. When you saw us in the kayaks, you thought we were the Lemurs, right? Darkness plays silly tricks. All we had to do was wait inside the cave and grab you off the beach. If you'd just stayed with your friends, none of this would have happened. Min Jun might still be alive."

The Lemur's name fell like an echo into a bottomless pit. Clipped memories of him came to Everly in tableaus—Min Jun gently carrying a tray full of bees, his thoughtful expression by campfire light, the look in his eyes when death was upon him.

"One thing isn't adding up," Everly said, an important detail coming into focus. "I get why you sent Arseniy after me, and I get why you went after Vashti. But why'd you attack us at the hives? That happened before everything else."

Arseniy looked at the ground.

"That was…improvised," Nikol sighed. "Funny enough, I hadn't actually made up my mind at that point. About the Dust. Then, at the bonfire, Tazeen told me my aunt's condition is getting worse. I begged her to let me visit her again, but the Umbo refused. She said it was too risky. Don't you get it? Tazeen forced my hand. I didn't have a choice."

"This is all the Umbo's fault," Arseniy hissed.

Everly shuffled through the new information, trying to form a timeline. At the hives, Micah and Nikol snuck off into the jungle. Which meant Arseniy must have launched the arrow. But why? If Nikol hadn't fully decided to work for the Dust at that point, there was only one explanation. He'd wanted to interrupt their love making. The attack wasn't about the Dust; it was about jealousy. And shortly after that, Nikol cut things off with Micah.

"But if Micah was a good source, why not keep seeing him?" Everly asked.

"I couldn't stand pretending anymore," Nikol huffed.

"Isn't that romantic?" Vashti said, vocals burnt with satire. "Love conquers all."

With shocking speed, Nikol slammed Vashti against the wall. In a menacing move, Nikol took a fistful of Vashti's hair and stuck the ends in the torch's flame. The hair sizzled as it burned and filled the cave with the stench of burnt feathers. Nikol dropped the torch. It rolled to Everly's feet.

Vashti shrieked. She dunked her head into a puddle of rainwater and came out of it looking like a singed panther. Vashti seethed beneath her eyelashes.

Off to the side, Nikol and Arseniy whispered with their noses almost touching. She was a venus flytrap. The further she beckoned him in, the more hopelessly imprisoned he became.

Everly picked up the torch. "It's this way."

After a while, the infamous boulder blocked their path. Someone had painted over the words, using blue mushroom juice to transform the letters into a troop. With tilted caps, the fungi watched with curious expressions as the group approached.

"I preferred my graffiti," Arseniy tisked.

"Me, too," crooned Nikol.

"We have to go around it," Everly explained. "Follow me."

Carrying the torch, she squeezed between the boulder and the wall. Arseniy snapped the leash and Vashti followed on Everly's heels.

Once both girls were pressed into the tight space, Everly paused. The obstruction offered a moment of temporary cover. Everly raised the torch between them. Her bandmate's lip curled, viciously. Everly motioned to the ropes. Vashti's eyes narrowed with suspicion, but she understood the intention and held her wrists to the flames.

"What's the hold up?" Nikol called from behind them.

"There's debris in the way," Everly lied.

Vashti grimaced as the knots ignited. She chewed on the pain as pieces of rope fell to the ground, still aglow.

With Vashti no longer tethered, the girls locked eyes. Everly mouthed a single word.

"Run."

CHAPTER 30

Everly tossed the torch into a puddle, and she and Vashti sprinted, hand-in-hand, into the velvety darkness. Their movements synchronized—racing footsteps, rapid breaths, pounding heartbeats—as they navigated by instinct alone. A blast of warm air hit Everly's arm, and she veered sideways, pulling Vashti into a smaller tunnel.

Nikol and Arseniy couldn't be far behind. The Naked Mole Rats had only taken this route once before, and their hunters knew it well. As much as she wanted to change course and throw them off their scent, the girls' only chance of survival was to get above ground, where hopefully, somehow, help would be waiting. So far, it felt like the tunnels were guiding them. They weren't lost. Not yet.

They ran for a long time. Was it an hour? More? When they turned down another pathway, Everly touched the low ceiling, the one that had forced Katak to walk with his head bent low. Inside, she was cheering. They were close.

The low tunnel led them the rest of the way to the Hangar. They ran into the middle and stopped, drenched in sweat, lungs on fire. The night sky was visible through the cracks in the vaulted ceiling. The glassy pools reflected the moonlight, replicating it over and over, filling the Hangar with crescent moons. Before Everly could speak, Nikol and Arseniy appeared, blocking the only known exit.

"That was stupid," Nikol sighed. "I was your best shot."

Frantic, Everly scanned the Hangar. Somewhere, hidden in the folded walls, was another way out. If only she still had her cast, with Min Jun's intersecting dots and dashes. Without his guidance, they were trapped. The only way out was through Nikol and Arseniy.

Everly turned around to face the spy. She was done running. "The Dust destroyed my family," she screamed. "I'll die a thousand times before I give them what they want."

"So dramatic," Nikol snuffed. "You'll only have to die once."

Beside her, Vashti used her teeth to roll the remaining fragments of rope over her wrists. She used the threads to wrap her knuckles. Everly was glad to have Vashti back on her side. At least they'd go down swinging.

With the last ounce of hope Everly could muster, she tried once again to reason with Nikol. "This is crazy," she yelled. "There has to be another way."

"There isn't, though," the spy shrugged.

"One way forward," Arseniy agreed, like it was a motto they shared.

"How many people are you willing to kill to save your aunt?" Everly scowled.

Nikol tilted her head, considering her answer. "As many as it takes," she replied. With long, powerful strides, Nikol crossed the Hangar. She leapt into the air and pushed off from a boulder, sending a flying kick into Everly's side. Everly buckled over. The spy climbed on top of her and hammered her with punches.

Vashti tackled Nikol from behind, grabbing a hold of her white ponytail. "You think you can mess with my hair?!" Vashti shrieked. Using both hands, she dragged Nikol to the ground.

Nikol scrambled to her feet and flipped Vashti, who landed with a thud on her back as Arseniy came running.

With blurred vision, Everly used a rock pillar to pull herself up. Nikol's foot came flying at her again, and Everly barely avoided it with a side-step. She grabbed a rock and whipped it, but it sailed past Nikol. The spy lunged, wrapping her legs around Everly's torso, torquing and sending Everly spiralling. In the air, Everly landed a backhanded fist against the spy's cheekbone. As they crash-landed, blows rained down, cracking Everly's ribs, bruising her insides, rocking her brain.

When Nikol grew bored of pummelling her victim, she grabbed Everly's foot and dragged her across the floor like a carcass. She chose a spot where two pillars grew with only a small gap between them.

Nikol hefted Everly's foot on top of the seam, flashed a beautiful smile, and dropped an elbow; her weight bent the bones and lodged Everly's ankle between the pillars. Everly's howls filled the Hangar.

"Leave her alone!" Vashti screamed. Arseniy took advantage of the distraction and landed a heel kick to her solar plexus. Vashti crumpled.

"String her up!" Nikol barked.

Arseniy hesitated. He looked at Nikol with a furrowed brow, like he couldn't quite figure out what she was asking of him.

"Do it now!" she blasted.

Obediently, Arseniy fashioned a slip knot from the long length of rope. He looped it over Vashti's head. While she struggled to get free, Arseniy flung the loose end over a u-shaped root growing from the ceiling. He stepped onto a boulder and jumped. As his feet hit the ground, Vashti was hoisted into the air. Her feet thrashed wildly as he tied the rope around a boulder. Her face turned crimson red. Her toes found the top of a pillar, taking enough weight off of her throat that she could take in shallow gasps.

The spy toyed with an invisible watch. "This is it, Everly. Clock's ticking."

Everly tried to move her foot, but it was hopelessly jammed between pillars. "Only Vashti knows the way," she screamed. "If you kill her, you'll never find the Cure."

"You're wasting time," Nikol said in a sing-song voice.

"I'm telling you the truth!" Everly cried. "I was knocked out when Vashti stole my badge, remember? She knows the way, not me!"

"Nikol…" Arseniy said. His voice sounded small compared to the vastness of the Hangar. He was looking at Vashti like he was seeing, for the first time, what he'd done.

"Shut up, Arseniy," Nikol barked.

"But…"

"Don't wuss out on me now."

"You said this was about helping people…"

"We're almost there," Nikol implored. "We're going to get the Cure and get off the island and be together forever."

"She doesn't love you!" Everly shouted, digging a trench with her free foot as she tried, in vain, to pull her trapped ankle from the pillars. "She's in love with Micah!"

Arseniy laughed, but there was tension in his voice.

"Think about it," Everly pushed. "Why else would she dump Micah the second she switched sides? Nikol was protecting him. You're the one she's using!"

"That's not true," Arseniy scoffed, unable to mask the insecurity in his voice.

"She's lying," the spy confirmed. "I'm not in love with Micah. I never was."

"Are you sure about that?" asked a voice from across the Hangar. Tazeen's grackle soared into the cavern and swooped in figure-eights between stalactites. Close behind, a shadow appeared in the mouth of the tunnel.

"Who's there?" Nikol demanded.

Micah stepped into the Hangar. "Just me, Nik."

"Micah," Everly screamed. "Help Vashti!"

Micah ignored her, keeping his focus locked on the spy. "What are you doing, Nik?" he asked calmly with his empty hands in plain view.

His presence visibly impacted Nikol—her brow creased with anguish, her frame softened, her eyes brimmed with tears. Micah was her person, the one who knew her ugly and her beautiful. The one who never looked away. Everly recognized the crumbling of form, the peeling back of layers. The same thing happened when Shelby walked into a room; it was impossible to pretend to be someone else when a mirror was standing directly in front of you.

Arseniy saw the shift, too. His head snapped back and forth between the spy and the mentor. "Nikol?" his voice quavered. She looked at him and sighed, unable to hide the truth any longer—she'd never belonged to him.

"I don't…" her words trailed off.

"After everything I've done for you?!" Arseniy wailed. "After everything I've sacrificed to be with you!"

"It's too late, anyway. You're in too deep now," she crowed.

"Arseniy, if you confess, Taz will forgive you," Micah countered. "She's forgiven worse, remember?" He pulled at the neck of his shirt and exposed his scar.

Irate, Arseniy grabbed fistfuls of his own hair. "I can't believe this!" he bellowed. "I'm done, Nikol. I'm out of here." Arseniy gave Micah a wide berth as he moved to the mouth of the tunnel, leaving his soulmate and her lover behind.

"Arseniy!" Nikol called after him. His footsteps quickly faded. The spy cursed in frustration.

"Let the girls go, Nikol," Micah hushed. "I don't know what you've gotten yourself into, but whatever it is, we can fix it."

"You don't understand," she cried. "I begged Taz for help. I begged her! Why won't she help me, Micah? Tazeen could save my aunt, if she wanted to."

"It's complicated—"

"It's not complicated!"

"We can keep talking, but I'm going to cut Vashti loose. You don't really want to hurt her."

"This is my aunt's only chance," Nikol sobbed.

"Nik, the Umbo got word from the Spearheads," Micah said, carefully. "Your aunt passed away shortly after the full moon. It's why Tazeen wouldn't let you go. She knew you wouldn't make it there in time. I'm so sorry."

Nikol's eyes turned black. "You're lying."

"I would never lie to you. Your aunt is gone."

"You're lying!"

"She died of pancreatic cancer, Nikol. The Bloodwood Society is not responsible."

"They are fully responsible! Don't you get it? They're hoarding the medicine. No one should have the power to decide who lives and who dies. It isn't right. It isn't fair." The spy turned her attention to Vashti, who was fighting to keep her toes on the pillar. Nikol walked over and put a hand on the taut rope.

"Nikol, don't," Micah pleaded.

"Vashti, I'll give you three seconds to tell me where the Cure is hidden."

"Please, Nik!"

"One. Two…"

Vashti's lips curled into a grin. Her fists gripped the rope, but she managed to raise a middle finger.

"Please, don't do this," Micah begged. "I love you, Nik. I've always loved you. I'd do anything to protect you."

"Anything," she repeated. "But only if Tazeen says so. You're devoted to her, Micah. How about, just this once, you pick me instead?"

Nikol heaved on the rope. Vashti's feet slipped from the pillar; she twisted and writhed as the rope tightened around her neck.

"No!" Everly wailed.

Nikol ran hard across the dirt, her ferocious gaze honed in on Micah. He jumped from boulder to boulder. They collided mid-air. Crashing to the ground, Nikol swung on top of him, choking Micah with her forearm.

"You have to choose," she cried. "Is it them, or is it me?"

"It doesn't have to be this way," Micah groaned. He looked over at Vashti. She was fading fast. "This can all be undone."

"No, it can't. It's too late. They killed her. My aunt is dead!"

Vashti's body went limp. Her hands dropped to her sides.

"Micah, look out!" Everly shouted.

Nikol smashed a rock across Micah's face. Micah bucked and sent her sprawling. He wiped his lip and examined his blood-covered hand, looking bewildered. Using a pillar as a springboard, Nikol threw herself onto his back. Micah flipped her to the ground and staggered sideways.

"I don't want to hurt you," he panted.

"How sweet," Nikol jeered. She spun around and landed a reverse roundhouse kick to Micah's temple. He fell to the floor and swept her feet out from under her. Micah twisted Nikol into an arm-bar and yanked on the joint. Her cry echoed across the Hangar as Everly's badge fell from the spy's shirt pocket.

Micah grabbed the badge and threw it. It landed in the dirt a few feet away from Everly. "Use it!" he yelled.

Everly blinked, unable to move. "What?"

"It's Lunar glass!" he replied before catching Nikol's forehead in the teeth.

Everly stretched to full length, but she couldn't reach the badge. The bones in her ankle cracked in response, but she was able to hook her finger around the loop of twine. Everly held up the badge, trying to form a coherent thought. Lunar glass. Lunar, as in moon. Above her, a moonbeam spilled past a fissure in the ceiling. The moon reflected sunlight. Sunlight started fires. It didn't make sense, but she had nothing left to lose.

Hugging the pillars for support, Everly used her free foot to thrust herself upward with the badge in hand, stretching for the moonbeam. It was too far. Gravity slammed her painfully to the earth. She tried again, holding onto the end of the twine and releasing the badge at the top of her leap. As the twine stretched to length, the glass cut through the moonlight with a glint. A white beam exploded from the glass. Across the Hangar, a boulder cracked with a deafening boom. Everly twisted her body, trying to comprehend what had just taken place.

Nikol and Micah stopped wrestling and stared at the blasted rock. "That's not possible," Nikol balked. She stared at Micah in disbelief. "Who is she?"

"One who topples giants," he gritted.

"No…"

Everly sent another blast across the Hangar, aiming for the root above Vashti. It connected with the ceiling. Dripstones dropped like spears onto the cavern floor. One of them landed across Micah's legs, pinning him to the ground. Another sliced Nikol's arm before she dived out of the way. She clambered to her feet and redirected her furious gaze at Everly.

"Nikol, no!" Micah shouted. He struggled against the weight of the dripstone which held him firmly in place.

With one final effort, Everly hoisted herself up, leapt as high as her breaking bones would allow, and let go of the badge. It cut through the moonlight. The part of the cavern that was holding up her bandmate exploded, and Vashti fell to the floor. Rocks and dripstones piled on top of her.

Nikol appeared above Everly. The spy's eyes were filled with bloodlust, fuelled by a disastrous combination of loss and failure. She gripped Micah's blade. "The Bloodwood Rebellion is not what you think," she rasped. "Let me save you some suffering."

Everly opened her mouth to respond, but Nikol didn't give her the chance. Instead, the spy drove the knife into Everly's gut like a colonizer claiming the land.

CHAPTER 31

Nikol left the knife in place. She stared, ribcage heaving, eyes raving. Everly coughed up a spray of red, which seemed to snap the spy back into focus. She looked at her own arm, noticing the open gash. Nikol stumbled back a few paces. Leaving behind her kills, she entered a shadowy crevasse in the far wall, headed for the open jungle.

The wound felt like it was expanding—eroding Everly's flesh, fraying her spinal cord, melting her bones. Her cries were soundless except for a bubbling deep in her throat. Blood spurted around the blade with each heartbeat. Everly's hands fluttered above the handle, but she couldn't bring herself to remove it.

Across the Hangar, Micah freed himself from the wreckage. He ran to Everly, screaming her name, but she read the hopelessness on his face when he reached her. Micah took off his shirt, steadied himself, and pulled the knife from her belly. Everly bucked. He pressed the fabric against the wound, but the blood soaked right through. His efforts were wasted, and they both knew it.

"Vashti…" she gurgled.

"You're sure?"

Everly nodded. "Go."

Micah's brow creased with grief. He grabbed her hands and held them, just for a second, before placing them on top of the shirt. "Press hard," he instructed. In her peripheral vision, she watched him clear the rocks and lift Vashti from the heap. Micah carried her to a patch of earth. He didn't bother checking for a pulse. Instead, he pumped his hands against her chest a dozen times before filling her lungs with his breath. The thing Vashti hated the most—human touch—was the only thing that might save her. She'd done the same for Everly not long ago.

Everly looked up at the ceiling. She watched a water droplet slide silently down a dripstone that had survived the blast. It plinked softly into a silver pool below. Water to water. Water to stone. Stone to water. Everything creating something, creating itself. It would be alright to die here, listening to the gentle orchestra of the cavern. There were worse places to be, worse ways to go.

Stronger than the pain was the lonesomeness. Everly and Shelby would die with half a world between them, both hurting, both alone. Maybe they'd be together again soon. Wherever the darkness led.

It was getting harder to stay awake. The ceiling glistened with last night's rain. Permeating through the jungle floor, tiny vertical streams formed, shimmering with a faint blue glow as they made their descent. Everly was hallucinating; the end must be close.

At first, the streams were as thin as threads, but as the water gathered, they swelled into ribbons that followed grooves in the walls and floor, reaching the spot where Everly had fallen. The water pooled around her. The earth at her back softened. She sank into it as her foot slipped free from the pillars. The water deepened, filling her ears, climbing over her rib cage. As it seeped into her wound, the edges of her parted skin glowed.

Everly writhed as the water flowed into her; it traced her body's pathways from the puncture wound to the soles of her feet and the palms of her hands. Arm shaking, she raised her wrist from the water. Her fingertips were aglow with the same clear blue light that enveloped her.

She convulsed as the edges of the wound came together, releasing a brilliant beam that shot into the night sky. The emptiness she'd felt as her blood ran out was replaced with a quiet resolve that life still belonged. The water drained from her pores; it spilled from her mouth and ears. It vanished into the earthen floor, leaving behind a pixie ring of glowing white mushrooms all around her.

Everly sat up. All that remained of her injuries was a hole in her shirt and a fresh scar beneath it. The grackle landed between Everly's feet. The bird used its beak to pluck a mushroom from the soil and dropped it into Everly's palm. The grackle cawed and took flight, disappearing into the tunnel. She twisted the glowing mushroom between her fingers as words delivered by the same bird drifted across her mind:

The warmer and wetter the weather, the better the fungi will grow; the closer two birds of a feather, the more that the moonlight will show.

Not a poem, but a clue. An answer when she needed it most.

Everly climbed to where Micah was still hunched over Vashti, trying to resuscitate her. He was grunting from the exertion and dripping with sweat. When Everly touched his arm, Micah recoiled. Mouth agape, he looked her over with shock and confusion.

"But how?" he panted.

Everly knelt beside Vashti and unhinged her bandmate's jaw, placing the glowing mushroom on her tongue. They waited. Seconds passed. Micah stepped toward Vashti, but Everly held out her hand to stop him. This was Vashti's only chance. It had to work.

Vashti was motionless. Her cheeks were sallow. Bands of bruises darkened her neck. Then, with a violent gasp, Vashti shot up, clawing at an invisible noose.

"Did we win?" she asked, deliriously, before losing consciousness again. Micah caught her before she hit her head on the hard ground. She was breathing.

"I don't understand," Micah hushed, cradling Vashti like a child. Micah studied the hole in Everly's shirt where his own knife had passed through. He met Everly's eyes and they stared at each other for a long time. Everly dropped her gaze to Micah's bare shoulder. Her mentor already knew a thing or two about impossible healing.

"Your scar…" she said, trailing off.

"I'd lost too much blood; I wasn't going to make it. My brother Ezra broke the rules. He had a glass vial. I found out later that he'd taken it from the package before the drop. The Spearheads were furious."

"Did they banish him?"

"No. They sent him to the desert. I haven't seen him since."

"I'm sorry."

"He's alive. I'm alive. It was worth it. I didn't fully understand his crime until now. This place…is this where the medicine comes from?"

Everly spun in a slow circle, beholding the Hangar in awe. "That day on the river, Vashti and I found something we were never supposed to find. A whirlpool, with water flowing in from all over the island. I think the healing power comes from the dripstones. The water filters through the jungle, gets charged by the dripstones, is absorbed through the cavern floor…"

"And flows into the aquifer," Micah concluded.

"I almost blew up the Cure," she said with a shudder.

Micah weighed her words. "Nobody knows the truth about this place."

"We need to keep it that way," Everly decided. From the corner of her eye, she caught a glint of metal on the cavern floor. She picked the badge from the dirt and tucked it into her pocket. Crossing the Hangar, she collected Micah's backpack and filled his empty canteen with mushrooms from the pixie ring. Hopefully, they'd keep for a while.

Micah picked up Vashti. Together, they turned to leave, only to find the Umbo standing in the mouth of the tunnel. Behind her, Arseniy was hunched between Ebimi and Andrew, with Maria Jose blocking his path from behind. The grackle fluttered above them.

"Micah," Tazeen greeted them. "Is everything alright?"

"Nikol didn't manage to kill the girls, but she sure tried," he replied.

"So, Arseniy was telling the truth. How disappointing. It seems our night of tribunals is far from over." She turned to Andrew. "Take him."

With his head bent low, Arseniy didn't struggle as Andrew led him away.

"Where is Nikol?" ask the Umbo.

"She escaped," Everly said. "She's hurt."

"She knows about her aunt," Micah added.

"I told you that information was volatile," Taz frowned. The

Umbo flicked her wrist and sent Ebimi on the hunt.

On her way by Micah, Ebimi stopped and looked at Vashti. She caressed her cheek with the back of her hand. "Maria Jose, take good care of this one, please."

"I've got her. Go catch us a spy."

Ebimi cracked her knuckles and jogged to the far exit.

The Umbo sighed, looking around the blasted cavern. "I don't know how everything got so out of control," she said, mostly to herself.

"Sometimes the truth is hard to see," Everly offered.

"And other times, it's too ugly to face," Tazeen said, solemnly. "I must admit to some bad decisions. The tokens were the perfect excuse to put trackers on everyone, and we used the Naked Mole Rats to try and lure the spy. But when the fire started, our plan quickly unravelled."

"I didn't start the fire," Everly stated.

"I know. The tribunals were a ruse, but I needed them to be convincing. I thought if the spy learned you were about to be executed, they'd try again. But Nikol outplayed us. I thought I was acting in the best interest of the Root, but I failed. I failed you and Vashti. I failed Min Jun. And I failed the rebellion. I left you completely unprotected."

"We weren't completely unprotected," Everly countered. "Vashti and I had each other."

"Gross," Vashti muttered from Micah's armpit. Everly chuckled, convinced her bandmate would make a full recovery.

"Maria Jose, make sure Miss Jahanara receives the very best of care," Taz instructed.

"Of course," the Lemur agreed. Micah and Everly moved to follow her into the tunnel. Tazeen stayed behind.

"Aren't you coming with us?" Micah asked.

"I will return in due time." Tazeen walked over to a stone pillar and touched a red smear that darkened its point. She spread the blood across her cheek with two fingers. "Right now, I am off to trap a rat."

CHAPTER 32

"Tell me again what happened," Inés demanded. "More slowly and with greater detail. You may begin." The girls were bathing in the waist-deep river water. Inés was busy working chunks of soap into her hair, trying to remove an entire season of dirt from her curly mane.

Vashti broke the surface. She was sporting a chic bob that rested at her chin. Somehow, the haircut made her look older and cooler, which was slightly annoying. "Is there going to be music and dancing at this party?" she asked.

"Most likely," said Inés. "It's the Blood Moon feast, after all."

Arriving late and wearing nothing but boxers, Katak sprinted along the shore and cannon-balled into the conversation. He emerged like a sea monster, spitting a stream of water in Vashti's direction.

"Katak!" Inés shrieked, covering her chest with her hands. "We're nude!"

"I'm not looking."

"Go away!" she shooed.

"It's not fair. I'm the only dude in our band. You can't discriminate. I'm not looking at you, okay? I mean, I am, but not like that. Okay, a little bit like that, but…"

"Katak," Everly laughed. "Stop digging."

"Fine, you can stay," Inés lamented. "But keep your face pointed the other way." Everly caught her smirking, and Inés quickly hid the expression. "Now if we're done with all the interruptions, Everly, you may begin."

Everly went about summarizing the wild events, even though she'd told her bandmates her version of things several times already.

Ten days had passed, but it would take years to tell the tale without feeling its effects. Everly left out the part about being stabbed and miraculously healed. She'd kept her shirt on to bathe, and the girls hadn't questioned it, but eventually, she'd have to explain the new scar.

"Do you agree with the Council's decision?" Katak asked, treading water with his back to the girls.

"Nikol and Arseniy got off easy. Other Death is better than actual death," Everly said.

"Wrong," Vashti sniffed.

"I think they got what they deserved," Katak stated. "I'm just glad you're both off the hook. Things got scary for a while. Anyway, what are you all going to wear tonight?"

Inés tossed a bar of soap at him. "My silk ball gown and glass slippers."

"Damn, that's what I was going to wear." Katak dived underwater. He swam over to where Vashti was floating and pulled her below by an ankle. She cursed and sputtered when they surfaced, but she was smiling.

Looking shiny and clean, the Naked Mole Rats climbed into fresh linen tunics and fisherfolk pants, provided by the Rooters for the special occasion. Inés revealed four strings of braided flowers to wear as headbands and passed around a thimble of coconut oil and beet juice to rub on their lips and cheeks. Katak insisted he wear some, too, and he came out looking glamorous in the best way.

"I also have something for you all," said Vashti. She walked over to a nearby rock and collected three packages wrapped in banana leaves.

"Aw man, I didn't know we were doing a gift thing," Katak grumbled.

"Me neither," Everly sighed.

"I called in a few favours," Vashti shrugged.

Inés unwrapped a wooden hair comb. Katak got a bracelet made of fish bones. Everly held up a soft strip of leather attached to a tiny pouch.

"So you'll stop losing your stuff," Vashti quipped.

Everly pulled the badge from her pocket and slid it inside. "It's perfect," she said, securing the pouch with the leather and tying the rest around her neck. "I'll triple knot it, so it's harder to steal."

Vashti laughed.

The sun dipped behind the trees as the Naked Mole Rats climbed the stone steps up the cliffs. When they crested the top, Everly stood for a moment with the canyon at her back, taking in the clearing where the Bloodwood tree used to stand. The Rooters had spent the days since the fire removing debris and building a structure above the exposed crater. Across the divide, they created a web using criss-crossed ropes. Next, they covered the web in burlap and a layer of soil. Within a few days, the jungle had taken over; moss and flowers had rooted, creating a green roof that flourished in the sunlight. The earth that had once held the ancient tree in place was now home to a lush green meadow with no hint of the subterranean world hidden below.

In anticipation of the Blood Moon, the meadow had been transformed further with colourful flags and streamers. As if they'd been invited to the party, hundreds of dragonflies zipped along, clearing the space of mosquitoes. A long harvest table was decorated with floral wreaths and flickering lanterns; old stumps, soft with moss, acted as chairs. Covered torches sent tendrils of smoke into the dusky sky, filling the air with the scent of lemongrass.

As the impressive red moon rose above the canyon, Rooters entered from the freshly-cleared footpaths, wearing floral garlands, elaborate braids, and big smiles. They all came together around a communal table. It was all so beautiful, Everly fought back tears. She and her bandmates followed the Rooters to the table and settled onto stumps.

At the edge of the jungle, the Lemurs appeared. The Umbo was holding a golden urn, while the rest of her entourage held tall candles. The Rooters quieted as their leader stopped at the head of the table. Tazeen held out the urn.

"The ashes of our beloved Bloodwood tree, in honour of our

brother, Min Jun," she said. Tazeen closed her eyes and moved her lips in prayer before spreading the ashes on the ground. Everly lowered her chin. She thanked Min Jun for giving his life in an attempt to save hers, sending waves of cosmic gratitude into the universe. Maybe, over the course of a lifetime, she'd repay her debt.

Tazeen wiped tears from her cheeks and looked out at the rising moon. "This has been the hardest season in living memory, but here we are, stronger than ever. Under the light of the Blood Moon, we celebrate our unity through the initiation of twenty-one new members. Of course, we had planned for a seventh trial, the Deal Breaker, but your actions during and after the fire more than proved your loyalty." The crowd murmured their agreement. "Now, it's up to our remaining newcomers to make a decision. Your final trial is upon you. If you wish to join the Bloodwood Society, you will now accept our mark and take the Blood Oath."

The table vibrated with anticipation. From the stump beside her, Katak clapped Everly on the back. "I've been waiting for this all summer. My first tattoo!" he beamed.

Everly groaned. She'd almost forgotten about the branding.

The Umbo must have sensed Katak enthusiasm, because she summoned him first to the head of the table. "You can place the insignia anywhere on your body," she said.

"Can I get it on my face?"

"Once it's healed, it will be invisible without the proper light, so that is an option."

Katak thought for a moment and snapped his fingers. "Put it on my butt!"

The Rooters chuckled, but Tazeen was unfazed. "As you wish," she said. Katak exposed a bare cheek to the crowd. The Umbo pulled her prism of glass from her tunic, angling it against the pinkish glow of the Blood Moon. A thin beam appeared, and she used it to burn the insignia on to Katak's bare flesh. The process didn't take long, but Katak yelped like a puppy from start to finish.

Vashti was next. She chose a spot on her ribs. Tazeen made quick work of it.

"Everly Dahl, it is your turn," Tazeen summoned. "If you would like to join the Bloodwood Society, that is."

Everly walked to the head of the harvest table. She stared at the Umbo's piece of Lunar glass. Her dad's badge, which had proven quite explosive, was safely tucked away in the leather pouch beneath her shirt.

"You and I have much to discuss," Tazeen said. "But for now, have you chosen a location?"

Everly took off her shoe and pointed to her heel. As Taz completed the brand, it felt like Everly was holding the bottom of her foot over an open flame, but the pain ebbed as soon as Tazeen was finished. The brand was the size of a silver dollar with lines creating the crescent moon and the Bloodwood tree's silhouette. Limping back to her seat, Everly crossed paths with Inés and smiled with encouragement.

After branding Inés at the base of her neck, the Umbo turned to the crowded harvest table. "I believe Inés has something to say."

"Yes, um," Inés looked at her bandmates and nervously picked at her bottom lip. "It's nothing big. It's just that, well…I am what I am. And I am the Moon Tracker!"

The Rooters sprung to their feet, howling and slamming their hands against the table. Water splashed and pinecones danced around its surface.

Everly, Katak, and Vashti stared at their bandmate in disbelief. She shrugged, bashfully.

"Congratulations to this year's champion!" said Taz. "Inés, what was your strategy?"

"Well," Inés smiled, "the best tracker tracks alone," which was followed by another round of applause for the unlikely victor of the game. Inés returned to her stump, flushed and grinning.

"Inés," Katak yelped across the table. "What?!"

"I'm so sorry! I wanted it to be a surprise. After the fire, when everything settled, I heard a rumour that Ebimi was back on the hunt. I figured we were the only two left. So, I followed her to the river yesterday afternoon—"

"Afternoon?" Everly blinked.

"Yes. You know when the sun and the moon come out together?"

Katak clapped his hands. "*Moon tracker hunts under the light of the moon,*" he quoted. "You sneaky little minx!"

"I used a rabbit snare and marked her before lunch," Inés beamed.

Everly considered her incredible friend with newfound admiration. "How do you know these things?" she marvelled.

"I'm a genius."

"And now you have an extra wish," Everly pointed out. "Do you know what it'll be?"

"I think I'll hang on to it for a while," Inés said. "You never know when we might need it."

After dinner, the rhythm of drums filled the night, and the swooning, spinning bodies of the Rooters moved together beneath the red moonlight as the slow shadow of a lunar eclipse waltzed across the Blood Moon. Everly's sore heel was a good excuse to avoid the dancing, so she stayed perched on a stump, taking in the festivities from a comfortable distance.

She watched Inés and Katak, twirling each other and chortling. Vashti was chatting with Ebimi, probably about her new bob, based on how much she kept touching her hair. Off to the side, Jolene clapped to the beat of the drums, and even Jax appeared relaxed. Everly caught his eye, and the Ghost Shrimp raised his glass. She smiled. They were good.

Everly pulled the pouch from her shirt and held it in her hand, slipping the badge out just far enough to see the rounded edge of the magnifying glass. A stump shifted beside her. "Micah tells me you were able to put that to good use," the Umbo said, pointing at the badge.

Everly blushed. Now that she knew what the glass could do, fiddling with it—especially under the light of a Blood Moon—probably wasn't the best idea. "There's something I don't get. Why did you give the Lunar glass back to me at the hearing if you knew it was a weapon? I could have used it against you."

"It was a gamble, I admit. But I knew you were innocent. And I knew I was putting you at risk. My hope was, if things went wrong, which they clearly did, it would be useful."

Everly raised her eyebrows. "It was. But if Nikol had the Lunar glass for weeks, why didn't she use it?"

"She didn't know how. My Lunar glass was given to me when I became the Umbo, and I'm still learning how to activate it."

"But, why did it work for me?" Everly asked.

"An excellent question. I caught a glimpse of your potential when you had a vision on the first night. Visions are common for Umbos. Perhaps leadership is in your blood."

"So, what, I'm destined to be an Umbo?"

"Only time and the tides will tell," Tazeen smiled.

Everly tucked the pouch away. "Taz, why did my dad have Lunar glass?"

The Umbo shrugged. "You will have to ask him."

The comment, spoken so casually, made Everly's heart swell with hope. She looked across the meadow to where her friends were swaying happily with the crowd. "You know, there was one thing Nikol said that I keep thinking about. Even if you get the one thing you want most in the world, it might not be enough."

"I know that to be true," the Umbo acknowledged. "There will always be another desire to take its place."

"So what happens now?"

"Funny you should ask. With the generator down, we will be needing some supplies, which means I have a special assignment for you and your friends. But, for now, Everly Dahl, let's sit back and enjoy the party."

Balanced on top of the moss-covered stumps, they watched the festivities late into the night. The Rooters cheered and kissed and sang, and when the Lunar eclipse reached totality, the Blood Moon transformed, if only for a moment, into a dazzling ring of red. Everything in the clearing took on a soft, pink hue. It was, undoubtedly, one of the best nights of Everly's life. She tried to take in every detail, so she could recount them all to Shelby, whenever she saw her next.

CHAPTER 33

The celebration lasted until dawn, when the Blood Moon finally sank into the sea. Tazeen gathered the Naked Mole Rats and told them it was time to go. Maybe it was the giddy exhaustion, but Everly felt oddly detached from the whole situation. The Rooters had transported her to the island without a scratch, so there was no reason to think they couldn't reverse the process. Clenched in her fist was a grey pill of Maria Jose's invention. The concoction was meant to knock Everly out for the length of the journey. The destination, however, was still unknown.

The Naked Mole Rats walked in silence, each lost in their own imaginations. A figure appeared from an adjacent tunnel; Everly's sternum tingled when she saw his outline. Her mentor had excused himself early from the Blood Moon feast—it was too hard to celebrate with a broken heart. After what they'd been through in the Hangar, Everly felt drawn to Micah in a way she couldn't explain. Their blood held traces of a secret that felt like a sacred bond. Did he feel it, too?

Micah waited for the others to pass before reaching out and wrapping a hand around Everly's wrist. When her friends were far enough ahead that their conversation wouldn't be overheard, Micah cleared his throat. "Before you go, there's something I've been meaning to ask you."

"Okay," Everly replied. Could he hear the tremble?

They walked slowly, keeping the distance between them and the others. "There are things Tazeen still hasn't told you. Things I think you should know."

"Maybe there's a reason," Everly countered.

"I'm done keeping the Umbo's secrets," Micah whispered. "I've learned the hard way. That piece of Lunar glass, it belonged to your dad, right?"

"Yes."

"Where do you think he got it?"

"I don't know. But my dad clearly knows more about the rebellion than he let on."

"Your dad was an Umbo," Micah stated. "Before either of us were born."

The air rushed from Everly's body. "How do you know?"

"I recognized your last name. Then I saw it in the logbook. Nathaniel Dahl's notes are all over it."

Everly thought back to the night she sat with Min Jun at the campfire; she'd rested her cast on the logbook while he drew her map. She was inches away from a vital fact about her own family—in another life, her dad was a rebel. "That's what you meant when you said I was only here because of the Bloodline Law," she recalled.

"The Bloodwood Society tries to recruit blood relatives, whenever they show potential," Micah explained. "Some Rooters are against it. They think it's unfair."

"Why are you telling me all this?"

"Because I saw what you did with the Lunar glass. I saw you bleeding out. And I saw…after. I don't know what it all means, but it's something we both have to carry. And for that to work, there can't be any secrets between us. I need you to trust me." He touched his shoulder, self-consciously.

"I read your file," Everly admitted. "I'm not afraid of you or what you've done. Your scars don't scare me."

Micah looked at her with a mix of surprise and relief. "Good. Your scars don't scare me either."

A lit entrance appeared up ahead, banishing the darkness and any hope for further clarity. The clock had run out. Tazeen's grackle zoomed past them, trilling loudly.

"Hurry," Micah said. "We have to go."

They took a long, complicated look at each other before catching up with the rest of the group. The small cave was cut in half by the aquifer. The river flowed in full force from one end and disappeared into a black hole at the other.

With the grackle perched on her shoulder, Tazeen stood at the water's edge. "Let's test your sense of direction," she said above the current. "In which direction does the water flow?"

The Naked Mole Rats looked at each other and around the cave in search of clues.

"South to the ocean?" Inés guessed.

"Incorrect."

Everly wished she'd paid closer attention. They were in an unfamiliar cave and had travelled unfamiliar tunnels to get there. "East," she hazarded. "Back to the Root."

"That is correct," Taz said. "But not always. On a full moon, the aquifer reverses course. Instead of moving east, as it typically does, the current does an about-face and flows west for twenty-four hours."

"That's impossible," Katak chuffed.

"The ocean follows the moon's pull every day. Tidal forces are some of the most powerful on earth," the Umbo reasoned.

From the walls of the cave came a chorus of cheeps, like tiny wind chimes. Everly followed the sound to a raised ledge and stood on tiptoes to see. Hidden in the shadows were dozens of nests, filled with newly hatched baby birds. Some lay helpless and wet on the straw; others were struggling to wriggle free from broken eggshells. All were calling out for food.

"Why are they all hatching at once?" Everly asked.

Taz beamed like a proud mother. "Aren't they marvellous? This particular species of grackle has a gestation period of exactly twenty-nine days. The females lay their eggs on the full moon, and one full cycle later—"

A gurgling sound drew Everly's attention to the walls of the cave. As if someone had turned off the tap, the aquifer dropped in pressure and then stopped completely. For a moment, the only noise came from the translucent beaks of the newborn chicks. From the opposite side of the cave, a rumbling began, growing stronger as an unseen force approached.

"Taz?" Everly shivered, feeling the rising instinct to flee.

Flying at top speed, a flurry of fully-grown grackles shot out of the wall, forming a tornado of oily black feathers. Tazeen's bird joined the throes as the grackles settled into their nests.

"Prepare the driftwood," the Umbo commanded.

The Lemurs appeared from the tunnel, lugging all-too-familiar coffins that made Everly choke on her spit. The long, slender boxes were disguised as logs, hollowed out and padded on the inside to safely transport a human. The Lemurs placed the vessels in a row along the empty channel.

"Katak, you're first," the Umbo summoned.

"No way!" Katak shouted.

"It takes faith to come to the island, and it takes faith to leave it. Someone will be waiting for you on the other side. You have my word," promised Tazeen.

It was happening. Right now. They were meant to travel through the subterranean world, following the whims of the current, hidden in the corpses of felled trees. A crazier plan had never been hatched. But, the portal was open, and it was now or never.

Katak turned to Inés, bending so their foreheads touched. "I'll see you on the other side," he said. Inés nodded, tearfully. Looking around at his friends, Katak added, "None of you die on the way there, deal?"

"Could you drag this out any longer?" Vashti griped.

"We'll see you soon," Everly said, trying to sound convincing.

Katak blew directionless kisses and hurried over to his driftwood vessel. Katak popped the grey pill in his mouth and looked over at Taz. "Hey, thanks for everything, eh?" he shouted.

"Peace be the journey, Katak Atta." With that, Maria Jose closed the lid, sealing him inside.

The Umbo called the next traveller: "Inés de la Rosa!"

Inés stood on tiptoes to give Everly a quick peck on the cheek. She offered Vashti an outstretched hand. Vashti slapped it away, but her lips crept into a smile.

"*Hasta pronto*," Inés said, rubbing her crucifix. "I'll see you soon."

Andrew ushered her into the box. She crossed herself before laying back. Andrew shut the lid with a bang.

Now that they were the last Naked Mole Rats in the cave, Vashti nudged Everly with her hip. "Thanks," she said.

"For what?"

"Saving my life. Twice. You're my only friend in the world. Did you know that?"

"Why do I not find that surprising?" Everly asked with a smirk. "Get going, you dirty thief."

Vashti snorted. Ebimi waved her over. The girls embraced and kissed a quick goodbye before Vashti sank into the vessel. Clearly, they'd worked things out at the Blood Moon feast, only to be parting ways hours later. Everly felt for them; she knew what it meant to long for someone.

The cave walls vibrated with a baritone hum. "Your turn, Everly Dahl," Tazeen shouted over the noise. Everly's feet were anchored in place. She looked at the row of boxes with her friends trapped inside. Were they panicking? Could they breathe? She was about to beg the Umbo for another option, but Micah stepped in her way.

"You got this," he said.

"I don't," she gulped.

"It'll all be alright." Micah took her by the elbow and guided her to the final log. Everly climbed over the sides and shimmied her feet to the bottom. Foam pressed around her on all sides, securing her in place.

"The pill," Micah said. Everly dug it out of her pocket and placed it on her tongue. A bitter powder coated her mouth as she chewed and swallowed thickly. She focused on her mentor's face, searching it for reassurance. Instead, she found something else. Mischief.

He leaned in and whispered with their noses almost touching. "My brother took two vials from the package. He used one to save my life. The other, he gave to your dad. When you see Ezra, maybe you should ask him why."

Everly opened her mouth, but her jaw felt tight, her tongue

heavy. "I don't—"

"See you around," Micah slammed the lid in place, sealing her inside.

"Micah!" she bellowed. She wanted to claw her way out of the vessel, to pummel the truth out of him, but her arms were pinned and the sedative was taking effect. Her vision spun like the whirlpool. She couldn't move. She couldn't breathe.

The moment the aquifer crossed over, her driftwood was hit by the surge. It lurched forward and began a weightless downward spiral. Everly was at the mercy of the aquifer once again.

Her pulse slowed, blood coagulating in her veins. Her thoughts blended together into a kaleidoscope of shades and textures. A storm cloud emerged, billowing, rolling toward her. As it took over her field of vision, the cloud transformed into a plague of grackles. With a cacophony of cries, the birds veered off path, violently crashing into each other mid-flight, becoming one gigantic bird with ghastly yellow irises.

Everly tried to cry out but her voice box was muted. Before she and the bird collided, she saw her own gaunt expression reflected in its huge black pupils. Before it flew down her throat, the giant grackle screamed the name given to her by the fallen Lemur:

Ever Moon.

CHAPTER 34

The world around her was blurry and far too bright as Everly's eyelids fluttered open. Fabric walls wafted against a warm breeze. The air felt dry. There was a plastic tube taped to the top of her hand with a line leading up to an empty baggie.

"Micah?" she groaned. "Taz…"

"Easy, killer. You're going to rip that line right out, and it was a pain in the ass to get in there," said a familiar voice.

Everly bolted upright. Shielding her eyes from the brightness, she instantly recognized the silhouette. "Shelby!" Everly tackled her sister. The fold-out chair beneath her collapsed and they crashed onto the sandy floor.

"Shit, I'm sorry, Shel. Are you okay?" Everly scooted away and looked her sister over. Shelby was transformed. Her head was buzzed, but her thick auburn hair was growing back. She was tanned and radiant. She'd gained some weight. The black circles under her eyes were gone. The sickness, whatever it was, had left her body. Everly burst into tears.

Shelby pulled her in close and rubbed her sister's back with warm, calloused hands. "Hey, it's okay."

Everly rocked with joyful sobs. "But how?" she hiccupped. "What are you doing here? How did you get away from the handlers?"

"Easy, easy," Shelby comforted. "I'll explain everything, I promise." She led Everly back to the cot and sat beside her.

"I can't believe you're alive," Everly sniffled. "I thought I'd lost you for good."

"I thought you were blown up!" her sister exclaimed.

Everly thought back to the moment at the fishery when Micah

threw a grenade and dragged her into the ocean. She hadn't considered what the moment would have looked like from Shelby's perspective. "I'm so sorry, Shel," Everly said, shakily.

"Don't be. You weren't exploded, and I wasn't locked up, so we're good."

"But how did you get away?"

"On the way to the prison, the rebels attacked the handlers. It was mayhem. The AUV crashed, and the rebels pulled me from the wreckage. They brought me here. It's called the Oasis. Look…" Shelby rolled the sleeve of her shirt and flashed a fresh brand on the inside of her wrist.

"No way," Everly gasped. "You joined the rebellion, too?"

"Yup."

"Well, isn't that just swell," Everly said, sarcastically.

"What do you mean?"

"It's just that…being a rebel, that was kind of my thing."

"Oh, I see how it is!" Shelby laughed.

"Couldn't you find your *own* thing?"

"Like rotting away in a Dust prison cell?"

"No," Everly tisked. "Not that. Never that."

Shelby sighed. "We made it, little sister."

Everly couldn't contain a fresh round of tears. "I wished for you," she cried. "You're the thing I care about most in the world."

"I wished for you, too," Shelby smiled. "And here you are. A truck dropped you and the others off last night. Your bandmates are here, too."

"Wait a minute," Everly scoffed. "You had the chance to wish away your sickness and you didn't? Why not?!"

"Some things are worth dying for," she said, eyes glossy.

"But how are you better?"

Shelby shrugged. "It's kind of a long story."

"We've got time." Everly leaned over and kissed her sister on the cheek. "There's so much I have to tell you. We need to find a guy. His name is Ezra."

"Speak of the devil, and he shall appear," said a young man as he entered the tent. He was ten years older than Micah, at least, but the resemblance was uncanny. They shared the same wiry build, high cheekbones, and self-assured smirk. He handed Everly another baggie. The water felt warm.

"Everly, meet Ezra, the Umbo of the Oasis," Shelby said.

"Umbo?" Everly repeated. "How many of you are there?"

"Half a dozen, spread out across the globe. Welcome to the home of the Bedouin. I've heard good things," Ezra said with a gap-toothed grin.

"Likewise," Everly replied, although the only thing she'd heard about the man in front of her was that he'd stolen vials of the Cure. She tried her best to hide the distrust behind a smile. Everly had an endless list of questions, but if she knew anything about the Umbos, they shared information on their own terms. Ezra checked his watch and shouted orders out the window. Answers would have to wait.

"Sorry to interrupt the reunion so soon, but we've got to get moving," Ezra said.

Shelby offered Everly a hand. "Can you walk?"

"I think so."

Shelby guided her out of the tent and into the blinding brightness of the desert. For as far as Everly's squinted gaze could see, they were surrounded by rolling white sand dunes. The camp was located beside a shimmering spring, complete with palm trees. The Oasis, a living mirage, was aptly named. Across the camp, a group of old-school military ATVs sat idling. Katak leaned his head out of one of them, screaming, "Everly! We made it! And look who's here!"

The back door swung open, and a scrawny kid with jet black hair leaned out. "I'm Jessie," he hollered. "Nice to meet you."

"Jessie?" Everly called back. "You're alive?!"

"Never better," he beamed.

"The Rooters aren't psychopaths after all!" Katak declared.

Everly pumped a fist and turned to Shelby, cheeks flushed with excitement. "We thought he was dead. Our Umbo drowned him on the first day."

"I guess Bloodwood gave him a second chance in the desert,

when the island didn't work out. Poor guy was so traumatized when he got here," Shelby explained. "But he came around."

A sharp whistle drew their attention to the top of a sand dune. The sun was directly behind it, and the figures standing at its crest undulated in the refracted heat. With whoops and hollers, they hopped on wooden boards and surfed the dunes, carving giant snakes in the sand as they descended.

Everly was mesmerised by their floating forms. They had scarves covering their faces. Their clothes were bleached by the sun. The tallest of the dune surfers picked up his board and jogged over to the girls. There was something about his gait that felt known, and Everly looked to her sister for clues, but Shelby was looking away, chewing her knuckles.

The boy stopped in front of them and unwrapped his checkered scarf.

"What the dust?!" Everly gasped.

"Watch your mouth, Dahl face." He pulled her in for a tight embrace. Everly leaned back and looked at Jordan Knockwood like she was seeing him for the first time. She took in the details of his goggle tan, the stubble on his jawline, the chapped curve of his lips. "How is this possible?" she asked.

"When the rebels ambushed the AUV, they weren't expecting to find two of us in the backseat, but I begged them to take Jordan, too," Shelby explained.

"So, instead of prison, I'm turning into jerky out in the desert," he quipped.

"You're really here," Everly said with disbelief. "Both of you. I can't…"

"Get a move on! We're rolling out in two minutes," Ezra shouted from the ATVs.

"We'll talk later," Jordan promised.

"Yeah," she replied. "We have a lot to catch up on."

As they watched him trot away, Everly elbowed Shelby in the ribs. "A little warning would've been nice! I smell like a rotten fish."

"You really do," Shelby teased, throwing an arm across Everly's shoulders. "He saved my life, you know."

"How?"

"His wish."

Everly's eyes went wide. "He wished for you to get better?"

Shelby nodded, tearfully. "The Bloodwood Society did the rest."

Everly pushed her curls away from her face, feeling the radiating heat of the hot, dry sun pulsing down on her. Jordan could have wished for anything in the world, and he asked for the one thing he knew would bring Everly the greatest amount of happiness. That had to mean something.

"I can't believe all of this," she sniffled, about to break down into sobs once again.

"There's one more thing."

"There's more?!"

Shelby's expression turned serious. "We're going to bust him out."

"Who?"

"Dad," Shelby said, her eyes focused and clear. "Ezra told me last night."

For a second, Everly forgot how to breathe. Sweat broke from her brow and evaporated instantly. "The Dust is not going to like that."

"Not at all."

The pouch concealing their father's badge felt warm against Everly's chest. She had a lot of questions for him. With any luck, she'd get a chance to ask them in person. Wiping grains of sand from her lips, she whispered the Bloodwood mantra: "The root of the root…"

"The salt of the earth," she and Shelby said together.

Everly grabbed her sister's hand. "Let's go get him."

ACKNOWLEDGMENTS

This book would not have come to life without the help of many talented, generous people.

To Rebekah Wheadon, my first reader, my friend and teacher. For poring over countless drafts, year after year, and patiently watching this story take form. For always coming through with the most insightful feedback and invaluable encouragement.

To Sarah Mughal Rana, Leah Lefort, and Siobhan Kellar, for your incredible editing skills. For seeing new paths and tying loose ends. For helping me to let go of scenes, characters, and words that no longer served. For lending your time, talents, and energy to these pages, while leading hectic lives of your own.

To Rachael Allen, Carrie Coad, and Ameerah Holiday, my brilliant beta readers. The finished product is very different from the versions you read, thanks largely to your honest and thoughtful responses.

To Sarah Bird, my first and most enthusiastic fan.

To Walid Alhindi, for brainstorming cover ideas with me as we hopped from airport to airport.

To Karolina Loboda and Eric Forest, for transforming this book into a beautiful work of art.

To my parents, Lisa and Tobin Doty, and my sisters, Tory Bishop and Leighton Doty, for taking this writer thing seriously and supporting me in every way.

To Lennon and Myles, for being magnificent, hilarious, and endlessly inspiring.

To my husband, Kev, for giving me time and space to make something, all while caring for our wonderful family and keeping all the balls in the air. You're my best.

And finally, to you, dear reader. For without you, I'm just a voice shouting into the storm.

Printed in the USA
CPSIA information can be obtained
at www.ICGtesting.com
JSHW012330101224
75106JS00015B/63/J

* 9 7 8 1 7 3 8 3 3 2 7 0 0 *